M

A Taste of Magic

Also from Tor Books by Andre Norton

A Taste of Magic

of Magic

ANDRE NORTON AND JEAN RABE

TOR®

A TOM DOHERTY ASSOCIATES BOOK

NEW YORK

A TASTE OF MAGIC

Copyright © 2006 by the estate of Andre Norton and Jean Rabe

This book is printed on acid-free paper.

A Tor Book
Published by Tom Doherty Associates, LLC
175 Fifth Avenue
New York, NY 10010

www.tor.com

Tor® is a registered trademark of Tom Doherty Associates, LLC.

Library of Congress Cataloging-in-Publication Data

Norton, Andre.
  A taste of magic / Andre Norton and Jean Rabe.— 1st ed.
      p. cm.
  "A Tom Doherty Associates book."
  ISBN-13: 978-0-765-31527-4
  ISBN-10: 0-765-31527-0
  1. Young women—Fiction. 2. Revenge—Fiction. 3. Magic—Fiction. I. Rabe, Jean. II.
Title.
  PS3527.O632T37 2006
  813'.54—dc22

                                                              2006005911

First Edition: November 2006

Printed in the United States of America

0 9 8 7 6 5 4 3 2 1

For Sue Stewart . . . who made Andre smile

Acknowledgments

This is the final novel Andre Norton worked on. The Grand Dame of science fiction and fantasy tried to finish this tale on her own. However, tired fingers and other unfortunate circumstances got in her way.

In the last days of her life, in March 2005, Andre plotted the end of this story with me. She'd given it much thought, and when she was certain I understood just what she wanted, she wished her characters well and bade us all good-bye.

What an extreme honor this was for me—to be gifted with the task of filling in the gaps for *A Taste of Magic*.

Only two words suffice for several people regarding this book: Sue Stewart, Andre's friend and assistant, who chose me to finish the manuscript; Bill Fawcett, who encouraged me and who packaged this project; Brian Thomsen, who made this a better book, and me a better writer, through his editing; Linda Baker, who shared her first-person wisdom, and who managed to find time to proof a good portion of these pages despite her own deadlines and dealing with the aftermath of a hurricane; and Tom Doherty, my publisher, for graciously saying yes to *A Taste of Magic*.

Thank you.

The Tale Behind *Taste*

IN OCTOBER 2002, ANDRE NORTON ENTERED THE HOSPITAL FOR surgery to repair a hernia. It was to be a simple procedure, but some things went wrong and it ended in serious complications, including Andre getting a vicious infection.

In effect, what was to have been a forty-five-minute operation turned into a two-hour operation. And what was supposed to be an overnight stay in the hospital turned into a six-week ordeal, some of it spent in intensive care.

Andre came close to dying then, but found the will to make it, especially when friends smuggled in a few of her cats for visits. When Andre finally returned home from the hospital, she tried to find some normalcy after all the "mass hysteria" of the past many weeks. But things were never wholly normal again.

It was mid-December 2002 when she decided to write the final novel for her "senses" series, and she began ruminating over various plots. (*The Scent of Magic* was published in 1999.) In January 2003, she began the outline for *A Taste of*

Magic. She'd read several books on the sense of taste and had done a little research. The outlining took her some time.

Then, in March 2003, she began the actual process of writing the novel. Unfortunately, Andre found it very difficult to concentrate. Her words didn't flow as easily as they used to. Everything seemed to have changed after her long stay in the hospital.

She finished a few chapters, and decided she would leave it a while, then come back to it at a later date. She carefully placed the manuscript into a brown leather zip-up pouch and put it into her filing cabinet. She did not take it back out to work on until I moved her into my home in May 2004.

One month later, after getting completely settled into her new apartment, she pulled the brown leather pouch out of her lower desk drawer and tried again to work on *Taste*.

Still, the words would not come, and she ended up frustrated and depressed. I came into her bedroom one day and found her with her head down, crying over the manuscript. This is when I put my arm around her and told her not to worry. I told her that her hands had made her a living all of her life through their creativity, and there was no reason why those same hands couldn't do another form of creativity.

I told her to start beading her necklaces again. It was a favorite hobby of hers. Susanne Hebden, a friend of Andre's, had taught Andre how to bead and had worked with her on the beading before she'd moved into my house. However, one of Andre's assistants at the time railed against the beading parties and discouraged Andre's newfound hobby. But in my house Andre could do as she pleased. The beading began in earnest.

Though Andre was having trouble writing, she became inspired by various beading projects. Andre Norton the writer became Andre Norton the designer and crafter of jewelry. From that point on, she never looked back, nor did she shed another tear over an unfinished writing project.

She gathered up her *Taste* manuscript, carefully stacking the papers and placing it back into the zip-up brown leather pouch and into her lower desk drawer. She then got into her upper desk drawer and pulled out the bead catalogs and began ordering beads and beads and beads.

In February 2005, *Taste* resurfaced again. Andre's health was failing, but her mind was clear, and she was thinking about that manuscript. Andre didn't leave things unfinished, and she insisted that I have her partial *A Taste of Magic* and lots of notes on how she planned to finish it. This was a book she wanted finished, one more wonderful story of magic and heroes. To allow me to handle the book myself, Andre generously sold *Taste* to me for the traditional one dollar on February 25, 2005. She then suggested that Jean Rabe, whom she had enjoyed working with before, could put it all together. Jean agreed, and the two spoke several times.

So this is the story behind *A Taste of Magic*. It includes both of those things Andre loved even in her last days, a good tale and wonderful jewelry. One of the necklaces mentioned in the novel is one that Andre made and sent to Jean as a Christmas present.

—*Sue Stewart,*
Andre's friend and assistant,
spring 2006

1

THE GREEN ONES FAVORED ME THIS DAY.

A brace of curl-horns, mates I'd tracked to a shallow den, lay across Dazon's saddle. No room for me to ride, they were so large! I knew they would pleasantly fill all of our bellies this evening and the next.

For the past five Oath Marks, and all the days between, our hunting had been disappointing. We'd been ranging farther north of the village and into the darkest parts of the Sabado Forest. Our families were proud and not known for depending on the elaborate rituals of either the Dawn Priests or the Sun Sisters, but lately there had been talk of seeking spiritual aid for our hunt. Perhaps if the Green Ones favored me again tomorrow, such prayers—and their expensive offerings—would not be necessary.

Lady Ewaren, our House Lady, was a weaver, and so I bowed my head respectfully as I led Dazon out of the thickest section of woods and past a large glow-spider resting in a dew-sprinkled net. Many minutes later the trees thinned considerably more,

longleaf pines and mature persimmons giving way to a scattering of sweetbays and young elms, signaling my approach to the
Village Nar. The afternoon sun stretched through the scant
branches and warmed my face and bare arms. I closed my
eyes and took a few blissful moments to enjoy this spring day,
and to listen to the birdsong and the other small sounds of this
undisturbed place—the chitter of ground squirrels and gray
backs, the soft chirp of insects.

Abruptly a bellow shattered the natural melody. The bellow
came again and again. I recognized it as a cow demanding
milking. The village cattleman was not one to be tardy to his
work and ignore our small herd. So I quickened my strides out
of concern and curiosity, tugging my horse to a faster pace until we cleared the woods completely. The recently sown fields
and the hedge of high brush that walled the Village Nar came
into view.

I stopped in midstep, listening to the repeated bellows and
smelling fire and burnt meat. I tentatively opened my mouth
and extended my tongue to confirm the scents.

I am a docent of Bastien t'Ikkes, a once-royal guard and near-
fabled Moonson who saved the Emperor's life during a bear
hunt many years past. His injuries from that incident forced his
retirement, his courage earned him a pension and a home in this
village, and his patience garnered me the post as his student.

Bastien taught me how to fight with a sword and knives and
how to taste the breeze and scent for danger and other things,
which was what I did now.

The tip of my tongue registered an unpalatable acridity, the
distinctive taste of death and the lingering scents of fear and
desperation.

There'd been a raid while I was hunting!

Our village is filled with farmers, hunters, and weavers, not warriors. Peaceful people! My heart seized with fear. I dropped the reins, knowing Dazon would follow me, and I rushed through a gap in the brush.

Who attacked us? And why?

I saw no one.

The gate to the courtyard swung in the wind.

Near Willum t'Jelth's house I spotted a snorter stretched on a frame over a now-smoldering fire, more than half of its carcass hacked away. I heard the bellow again, and I slipped along the hedge to the north, drawing upon all the stealthy skills Bastien had taught me and trying to force down the dread threatening to overwhelm me.

"Willum? Gerald?"

No answer.

I raised my voice. "Maergo? Lady Ewaren? Lady Ewaren!"

Now I could see a section of the yard beyond the gate, the Great House and its various attendant buildings essentially forming the walls of the courtyard. Inside, a large cow tramped across the soft loam of a newly seeded herb garden and continued to bellow loudly, two smaller ones trailing behind it. Another cow leaned against the side of the Great House. The sun caught on shards of metal protruding from its black hide, as numerous as the pins in Lady Ewaren's sewing pillow. Blood dripped from its wounds. I vowed to end its suffering—after I saw to the village.

I looked elsewhere, cupping my hands over my eyes, shutting out the light and focusing on my wyse-sense and on my tongue and what the wind was telling me.

Death.

The wind spoke of death and suffering and confusion.

I thought I saw a foot and a torn piece of material just under the shadow of a jutting second story.

A foot . . .

"Willum! Maergo! Lady Ewaren!"

Loosening the web of my backpack, I sat it on the ground and placed my blowpipe and quiver of bolts next to it. I did not want to be encumbered when I faced the enemy, but I wanted to be prepared. I drew the longest of my knives and fought to keep my senses sharp. Fear and grief threatened to overwhelm me.

It was easy to suspicion all manner of horrid things, especially after seeing the throwstars in the cow's side and finding no one outside and no one to answer my call. I wanted more than suspicion to work with, and so struggling desperately to keep panic at bay, I again tasted the air, urging my tongue to find the scents.

Blood—blood is always strong enough to make itself known first. There was more blood than I had ever scented before. And I picked up a touch of sweat—of men and mounts—and the fire I smelled earlier, and ashes. Then I strained my senses to the limit, barely able to reach and identify emotions. I tasted terror, pain, and hate. And above all of that, I tasted my own horror, choking and dreadfully nauseating.

"Willum." My voice grew weak, a whisper. "Lady Ewaren."

Still, nothing stirred in the village.

The foot I spied in the distance did not move, and somehow I knew it belonged to a corpse. How many dead? I knew I would have to search the entire village to learn what had happened.

My stomach churned with the grisly possibilities, and my heart hammered with each step I took. I was feeling faint from the scents and the notion that I wouldn't find a soul alive, that everyone I knew and loved had been brutally butchered.

But slain by whom? Slain why?

And why had I gone hunting so early this morning? Had I lingered, I could have defended this place.

"Willum!"

The coughing sickness had taken Bastien this past winter. The village had no guards, the elders thinking Bastien's presence enough protection. But after his death, the elders still took no steps for defense, thinking our world oh so peaceful and safe, and thinking that I could be sufficient defense, given the skills Bastien had taught me. Too, there had been no rumors of invasion from the Twisted Lands, and Lady Ewaren seemed held in favor with the neighboring countries to the west—even though it was said she was descended from the long-outlawed House of Alchura.

I sheathed my knife and tugged a long, thin chain free from my belt. I preferred it as a weapon because of its reach. Then I started down a gentle slope, making use of the shadows from buildings to provide me some cover. Within heartbeats I stood in the gate road. Once more I tongue-tested, finding more blood, ashes, terror, and hate. Oddly, hate was the strongest here, almost overwhelming. Darting around the corner of the gate, I came into the courtyard.

The foot . . .

The rags that had been her spring-green gown lay torn on the ground between myself and where the body lay. Her ripped undergarments were saturated with blood. Something stronger than anger welled from deep within me, and a horror I'd never felt overcame me. I grabbed on to a post to support myself.

I edged closer.

The foot . . . it belonged to Lady Ewaren, our House Lady. My breath caught and I went down on my knees beside her body, fighting for air.

"My lady!" The first words I'd spoken since entering the village were filled with grief. "By the Green Ones, my lady!"

Lady Ewaren had taken me in after the death of my mother ten years past. Hers was the only home I truly remembered. Her face . . . now a broken ruin. Sobbing, I tugged down from her curve cap a length of lace veil. It didn't hide all the blood, but it softened the worst of it around her face. Then I noticed her other injuries. Each and every one of her fingers—which she had used to weave such beauty that nearby lords and ladies begged for her work—every one had been broken. Deliberately, cruelly, I knew, broken while she'd lived.

Once more I heard the bellow of the cow. Though the mournful sound was muted now by the intervening buildings, it was nonetheless demanding. In the intervals between the bellows, I heard an incessant buzzing from the bees in the hive housed on a balcony above me. I noticed the sound of flies, too. They were drawn to Lady Ewaren's body.

Lady Ewaren, I should pray for her.

I hesitantly touched her broken fingers and under my breath, in the thinnest of voices, I uttered old, old words.

"Nesalah dorma calla—"

"Yaaaaaah!" The scream spun me around so quickly I nearly

lost my balance. I saw a slip of a girl, just a heartbeat before her knifepoint flashed down and sliced my tunic at the shoulder. I moved fast enough that the blade only drew a thin line of blood. Without pause, I lashed out with my chain, whipping it around her arm.

She cried in surprise and pain, and dropped the blade as I dragged her close. But she didn't give in. Her wide golden eyes flashed with madness, and her teeth snapped at my throat. It was as if I held a night fiend instead of the slight girl that Lady Ewaren had taken as an apprentice almost a year ago. Lady Ewaren had hoped I'd be like a sister to this girl, but that hadn't happened. I didn't want to hurt the girl if I could help it—and it would be so easy for me to end this fight with a single blow. I was that much stronger, and she was half my age . . . at most ten years old.

"Demon!" she spat. "Thrice-damned demon may you be!"

I dropped my chain and grabbed both her wrists, shaking her roughly in an effort to bring her to her senses. She kicked at me now, her heavy boot landing a solid blow against my shin. I cringed and dragged her so close against me she had no room to kick again, while at the same time I twisted her arms behind her in a hold Bastien had taught me early on. I crushed the air out of her, and she swayed and gasped. I truly hadn't intended to hurt her, but she'd given me no choice.

I bent my head to her ear, as I stood several inches taller. "Alysen, what happened here?"

She went limp, and I held her up now.

"They came for you, Eri," she said after a moment.

"Who? Tell me, Alysen!"

She didn't answer this, saying instead, "They came for you because the Emperor's dead. And so is your father. You and your kin, the Empress has had you drummed!"

I loosed her then and she staggered back, stumbling toward one of the slender pillars that held up the outer edge of a narrow roof. Catching at the pillar with both hands to support herself, she faced me. Alysen's smooth face was a scarlet mask of hatred.

"They came for you!" Her voice was stronger now, spittle flecking at her lips. "You they wanted! And all this death, Eri, is because you weren't here! Everyone died because of you!"

Me? All this because of me? A wave of dizziness crashed against me.

"Everyone is dead, Eri!"

Except her. I noticed then that there wasn't a mark on her, save where my chain had reddened her arm. Her dress was soiled slightly at the hem, which brushed across the ground, but it was obvious she'd not been touched in this assault. Her long black hair was clean and shiny, as if she'd just combed it.

"You! It was only you they wanted! In all of Nar, only you! And had you been here, they might have slain you or took you away and left everyone else alone. One life—yours—for all of these."

Alysen glared at me, her chest rising and falling rapidly as she sucked in gulps of air. "The men . . . they said she . . ." She gestured at Lady Ewaren's corpse. "They said she warned you that they were coming. That she sent you away to keep you safe." She released the pillar, only leaning against it now. "The Lady argued, said she hadn't sent you anywhere. But they didn't believe her."

"Who?" I asked. "Who didn't believe her?"

"He . . . he told them to take her fingers. One by one, her left hand, snapping them like twigs until she passed out from the pain. When she came to, they started on her right hand."

I stared at the girl, then dropped my gaze to Lady Ewaren's corpse, trying not to imagine what she had felt, trying to wish all of this away.

"This man, Alysen, the one who ordered this, who is he?"

Alysen didn't answer me, just continued to glare, her eyes trying to pin me in place.

"Tell me the name of this man, Alysen."

"They killed everyone, you know, save two servants and a few children who ran toward the lake. They might have got the children, too, I didn't see. Two men with swords rode off in the direction of the lake. Two more took toward Mardel's Fen and . . ." A pause. "When the killing was finished here, they went searching with swords drawn."

I reeled at the news, her words pummeling me. *All this death . . .*

"The bodies are in the houses, some in the barns, Willum and his family are all in that barn. Butchered and covered with hay. Lady Ewaren . . . they didn't give her even that bit of respect. They left her for the carrion beetles and the crows."

All this death because of me . . .

"Where were you, Eri? Why couldn't you have died instead?"

There was a longer pause, and in it I again heard the buzzing of flies drawn to Lady Ewaren's body. There was another swarm of sound, a soft, constant drone that came from the nearest house.

Because of me! I would eagerly have died to keep these people safe.

"They killed Willum and Sela and everyone," Alysen said. "And all they wanted was you, Wisteria. Where were you?"

My mind swirled. I'd left the village long before dawn, not telling anyone I was hunting so early, and not telling them where in the forest I intended to go. I'd planned to range far, and so needed to leave early so I would have the time for travel. Had I been closer to the village I would have heard the horses, the men, and the desperate screams that must have filled the air.

"Purvis," she said at last. "The men called him Lord Purvis. He's the one who ordered her fingers broken, and then ordered her killed."

The village dead, Lady Ewaren dead, before that the Emperor and my father—if what Alysen said rang true. I dug my fingernails into my palms, the pain helping to keep me from swooning. My father . . .

My only contact with my father had been more than a year ago. He'd sickened from a summer fever. They'd called me to his side in the great southern city, and he ordered me to hold myself ready to take his place as taster at the Emperor's board. My brother was summoned, too, but he was several years older and serving in some lord's army. He never came. My father had written me a letter, which he'd pressed into my hand. It was the only thing he'd ever given me. A single sheet, it said he hoped that if I were called to my life-duty, I would serve the Emperor well. I returned to this village, without the letter, and weeks later I'd received news my father had recovered. Now here came news of his death, and the Emperor's.

"Lord Purvis," she repeated, the words spit out like they were pieces of spoiled meat. "He ordered all of this, Eri."

I'd never heard of Lord Purvis. A chill passed down my spine and the intense tragedy of this day finally settled deep, deep in my soul. My knees buckled and the darkness claimed me.

2

I AWOKE WITH AN INTENSE SOURNESS IN MY MOUTH. UNTIL THIS day it had been an unfamiliar taste to me. Loss, grief, utter despair—that was the taste, and it radiated from me and from Alysen, who hovered above me. Most of the hysterical fury had faded from her face, and she stared at me in puzzlement. Then, she repeated slowly, as if I might not have heard her the first time, "Wisteria, are you listening to me?"

I gave her a nod.

"Lord Purvis of Elderlake. He's the foul demon-of-a-man who ordered everyone killed. Didn't even have the nerve to do any of the killing himself. Lord High-and-Mighty Purvis of Elderlake."

Indeed I heard her, but I couldn't build the image of a man from the name. I was still consumed by the disbelief that the Village Nar was dead . . . and I was the root of it.

"Lord Purvis of Elderlake, Eri."

Elderlake sat in the country Rhinardrelle to the southwest, the largest country on our island continent. Elderlake was in

the narrowest part by the coast, where the villages were large
and where the seat of the Rhemra Empire wrapped itself in
tall buildings and a fortified wall. Lord Purvis had quite a ride
from there to our Village Nar. But he would ride to hell if I had
my way.

Alysen helped me sit up and repeated the name twice
more.

"Purvis. The demon-of-a-man is—"

Abruptly I stood and pointed a trembling hand toward an
open doorway.

"Lord Purvis. I heard you, Alysen. The cloak stand within."
I caught at her shoulder and turned her a little. "The cloak
stand. Get whatever you can find there. And hurry."

The stare Alysen had locked upon me finally broke, but she
made no move toward the door. Instead, she dropped her gaze
to Lady Ewaren's corpse.

"Do it now, Alysen. The cloak stand."

Numbly, she nodded, then she ran to the main door of the
manor house. After she'd disappeared inside I grabbed up the
torn dress and spread it over our House Lady. Then I resumed
my prayer in the old, old words, barely finishing when Alysen
returned. She held two weather cloaks, one forest green that
had been handed down to her from me, the other mist gray
that had been Lady Ewaren's favorite. She helped me wrap
both around the broken body, then watched as I picked it up
and carried it inside the manor house. Alysen followed closely
on my heels as I went to the great hall and laid the body in the
center of a long table.

"Where did they go?" I asked her.

Again, she'd lapsed into silence.

"Where, Alysen? The men and Lord Purvis?"

She stared at the bundled form, then after a moment shook her head slowly. "Lord Purvis and his men?" She shrugged her narrow shoulders. "There came a speaker bird, a summoner, I think. It landed on Lord Purvis's shoulder and spoke so softly I couldn't hear. But when it was done and flew off, they all rode away in a great hurry. They took the two servants they hadn't killed, and—"

"And they left you here. Why? Why in the name of the Green Ones did they leave you alone? Why leave you and kill everyone else?"

Her eyes, so like the huge ones of a tree-cat, even down to the golden coloring, would not meet mine. But at least this time she answered me without pause.

"I was with Nanoo Gafna when the raiders came." Alysen ground the ball of her foot against the hard-packed dirt floor. "She—she put a ward spell upon me, a no-see and—" She hesitated, and then ended in a rush of words. "It worked! By the Favor of Ostare, the ward spell worked. Nanoo Gafna slipped away, probably to the fen. I didn't see them catch her, didn't hear her scream. She must be safe, right? Safe like me. The riders looked straight at me and did not see me. The Moonsons did not know I was standing in the doorway. They could not see me, but I saw them. By all that's holy, I saw everything they did!"

I swallowed hard. "Moonsons. You said Moonsons rode with this Lord Purvis?"

"The demon-of-a-man."

The confusion must have been evident on my face. "Moonsons, but—"

"Some of them were Moonsons, they had the symbol on their shields and helms. I recognized the symbol from Bastien's shield that hangs above the fireplace." She gestured to the shield, gloriously battle-pitted. "And from the shields of the Moonsons who've come through the village before. The rest of the men, I guess they were Lord Purvis's household guard. They were wearing the colors he wore, green and black with a lion on the shield laying down and looking over its shoulder."

"The Moonsons?"

"They stood apart, and I do not believe they took part in the killings."

"But they did not stop it."

"No. They didn't stop any of it."

"Was one in charge?"

"Of the Moonsons? None I'd recognized from their visits here. And no officers that I could see. No braids or medals or finery to mark one above the rest. And none of the Moonsons wore officer plumes. But they all seemed to answer to Lord Purvis."

She raised both hands to push back long strings of inky black hair from her face. Suddenly she swayed, and I moved to catch her. I set her on one of the chairs by the table, turning it so she couldn't look at the wrapped body. Her breath came unevenly, as if everything had finally caught up to her, and her anger started to fade, taking her strength with it.

"This bird messenger," I prompted. "The summoner." Alysen needed rest, but I needed more answers, among them why Nanoo Gafna would cast a no-see ward on the girl before she would do so on Lady Ewaren. What could be so special about this child? . . .

"I am of the House of Geer." Alysen's words shattered my musings.

Was the child able to work her way within my skull and read my thoughts?

The girl stared beyond me and at the wall, and she spoke deliberately, as if she fully expected some sort of startled reaction from me.

"Only Nanoo Gafna and our House Lady knew me as a firstborn from the House of Geer. That's why she gave me the ward spell."

House of Geer—indeed, no wonder Nanoo Gafna had spun a protection spell for her. The Nanoo, who for the most part lived reclusively in Mardel's Fen, claimed no kin of this world and embraced the House of Geer's otherworldly ties to arcane power. The House of Geer had long supported the Nanoo, but the House's members had dwindled through the decades, many of them dying of disease or various maladies that were whispered to be acts of murder. The dwindling House's surviving members, known to be in disfavor with the Emperor, had a rich history dotted with seers.

And those seers were all firstborns.

Nanoo Gafna would have recognized any power within the child Alysen, and she could have convinced Lady Ewaren to hide the girl here as a simple apprentice. Lady Ewaren had certainly helped me, and had nudged me to Bastien for teaching.

So the girl had been protected because of her blood, placed by Nanoo Gafna before Lady Ewaren. Saved when Lady Ewaren was brutally murdered.

I nodded to the girl and took a chance. "Lady Alysen, strong be the wyse."

She smiled. "*La yulen t' Korus.* You and I may be two of a kind, Eri. But that is yet to be proven."

"And now is not the time, and this is not the place to prove anything." I would learn more about her later.

The Emperor, a man obsessed with individuals possessing arcane talents, was dead. My father, who had been forced to serve because of his wyse-sense, was dead, too. I prayed my brother, wherever he lived, was safe.

"*Is* safe," I whispered. My brother lacked wyse talent, and so might be spared. But me? The wyse flowed in my veins.

A force had come to this village looking for me. Why? Because of my wyse abilities? Because of my blood? And why kill everyone here? I looked at the wrapped form of our House Lady, and again the bitter tastes of grief and confusion settled strongly in my mouth.

Did they truly seek me because of my father? Did they want to use my inherited wyse-sense for their own dark purposes? Or did they want to make sure—with my death—that the magical ability from our family tree ended with this last feeble limb? There were those in this world who wanted magic to die.

"Eri, do you think they will come back here looking for you?"

I shrugged, my gaze still locked on the covered body. If the men thought I might return, they could return as well. And why wouldn't I come back here? It was home. A great part of me had a strong desire to wait here and see, to fight all of them. Bastien had trained me well.

But the wisest part of me knew I couldn't take on any sizeable group of men alone—not if I wanted to protect this girl.

"We cannot leave our House Lady here, like this."

"Do you, Eri? Do you think they will come back?"

Alysen and I were making a habit of not readily answering each other's questions. However, I suspected she could pull the answer of yes from my mind if she tried. I picked up Lady Ewaren and carried her to the kitchen. Alysen washed her body while I searched for something presentable to dress her in. I returned with one of her court robes, a miracle of color with tiny gems sewn into the braiding along the neckline and sleeves. Our House Lady suitably attired, we brought her body to a great carved bed and laid her in the center. Then Alysen sprinkled dried flowers and herbs around her, as was a wyse custom. She was about to draw a gauzy curtain over the still form, but I signed for her to wait.

I was not a Moonson—only men of noble birth were allowed that. But because of Bastien's teaching I had long lived by their covenants. The two knives Bastien had passed to me on his deathbed rested in sheaths at my waist. I pulled one free and held the tip even with my eyes.

"What are you doing, Eri?"

I leaned over Lady Ewaren and set the blade to the back of my left hand.

"Wisteria . . . what are you doing?"

I sliced my skin and recalled the words I'd heard Bastien utter only once. I hoped I had them correct.

By salt and bread, water and wine
By steel and rope, hand, foot, and breeze
By the ancient and the elder, master, and man
This bloodoath I so swear.

There was no Moonson to hear the oath and vouch for it and me, but it didn't matter. As blood dripped down upon the bed and the body, I committed myself physically and spiritually. I would never stand free until the blood price for Lady Ewaren was paid . . . until the man responsible for her death was slain by my hand.

Lord Purvis.

Alysen pulled the gauze over the body, and I repeated again the prayer in the old, old words.

"Nesalah dorma calla aloran se. The world holds its breath at your passing. *Nesalah dorma entare se ren salma.* The world holds your memory for all time."

"May your spirit be at peace," Alysen added. Then she turned from me and the body, her shoulders shaking as she sobbed.

3

ACCORDING TO ALYSEN, THE ONLY NANOO IN THE VILLAGE AT the time of the attack was Gafna, and I could not find her body. She didn't live in the village, and she only came on the middle days of every other week to see Lady Ewaren. She lived in the fen, as nearly all the Nanoo did, and it was a good distance on foot. Alysen thought perhaps Gafna had escaped the carnage and fled to her home.

I agreed to search for the old woman, as she might provide more information about the raid and about the vile Lord Purvis. Too, I intended to leave Alysen with Nanoo Gafna while I pursued my bloodoath, though I did not tell the girl this. I needed to be rid of the child to pursue my bloodoath.

It was not in my nature to be motherly.

A sharp thought pierced me—Alysen said the riders had searched for and chased down those running away or at the very least looked for those who had fled. Had the men caught and killed Nanoo Gafna? Would my search end in one more friend to mourn? Had the searchers traveled into the dark heart of the woods and found the homes in the fen?

When we ranged from this village, would I find her body as I had found Lady Ewaren's? One more to mourn, I thought again.

No! I held tightly to the knowledge that Nanoo Gafna knew the fen and magic and that both would keep her and her kind safe. Still, the fear burned in my belly that some ill had befallen the old witch. And from the look on Alysen's face, I could tell she was reading my thoughts and wondering the same thing.

I knew I could not return here, certainly should not if I wanted some time to think things through and to properly grieve for the slaughtered villagers. Alysen couldn't stay either—little more than a child, she couldn't make her way alone in a village of the dead. Her eyes were fixed and glassy, and I wondered what thoughts twirled in her head . . . she'd witnessed all the villagers slaughtered. And cloaked by a no-see spell, she could do nothing to save them.

"There will be no open door for me at the Geer House, Eri. I would bring danger to my family, and likely they would turn me away." She paused. "They sent me away before."

Gave you to Nanoo Gafna and Lady Ewaren.

She nodded.

She was indeed picking through my mind. A firstborn and strong in the wyse, I knew she wasn't safe even with her own people; this village had been a good hiding place for her.

"Do you have distant kin, Alysen, or friends in a far village who you might . . ."

She shook her head, eyes still glazed. "But I believe in the Nanoo to keep me safe. Whatever course Nanoo Gafna chooses for me, that I will accept."

"Then we must find her, eh?" *If she lives.*

I wanted to bury all of the villagers or burn the bodies, the latter being the custom of some of the families. But that would take time, a few days likely if we took care of all of them, and we could not risk the chance the men would return during that time. Oh, a great part of me wanted to face Purvis and his men as soon as possible. But again I reminded myself that now was not the time for revenge.

I needed to prepare.

I needed to know more about them, Lord Purvis especially. I needed Alysen safe. So I prayed to the Green Ones that merchants or herders would pass through this village soon so the bodies could be taken care of.

"Bury no one, Eri?"

I fought back tears as I shook my head.

"That is wrong. We should—"

"We take things only from the House of Ewaren, understand, Alysen? These other folks have relatives in nearby villages and cities to the south, and their goods should be willed to them."

Alysen hurried into the manor house. I waited a few moments, tasting the breeze again, making sure nothing was stirring and that there was no hint of the men returning. There remained only the tastes of blood and death and sorrow.

Satisfied we were alone, I followed her, taking a winding staircase to the second-floor chambers, my knees shaking and threatening to spill me. I knew Alysen had come this way, as I heard her moving around behind her closed door. I knocked and opened it.

She was folding clothes into a satchel. "About Nanoo Gafna, Eri, will you please—"

"Aye, I will go in search of the Nanoo with you. I promise. I'll not abandon you."

"Because the wyse is strong with me? Like it is with you?"

"No. Because keeping you safe is the right thing to do."

"Even if I had no magic about me?"

I didn't bother to answer that.

I left her for several minutes, retreating into my own room and collecting a few changes of clothes. These I put in a heavy cotton bag, adding to it a comb and brush, three strands of beads Lady Ewaren had given me, two of them woven of a thick yarn, looking like lace speckled with shiny stones and miniature carved wooden animals and flowers. The third was a strand of polished carnelian stones, carved into half-moon shapes, that I treasured.

My favorite necklace I put on. This was a gift from Bastien, and I suspected it had belonged to his mother, as he'd had no wife, and with no lady-friend he'd had no cause to purchase such jewelry. This strand was made of moss agates smoothed into the shape of teardrops. Each stone was a slightly different shade of green and was shot through with veins of brown and gray so dark they looked black to one who didn't inspect it closely. I'd mourn the dead with the moss agate tears now. I would properly cry my own tears later, when we were well away from this blood-drenched place.

I had only a handful of gold coins to my name, these willed to me by Bastien. I kept them in a small pouch, which I thrust deep into the bag. I paced around the room, tugged a gray wool blanket down from a shelf and rolled it, tying it with leather hair cords.

There were other odds and ends I gathered—two cakes of

precious oatmeal soap, a soft pair of slippers, and a leather-bound journal I'd kept while I studied with Bastien. I added an earthen jar filled with skin cream Willum's mother had made, and a dozen ivory ribbons I'd traded a wolf pelt for on a trip to Mamet two years past and had never put in my hair. My hair was far too short, as I always kept it trimmed close so it was easy to wash and comb and wouldn't tangle in the tree branches. Bastien said my head looked like an acorn, my skin smooth and tanned and my hair looking like the cap. But I thought I might grow my hair longer someday, and so I'd wanted the ribbons. Was it foolish of me now to take them with me?

I also took a section of lace I'd woven when I was Alysen's age—the first piece I'd made without Lady Ewaren's help. There were other treasures in my room, certainly, but I wanted to travel lightly and quickly and not be slowed by precious burdens. A last look around my room—the place I'd called home for the past ten years—then I returned to Alysen.

I saw that her door had a lock. Odd that I'd never noticed this before—but then, I'd not spent any amount of time with the girl, other than to greet her at the evening meal or to nod to her in passing. We were years and interests apart, though she called me Eri, a familiarity that bothered me a little, as that was what Lady Ewaren and Bastien had called me.

. . . But a lock on her door? I'd never found the need for such. Lady Ewaren had no lock on her door. That the child would lock her room in refuge made me aware that I knew very, very little of Alysen t'Geer.

She'd finished stuffing a second satchel. Both were small, and therefore acceptable. She, too, looked at her room a last time, tears threatening the corners of her eyes. She slipped a cloak on, while I took a blanket off her bed and tied it as I had mine. Then I handed it to her, though she had trouble managing it and her two satchels. I did not offer to help her; she would have to make her own way.

I glanced out the window of her room, then out the window at the end of the hall, watching for any sign of riders. The only thing stirring was my horse, Dazon. He was drinking deeply from the trough at the stable.

Alysen followed me to the kitchen, and we took what we could fit in a backpack hanging on the back hook—dried provisions that would not spoil and two jars of strawberry jam one of the cooks had put up a few days past. I pulled two traveler's water bottles from a high shelf.

"We'll fill these at the fountain in the courtyard." After a moment, I took a third, then Alysen and I crossed the courtyard to the barracks.

Since Bastien's death the barracks had been empty, serving mainly as a place wayfarers could rest between villages and where traveling soldiers could stop during their patrols. His room had been left largely intact, in the event distant relatives came by to claim his things. This is where I went.

"Wait outside and be wary," I told Alysen. "Call out if anyone approaches." Then I sat my bag and blanket at her feet and let the shadows of the barracks claim me.

If Bastien had distant relatives, I didn't know of them. And if they existed and knew of his passing, they would have come for his things by now—if they were interested. There were so many things I would have claimed. But I tried to keep my burden reasonable, and so I passed over his weapons, hanging dusty on the rack. A few were missing, and I wondered if some of the villagers had come in here and grabbed them in an effort to fight off the riders. I could have searched through the homes and the field, looking for such evidence—but the knowledge would be useless and would do nothing for either me or the dead.

I looked through the corner he'd considered a den and hesitated over a small, fancifully carved wooden box. It was no larger than an apple, and it held a secret, as I had never seen it open. I knew it was my mother's, and that Bastien was holding it for me. I'd tried opening it many times through the years but was never successful. Perhaps if I'd been closer to my mother, it would have intrigued me more. But, as it had been with my father, my mother and I'd never been close.

Oh, I could have bashed the thing open with my fist or a hammer, or forced it somehow, but Bastien had talked me out of that. He said I must discover the "key," or else I was not ready to see its contents. I balanced it in my hand a moment, considering leaving it. But after a moment more I put it in a belt pocket.

I took Bastien's cloak from the hook. It was too large for me, but was well made, lightweight wool dyed dark green. Another remembrance of him, this cloak. I folded it and tied it with a piece of twine. Then I took down a woodsman's hatchet, fitted in a leather pocket. It might come in handy.

"Eri!"

I rushed outside, fearing the return of the men. But Alysen was merely anxious.

She took the lead as we hurried to the stables. There were eight more horses inside, marking our village as quite prosperous. I selected the three best—a draft, a cob, and a dappled gray fell pony, and saddled them, then released the others knowing they could survive on the hay in the barn and the grass in the fields and at the edge of the woods. Too, I asked the Green Ones to let merchants or passing farmers find them and give them good homes.

I opened the gate to the field so the cows could also graze farther and get water. The one with the throwstars in its hide was down, already dead. I felt sorry that I had not ended its suffering immediately, that it had to feel such pain for so long, but so many things had flooded my mind.

I tied the backpack filled with food, Alysen's two satchels, and my satchel to the draft's saddle, adding Bastien's folded cloak and the three filled water bottles. I checked the curl-horns on Dazon, and added my small backpack and blowpipe and bolt quiver. When I was certain that everything was secure, I handed the reins of the fell pony to Alysen, pleased she was quick to get on its back—though was not at all graceful doing so. I took the cob.

Dazon was clearly fatigued, as I'd had him up so early and had traveled with him far this day and two days before. I wouldn't leave him, but I wouldn't ride him again until tomorrow. Nor would I give him anything else to carry the rest of this day. Dazon was seven, foaled by Bastien's prized mare, one of the horses I'd turned loose. Given to me as a Harvest Day present, there had not been a day I had not spent time with Dazon. The horse knew my moods as well as anyone who had lived in the village—as well as Bastien and Lady Ewaren had.

"Does she have a name?"

I turned and saw Alysen's gaze riveted to the woods beyond the gate.

"The pony, Eri, does she have a name?"

The pony had been in the village for nearly a dozen years, and I suspected it was a few years older than that.

"Spring Mist," I told her. The pony had been named for her hide and mane, both the color of early morning fog. Despite living in Nar for a year, Alysen obviously had not been around the village horses much—I could tell that from the unsure way she rode.

"Spring Mist. I like the name." She twisted her fingers in the pony's mane, a gesture I suspected was meant to give her more security on her mount.

"We'll travel slower than I'd prefer, Alysen. I want to keep Dazon from coming up lame or from suffering exhaustion." By the Green Ones, I'd not leave Dazon in this village of the dead!

Less than one hour after I'd come home to discover the massacre, I was leaving the Village Nar. Without looking back, Alysen and I made our way out the main gate, heading northwest.

I wondered if I would ever see home again.

4

NO PATH LED TO NANOO GAFNA'S HOME—TO ANY OF THE HIDDEN places of the Nanoo. Those who would deal with the witches had to watch the trees carefully for artfully crimped branches, symbols in the whorls, patches of gently scraped bark—all of those things serving as well as carved signs along the road to one who knew how to read them.

The way to Nanoo Gafna's was entrenched in my memory, and so I took barely passing notice of the signs. I was too preoccupied with visions of the Village Nar to pay much attention to my surroundings, too guilty that I'd buried no one . . . more guilty that I could well be to blame for all their deaths.

The way to the Nanoo's fen was seemingly known to Alysen as well, as she'd taken the lead. Or was she dipping into my mind and tugging the directions from me?

When I pulled myself back from the horror and grief and looked to the ground, I could tell that none of the riders had come this far into the woods. They'd turned around shortly after entering the treeline. I saw no signs of a scuffle where they'd stopped, and so I breathed easier about the fate of Nanoo Gafna. I did not believe they'd managed to catch her.

Before we took the first twist in the unseen path I signaled Alysen to stop, and I led Dazon well away and loosed his burden. I let the curl-horns lay stiff-legged on the ground. It was hard for a hunter such as myself to waste that supply of fresh meat. Still, to have left it at the village would have betrayed my return, and to carry it to the Nanoo was to invite evil to the witches. Slaughtered animals were a bane to them and dishonored the gods they revered. No trace of animal flesh passed their lips, lest they risk losing their arcane powers. I knew woodland creatures would rejoice to find the curl-horn carcasses and would feast—at least that was some consolation for my morning's hunting efforts.

I cut off a strip of meat and wrapped it in a piece of hide I pulled loose.

Alysen watched me, curious.

"I will cook this later, when we stop for the evening," I told her.

I raised my head and stared into the growing shadows, as the afternoon continued to advance. I got on the cob and nodded for Alysen to continue, Dazon and the draft drifting in behind, neither needing a tether. Sometime later, as the sun edged lower, its rays turning the water standing in a marshy land golden, we passed a lone willow birch.

"Wait, Alysen." Not speaking the ancient words above a whisper, I repeated the Gift-Give ritual Nanoo Gafna had taught me years ago.

"*Haltha yorin tildreth.*" I traced a pattern in the air that symbolized a weeping branch stretching to the ground. "*Drathra*

yorin soldreth hal." I held my hand parallel to the earth and
blew across my palm.

Alysen slipped from the back of the pony and watched. Her
eyebrows were raised, but she didn't ask any questions. Perhaps she knew I spoke a salute to the spirits of the Nanoo who
rested beneath the earth. I was certainly not inclined to share
this particular bit of wyse knowledge with the girl—I doubted
she knew it. And I concentrated to keep my thoughts hidden
from her prying mind.

I dismounted and took the reins of the cob, and signaled
Dazon to follow; we treaded softly now along the hidden way.
It was nearing sunset, and I believed that a storm was gathering above the forest canopy, intending to add to the wetness of
this place. I could smell the water heavy in the air, stagnant
pools lying beyond my sight, the dampness thick in fallen, rotting trees. The scent of this place was strong, and while not
pleasant, it was not odious. It was full of life and magic and old
things, and I breathed the air deep into my lungs and held it as
long as I could.

"We're being watched," Alysen said. "I can feel it."

"Aye, girl. We have been for quite some time." I breathed
again and noted that Alysen tried to copy me. "The forest itself watches us."

All ancient woods had inhabitants, guardians who did not
share the life span of humankind. The guardians were as old
as the eldest trees, perhaps were the trees themselves. They
didn't worry me, rather they gave me a measure of comfort. I
led the horses between the trunks of two gray ash trees that
stretched so high above I lost them in the canopy and the
darkness.

"I will help you!" The cry came from Alysen, and startled me. She repeated it, sundering the silence of the woods.

I whirled to face her and get her to hush, but she dropped the reins of her pony and was by me in an instant, crashing through the brush ahead, feet slapping against the marshy loam. I had not been prepared for her to shoulder me aside, and my attempt to grab her came late, my fingers closing only on damp air.

I knew the Nanoo's clearing was roughly two miles away, and I worried that Alysen might reach it before me and break the witch's protocol if she charged in uninvited. So I dropped the reins, too. I knew Dazon would follow me, likely causing the other horses to join him. I chased after her, intending to reach her and bring her down before she made the clearing.

I caught up to her quickly, but she was nimble and dodged me, racing ahead despite the shadows and the danger laden in this venerable fen. She narrowly avoided slamming into a stone pillar greened with thick moss. The ground was terribly spongy here and sucked at my feet.

Dazon nickered inches behind me, and I slowed. I wanted to catch Alysen, but I'd do neither of us any good if I stumbled into a bog.

"Easy, my friend." I repeated it, slightly louder. "Careful."

Dazon complied, planting his four hooves heavily. I knew the horse well, and knew his will agreed with mine at the moment. I drew my fingers down his neck, where the hair was roughened by sweat. He wuffled softly.

Moving steadily, I led him through a stand of trees, the draft, cob, and fell pony plodding behind. I couldn't see Alysen's boot prints here, but I could see where bushes and low-hanging tree limbs had been disturbed in her haste.

We traveled a little more than half a mile before I slowed the pace further. It was getting difficult to see, because of the numerous trees and dense canopy, and more so difficult to spot Alysen's signs. Still, I had no worry that I would find the girl, as I knew where she was headed. But I knew reaching her before she got to the Nanoo was unlikely now.

With each step, I thought about the dead Village Nar and Lord Purvis, and I prayed that he would pay in blood for what he did this day. At my belt swung the two sheathed knives of different lengths, and my chain was hooked there, too—one of these weapons I would use to kill Lord Purvis, the demon-of-a-man.

I could use a sword, Bastien had taught me well, and now I wondered if I should have taken one from his office. But a sword was considered a noble's weapon, and in some places there were laws against carrying such unless your birthright permitted it. Should I have taken a weapon for Alysen? Or a leather vest to protect her like light armor would? Her cloak was bulky, but would not suffice against weapons.

No, she wasn't trained with weapons. Carrying one might only put her at risk. She wouldn't need weapons or armor if I could get her safely into the hands of the Nanoo . . . or at this speed, if she could get herself there.

I heard her then, moving clumsily through the brush ahead and to the south—not toward the Nanoo village. Where was she going?

I listened intently to make certain she hadn't gotten too far ahead. Then I couldn't hear her any longer. At first I thought she must have stopped, hopefully waiting for me.

I looked over my shoulder to Dazon. He'd started to snort

nervously. I felt a prickling sensation on the back of my neck, and I glanced at the fell pony. She was nervous, too. The cob and draft had found sweet grass to eat and were unaffected. I turned to face the woods in front of me again and tentatively opened my mouth.

I tasted the heady loam of the spongy earth beneath my feet, rich from recent rains. I tasted the moldy, fusty scent of rotting wood. Nothing seemed amiss. But something looked wrong. Straining through the shadows, I saw the way ahead was blocked by a tight weave of thorny branches.

Had Alysen found a way through that weave?

I praised the Green Ones that I'd thought to take the hunter's wood ax. I retrieved it from the half-pocket in my pack and faced the wall of thorns. Close to it, I could see that there was a wide path that ran parallel to it, heading west. Perhaps the woods wanted me to follow this path. I knelt and felt boot prints—Alysen had come this way. I thought I'd been through every bit of these woods before, and I had not remembered such an impenetrable thicket. But I had not been this way for nearly a year.

Suddenly I heard a sharp cry—and yet I didn't hear anything.

The call had been within my head, an eerie, inhuman sound that was repeated.

Then there was a profound silence.

I took a step back from the weave to get a better look at it, and I stumbled against Dazon. My eyes grew wide to see the very grass acting like hundreds of miniature serpents, stretching up and writhing around my ankles. The enchanted grass couldn't hold me fast, I was too strong for it. I turned to look at the other horses. I would lead them out of here, return for

Alysen, and . . . Something stopped me, a shiver that raced down my back.

I didn't *hear* anything, not Dazon breathing, not the rustle of the branches in the breeze, not even the thundering of my heart. The unnatural silence festered within me and I sucked in a great gulp of air. I didn't hear my gasp. I truly didn't hear anything.

Dazon's nostrils flared, and he swung his neck, snapping with his yellow teeth. He raised one foot, tearing the grass around his shank, then slamming the hoof down as if he were a war horse with pointed battle shoes meant to savage something on the ground in front of him.

I swung the small ax so that its flat head smacked heavily against the palm of my hand. There was sound, I heard it, though it was far softer than it should have been.

Dazon showed his teeth again and lifted both hooves, rearing back, tearing more grass, and slamming them down, sending up a spray of water from the marshy ground. The other horses were agitated now, too.

"No!" I put all the volume I could muster into the word, and though it came out as a whisper, the horses held. Bastien had trained them well, lessoning me along with them. Moving deliberately, with no betrayal of haste, I placed my free hand on Dazon's head so that my fingers were flat against the blaze between his eyes.

Then I searched within myself, calling on my wyse-power so I could communicate with him.

Again I heard the cry, and again it came from inside my head and far from this clearing. Still, my ears took in only the odd silence of this place.

I studied Dazon, standing as if he'd been carved from wood, allowing the grass to wrap around his shanks again. The other horses copied his pose, keeping their eyes on me, though their nostrils flared with worry.

"Wait here," I mouthed, intending the order for all the horses and praying they would not bolt.

I approached the weave, nearly stumbling again when the vine of some creeping flower twisted up my ankle. I hacked at the vine with the ax and continued, stopping just before the weave. I looked to the parallel path, which I could tell ran straight for only a few yards. The failing light made it impossible to see more than a dozen feet.

"I will be back soon," I shouted to the horses. I prayed they heard the whisper that came out. Then I took the path, intending to follow it along the wall of thorns for only a few minutes, just until I could find the girl.

Why did Alysen rush away from me? And why charge down this path? How could she not have seen the oddness and the danger in these woods?

I cut around one curve and then another and another, realizing I was almost doubling back on myself and worrying about the horses—and Alysen. Then I called upon the wysepower, channeling it rapidly. I extended my tongue just beyond my lips, tasting the air. I detected a sharp sourness and the sickening foulness of old death.

I looked to the wall of thorns and crouched at the base. It was as if they'd been deliberately planted and nurtured by magic. I turned to retrace my steps, discovering that another wall had sprung up behind me. I felt my chest grow tight and I spun back, discovering that the path ahead now led to the edge of a sunken cup filled with short growth still yellow from a harsh winter. At least the light was better in the cup, from a gap in the canopy above it.

Alysen knelt in the center of the depression, only partially cloaked in the shadows from the wall of thorns that grew higher at the margins.

A mix of emotions flooded me—anger that she'd run ahead, terror that something would happen to her in these woods before I could get her to the Nanoo, concern for Dazon, and wonder at the enchanted thorny wall.

I called her name, but no sound came out. I called again, louder, detecting a whisper that couldn't have carried beyond a hand's breadth in front of my face.

I edged closer, drawing a knife with my free hand and looking furtively to my right and left, hoping to spy something in the weave to explain the silence—and at the same time hoping nothing was there. Each step was difficult, as the grass was thicker and taller here, and it fought with unnatural strength to hold me in place.

Eventually I reached the edge of the cup, looking back to confirm what I'd feared—the wall was growing behind me, shutting off the way to Dazon and the other horses.

I heard sound now, faint as if it came from afar, far distance. It was a cry, like I'd heard in my head minutes ago, filled with pain and panic. Now, however, I could hear it with my ears, though barely. And I could tell it was coming from a small creature in front of Alysen.

I stepped into the cup, walking down the side and struggling with each step against the grass and vines that continued to grasp at me. Closer to Alysen, I saw that she wore gloves, and that they were torn from a tangle of vines she pulled at. Like the wall, these vines had thorns but appeared far more supple. As I came closer still, I stared unblinking. She pulled one vine loose and held it as it twisted vigorously and tried to wrap back around the creature.

A moment more and I was in front of her and the small beast, bending over and sheathing the knife, then gripping the whip length she held. She did not look up at me, but nodded to confirm my presence. She pulled another vine away and shouted. I strained to hear her.

"Watch for the white thorns. I think they carry some poison. Look to the creature's leg."

The stem broke away from Alysen, writhing back and forth as if the dark green length was part of a sentient thing. I brought the ax down on it and was rewarded with a shower of sticky, stinking sap. The smell was so strong that it settled firmly in my mouth, causing me to gag. The horrid scent was nearly overpowering, and I had to concentrate to keep on my feet.

I brought the ax down again and again, cutting all the way through the wicked tendril. I picked up the broken vine and hurled it away, feeling a thick, oily sap running down my arm. The sap was the source of the overpowering smell, and I felt myself swoon. I pulled on the arcane strength of my wyse-power and barely managed to force the scent away before it completely overwhelmed me.

By the Green Ones, how could I best this . . . thing?

5

THERE WAS CONSIDERABLE MAGIC — AND MALICE — IN THE VINES, else their odor would not have struck me so. I continued to use the wyse, but this time rather than scenting and tasting for danger, I implored it to keep the oppressive scent from rendering me unconscious. I could not force it away altogether, nor could I get the taste completely out of my mouth. So I worked faster, hacking at the next length of vine Alysen pulled free. A few more vines sheared, and I could better see the strangeness of the creature.

A bird? Not like any I'd seen before.

The creature's fear was palpable. Round eyes looking too large for its diminutive, feather-covered sphere of a head stared up at me. Stared through me—as I did not believe the little beast actually saw anything, so terror-stricken it seemed. From an oddly curved beak came a sound that was close to a whimper, the mewling I'd heard earlier in my head.

Blood-crusted silvery feathers covered its head, shoulders, and webbed wings. Fur covered the rest of it, a mottled gray-white not unlike the dappling on Alysen's pony. It had sharp claws at the ends of its wings, and at the ends of its stubby legs. Its body was the size of a rock melon, though tapering near its neck.

Alysen leaned forward a little, carefully working to detach another confining stem that had wrapped around its chest. I hacked at the offending vine with the ax, cringing when the potent sap threatened my enhanced senses again. I don't know if Alysen realized I was in distress, but she worked faster now, pulling away the smallest vines, yanking them out of the ground and throwing them over her shoulder.

When nearly all these threadlike vines were pulled away, she reached into a pouch at her belt and pulled out what looked like a pinch of withered leaves. She held it over the bird-creature, a scarce fingernail distance from the formidable-looking beak. At the same time, she started rocking back and forth and crooning, the sound so soft I was certain that I only imagined it. Some of the thread-vines had wrapped around my legs, but there was none holding Alysen. I cut at the vines that held me, while I watched her and the feathered beast.

The creature did not blink, just kept staring with those wide, frightened eyes. But it moved. It snapped its beak, making a grab for Alysen's fingers. My hand shot out to snatch Alysen's arm away and pull her out of reach of the creature. But she struck back at me with her other hand, then pushed. I tottered, weak from the malign smells of this enchanted place.

Once more the beak made a move to grab her fingers.

"Alysen," I shouted. "Get away!"

I could visualize her hand being torn into tattered strips of flesh, in spite of the glove she wore.

Alysen might not have heard me, for she didn't look in my direction. She shook her head violently as the beak scraped her gloved palm. What she had offered the beast was gone, save for some fragment of a dried leaf.

The creature stiffened, and Alysen tried to pull away the rest of the thread-vines that held it around what passed for its shoulders. Finally she looked my way.

"Eri!" Her shout was a hush. "Cut it free!" Despite its softness, her voice had the same commanding tone as Bastien's had held on occasion.

I didn't argue; this wasn't the time or the place for it. I used my ax to slice through the rest of the plant, the stench from the sap growing stronger with each cut. I coughed once, breathed deep, and started coughing again as if I were in the throes of a lung sickness. I drew back, coughing deeper still and feeling as if my chest had caught fire, growing weak. Still, I fought the vines, crushing some under my boots as they writhed back toward the creature.

A moment later, struggling for breath, I helped Alysen lift the creature. I dropped the ax and cradled the thing in my arms. Alysen picked up the ax and walked around me and up the side of the cup. She hesitated a moment at the wall of thorns that had grown up to block the path we'd taken to get here. Then she followed the lip of the cup around to the east, pulling with each step as small vines clutched at her feet. Though I was fatigued and nauseous, I now had an easier time pulling free of the brush than I had before.

She found a gap in the wall and slipped through it. There was so little light—just a world of shifting bands of blacks and grays, the tree trunks the darkest slashes. I'm not sure how we found our way back to Dazon and the other horses. It took us quite awhile, and maybe it was only luck that brought us to the clearing. Alysen used the ax to cut at the thickest vines that twined around the horses' shanks, then she and the horses followed me away from this horrid place.

I didn't stop until I could hear my ragged breath and the grass no longer whipped around my feet. Then I sagged to my knees, still holding the creature close and feeling its warmth through my clothes. The shadows were not so thick here, as we'd found our way to another clearing, this one a little wetter than what we'd already crossed. At its edge ran a stream that had overflowed its banks.

I sat the creature on the soggy ground in front of me. Alysen was quick to join us, but she stood, bent over and staring at the thing. I could see it far better here, and its appearance sent a shiver down my back. It was a singular creature, like nothing I'd ever glimpsed before.

The claws at the ends of its wings were actually tiny hands, like some primate's. And the feet at the ends of its legs were not birdlike, in fact they looked almost human—save for the curling talons, which withdrew and extended while we watched.

Alysen sprinted to the draft horse, searching through one of her bags. I returned my attention to the creature. What I'd first thought wings were actually membranes like those a tree squirrel possessed. So the creature could glide and grip branches.

"What manner of beast are you?"

It looked at me and made a mewling sound, which I could hear plainly. The noise echoed inside my head.

"And what caused the deadness in those woods, making it so difficult to hear? Why the writhing grass, and the vines with the foul sap? Why did Alysen run from me and to you, little beast? Did she hear you calling out? What magic is in her? Is there magic in you?" The last two questions I'd asked softly so Alysen couldn't hear.

A moment more and Alysen ran back, squatting opposite me and trying not to get her dress soaked—a futile attempt, as it was already damp and dirty. She started crooning again, louder and musical, and I found myself enjoying it. She held a small jar, uncorked it, and put some paste on her fingers. Crooning a different tune now, she began rubbing the unguent on the creature's worst wounds. I had not known that Alysen possessed wyse healing magic. But then, I didn't know much about her at all.

As I listened, I looked skyward. The sun had set and twilight was nearing, and I wanted to find someplace safer to stay. This clearing was too close to the thorny walls and twisting grass, and the place of unnerving silence.

We must have shelter of some sort, I told myself. I did not believe we could reach the Nanoo's Standing Stones soon enough for my satisfaction now, even though they were only a few miles from here. We'd have to find a way around the thorny walls, and that would take quite some time. I decided to scout for something suitable closer; perhaps one of the massive willow trees that dotted the woods could provide shelter enough.

"Alysen, stay here with . . . that creature and with the horses. I will return."

She didn't look up or halt her crooning, and I refused to wait until she gave me her full attention. So I headed west, following the swollen creek. I wanted to stay near fresh water—that would be a necessity for the horses. I listened to the creek's pleasant babbling, and I breathed deep. The stench from that malicious weave and the grabbing vines was lessening. A dozen steps more and the stench was nearly gone. I took a few more long steps, inhaled, and extended the tip of my tongue.

I shivered.

By chance I'd thought to bring the ax with me, and had stuck it in my belt. It could be useful if I came across any more thorny walls. Though against the peril I scented now, the half-size ax would be as useful as trying to bring down one of the ancient, giant trees with it.

The scent I tasted was a fose-bear.

Of all the dangers in the depths of this old forest—the dangers known to most of those who lived near its boundaries—the fose-bears were the worst. Mountains of dusty brown fur, they held rule here. There were tales of other strange and monstrous creatures, glimpsed here and there, set to song and stories. But the fose-bears were more than tales; they were horribly real, intelligent, formidable, and always hungry.

I began to retreat, one cautious backward step at a time, keeping my gaze on the westward flow of the creek and continuing to taste the breeze. Had the air not been so fouled by the weave of plants, and had the sap from the vines not so choked my senses, I would have tasted the bear sooner.

I shivered again.

And if I could detect the presence of that monster by using my wyse-sense, no doubt it could smell me in return. The senses of beasts are far superior, I believed, to my magically enhanced abilities.

Again I entered the slight clearing. Alysen had stopped her

crooning and spread more healing salve down the bird-beast's shoulders. She noticed me, and I gave her a warning signal, then I went directly to Dazon. I reached into my pack and re-trieved a thong attached to a cylinder. I scowled as I carefully unscrewed one end. Bastien early on had impressed on me the need for keeping weapons always ready at hand. But never before had I cause to use this one. There existed a chance that the contents had suffered through age.

"A fose-bear?" Alysen kept her voice low. It was clear she had pulled the worry from my mind. "There's a fose-bear out there?"

The feathered creature in front of her made no attempt to copy her quiet. The crook bill opened, and it was far from a silent cry that issued forth. The sound was harsh, high-pitched, and it cut loudly through the clearing.

6

EVEN THOUGH THE BIRD-CREATURE WAS SLEEKED DOWN WITH the healing salve, the feathers stirred and puffed until its face seemed twice as large as it had a heartbeat before. The creature struggled to free itself from Alysen's hold and managed to sit up.

I don't know why I then made the choice I did.

I raced toward Alysen and knelt in front of her, cylinder in my hand. I looked nowhere but straight into the great round eyes of the feathered beast. I drew upon that same fraction of talent as I had to calm Dazon earlier. This time I visualized something that might enthrall a bird, as the creature was part that. I had to quiet it, lest it bring the fose-bear directly to us because of its high-pitched squawks.

I quickly coaxed my wyse-sense in the growing darkness, and in my mind it manifested as a bright beacon of light. In the air in front of me, however, it blossomed as a pale blue globe the size of a large apple, with undulating tendrils. Motes of a darker blue light flickered at the margins. I took the cylinder and touched it to the globe, then I raised the cylinder and poured out its contents. The globe flickered and crackled and popped like a diminutive fire.

The creature's bill opened again, but this time no cry issued forth. It was captivated by the simple magic of the light-ball, and its beak was open in surprise and awe, and its great, dark eyes locked on to the glow.

Alysen slid an arm around what passed for the creature's shoulders. It did not break its gaze upon my magic, but it settled back a little, accepting Alysen's gentle grip. Then it slowly raised a webbed arm, its small hand held out, palm up and talons flexing, reaching for the ball.

I wrapped my mind around the blue glow and tugged a piece of it away, shaping it into a ball the size of a cherry and letting that piece come to rest on the creature's upturned palm. It purred softly and studied the small glow.

"Leafbud," Alysen whispered. "Protect my new friend with a leafbud."

"That is what I intend to do," I returned, "if the powder Bastien gave me is strong enough. There is a fose-bear out there and . . ." I tasted the air, trying to determine how far away the bear prowled. I scented the monster, but it was not yet threateningly close. Perhaps it hadn't picked up my own scent and I'd worried for nothing. Still, I'd already emptied the powder into my wyse-globe.

I sucked in a breath and looked to the larger blue glow. I changed its shape, forming a pointed stick that dripped dark blue motes and resembled a quill pen. I slid one hand under the creature's left paw to steady it, then I mentally touched my magical pen to its right paw, outlining a leaf with a faint pulse of color. The sigil flashed bright then melted into its skin, leaving no trace. The intent of the leafbud enchantment was to cover the creature's odor, replacing it with the scent of a fresh, green, uncurling leaf.

I did not stop there. Next I directed the pen to draw a similar symbol on Alysen's forehead, then on mine. The horses across the clearing, my magic could not reach. Too, I sensed the powder had been used up on these three sigils, and so I let the pen dissolve.

The creature remained entranced with the small glowing orb on its right palm, apparently oblivious to the arcane mark I'd placed upon it.

"I've named it," Alysen said. "Grazti."

If the name carried some meaning or significance, I didn't know it. I released the magic behind the small globe in Grazti's hand. The creature blinked furiously, surprised and disappointed, then turned its attention to the other palm, sniffing where I'd penned the image of the leaf.

"The fose-bear." I drew Alysen's attention away from the creature. "The horses still carry scent, and—"

"I trust your leafbud, Eri." She looked to the horses, then back to the creature. "Grazti is beautiful, don't you agree?"

I didn't answer that, but I stretched out my hands. The small beast did not avoid my touch when I set my fingertips against the greasy feathers just above and between its eyes. As with Dazon, I strove to communicate, desiring to learn the creature's intelligence. I tried to pick up its emotions and the concepts it thought about. Words were meaningless, but I detected goodwill, the need for fellowship, uncertainty of the future, and the sense that it had made a promise. To Alysen? To another of its kind? The thoughts seemed distorted, like speech that sounded muffled. I picked up the hint of urgency or purpose.

I formed a message as best I could, that I would try to keep it safe, as I intended to keep Alysen safe. Perhaps I also would take the creature to the Nanoo.

"We will leave this place," I told the creature. "Despite the coming darkness, we will travel around the weave and toward the Nanoo."

I rose, and Alysen clutched the creature to her with one arm. With the other, she pulled a tuft of grass from the ground and rubbed it between her fingers and across her jerkin, then extended the blades to me.

I shook my head, and she looked perplexed that I didn't understand whatever magic she evoked. I touched her forehead, flicking back the end of a wandering curl.

"I am remiss in my task to protect you, Alysen. I have let us tarry here too long, given the presence of a fose-bear."

"I am not afraid of that, Eri. You cast the leafbud, and I have this." She gathered more thick blades with her free hand, her mouth working as she did, reciting a spell.

Alysen stood and stepped close, brought the broken grass blades up, trying to wipe them across my forehead. Again I shook my head, wanting no part of magic I did not understand, or if it wasn't magic, an unknown ritual. Perhaps grass-rubbing was a significant thing for the House of Geer.

I went to Dazon, opening my mouth and searching for evidence of the fose-bear. It was a little closer, and I knew Dazon sensed it, too; his nostrils quivered nervously and he made a soft snorting sound. I tasted his fear, then the fear of the other horses. They started nickering anxiously.

Would the monster come into the clearing? Was it tracking me, though it could not pick up my odor now because of the leafbud? Was it following something else or nothing at all? Had it heard the horses?

"Kyrols, neme're. Kyrols." Alysen spoke words unfamiliar to me, yet with the familiar ring of wyse magic.

She rubbed the grass blades against the forehead of her pony, Spring Mist. Then against the blaze on the muzzle of the draft and then the cob, all the while her mouth working, and all the while clutching the feathered creature to her. The horses whinnied and tossed their heads, the cob pawing at the ground. Certainly the fose-bear would have heard that.

Alysen came toward me, then past me, walking to Dazon's front and extending the crumpled blades. Without asking my permission, she wiped the grass against his muzzle, then she whirled and brushed the grass against my exposed arm.

She might have held an icicle in her hand, so did that thrust of cold arc into my skin and travel up my arm and over my shoulder, settling in my head and causing it to ache briefly. It was a ward, not a ritual or simple magic she'd called. That a girl her age knew such startled me, as did her method of delivery. Had she proper manners in the wyse, she would have explained what the grass and her words were for . . . and the purpose behind the ward.

I caught my lower lip between my teeth, anger flaring at Alysen, then anger at myself—for I had a fleeting thought that it was wrong to spare the life of a rude girl like this over the life of Lady Ewaren.

Alysen's eyes were slits staring at me.

How much of my mind was she reading?

7

"GREEN GROW THE LEAVES, STRONG GROWS THE TRUNK." ALYSEN was speaking the words in a singsong fashion to finish her warding. "Roar on, dread flyer, roar on needled wings. Ready your fangs to promise death. Breathe, breathe the cloud come to ground."

I listened to her, hearing something else intrude, a chittering, light and distinct, like a squirrel might make. But it held to a pattern, and I realized it was part of the warding. Bastien had never taught me a ward spell; that magic was more the badge of the Nanoo. No doubt this was something she'd learned from Gafna.

> *Green, green, green grow the leaves*
> *Strong, ever stronger grows the trunk.*
> *Roar on loudly, dread flyer of the loam.*
> *Roar on sharply needled wings.*
> *Ready your fangs to promise death.*
> *Breathe, breathe, breathe wildly the cloud come to ground.*

I heard her whisper, "Protect us." But I did not see her lips move. Then the chittering grew louder, and she hummed and rocked on the balls of her feet.

I had no clue what the chitterings and music meant, bonded to this ritual of hers. The horses were silent, engrossed in Alysen. The creature she'd named Grazti had its beak open, eyes fixed on the girl's mouth.

Alysen repeated the words, varying them slightly and slowing the cadence. Around us a fog rose, thickening as it spread outward. I had no doubt it was caused by Alysen, but I did not know its purpose. A ghostly light shed from her eyes and flowed down her arms, then her legs, moving away from her and joining the mist, lightening it.

That the fose-bear had not yet reached us was strange. It must have picked up my scent when I followed the creek. There! At the far edge of the clearing the brush was quivering.

A roar deafeningly loud filled the clearing. I felt the earth rumble beneath my feet when the roar sounded again. As one, the horses reared. I lashed out, grabbing the reins of the cob and Dazon, seeing Alysen snatch the reins of the pony with her free hand. I called to the draft horse, demanding that she stay. She reared once more, then tossed her head back and whinnied fearfully. She held . . . but for how long?

I looked to the far edge of the clearing, just as the monster tramped through the bushes, cracking twigs and limbs and making the earth shake with each step. My throat tightened and my limbs went numb. Never had I felt such bone-chilling fear.

Giant eyes blazed red-orange like leaping flames, and when

it opened its cavernous maw, I smelled an intense sulfurous stench. It had teeth longer than my hand, curved and yellow and shining dully in the lightened mist, and I knew one bite would spell the end of any creature. A mountain of furred flesh, it rose on its hind legs, more than a dozen feet tall and half again that wide.

The ground continued to tremble, the horses reared, and Dazon and the cob tore the reins from my numb fingers. I didn't turn around, I knew they'd bolted. A great part of me wanted to flee with them.

I opened my mouth to say something, but no sound came out.

The monster roared again, spittle flying from its massive jaws, saliva dripping down to the ground and hissing in the magic fog. Its fur was at the same time brown and black, bands of darkness that shifted when its muscles tensed. Its forepaws crooked before its heavy paunch, revealing knifepoint claws.

At my side, Alysen fell to her knees, still managing to hold on to Grazti.

Every tale I'd heard about the fose-bear paled beside the real monster. I knew that the stories could not have been told by someone who'd been this close to one of the bears. Walking on its hind legs it took a step toward us, then another. My body shook, though my mind demanded that I act.

Run, I screamed to myself. *Grab Alysen and run.*

But my feet would not cooperate; they were rooted to the ground. A thought flickered—perhaps the magic of the monster let it trap its prey thus, deafening them and scaring them into total inactivity.

Somehow, over my pounding heart and the thrumming of the fose-bear's footsteps, I heard Alysen.

Green, green, green grow the leaves
Strong, ever stronger grows the trunk.
Roar on loudly, dread flyer of the loam.
Roar on sharply needled wings.
Ready your fangs to promise death.
Breathe, breathe, breathe wildly the cloud come to
    ground.

This time when the fose-bear roared, it sounded different, menacing still—as even the exhalation of breath would sound menacing from such a mountain. But it had a different tone, and were I not frozen so, I would have used my wyse-sense to learn what that tone meant.

A moment more, however, and I guessed the roar was one of consternation and shock. Fear, too? No, I knew such a creature incapable of that.

The mist was losing its translucency. In the passing of a few heartbeats it became opaque, and it started changing from a pale white-gray to the dark gray of a rain cloud. It curled around the fose-bear, which had stopped walking toward us. It curled higher, wrapping around its huge waist and rolling higher still, thickening and climbing until only the enormous head of the monster remained clear to my sight.

Never did the fose-bear's fiery red-orange eyes blink. But they simmered with fury, shining like glowing coals.

My tongue smarted under the heat of rage that emanated from the bear. Its fiery anger stretched across the clearing to hit me like a hard fist. The monster's fury at its misty prison was boundless and as palpable as anything I'd felt.

Lines of light spiraled around the fose-bear in the solid mist, then spun faster and faster, wrapping tight and urging the mist up to cover the head and the blaze-bright eyes. I blinked and gasped, steadied myself, and pressed a palm against the heart thundering in my chest.

"Alysen." It took me effort to get the word out. "Alysen, we need to . . ."

The mist had become a pillar, nearly twenty feet tall and looking like stone, cored by the fose-bear, which continued to roar, muted now but no less angry. The ground still trembled from its wrath.

The leafbud I'd fashioned kept the monster from smelling us, but it had sighted us. The magical ward Alysen had conjured was incredible, but I knew the fose-bear would break it down.

"Alysen, we must move. Now." I tugged her to her feet and pushed her ahead of me. The fleeing horses had made a path, one easy to follow. "Hurry."

She didn't argue, just clutched Grazti tight and ran as fast as her legs could manage.

8

FINDING THE HORSES PRESENTED LITTLE PROBLEM. FOLLOWING the trail they'd made, we came back to that part of the woods with the twisting vines and the wall of thorns. They were grazing on the very strands of grass that sought to hold them tight to the earth, and I wondered what the grass would do to their stomachs.

Alysen tried to hold Grazti, while at the same time pull at the grass around the pony's hooves. I watched her hacking at the grass with my ax, then leading Dazon far enough away where the grass stopped grasping. I worked quickly to free the cob and the draft, then I helped Alysen with the pony.

"We need to move." Again, I had to shout the words so she could hear them as whispers.

What was amiss with this part of the forest?

Again my mind whirled with the thoughts of what magic so possessed this place that it deadened sound and turned the grass into tiny snakes.

"That ward you called is powerful magic, Alysen, but I don't trust it to hold that monster much longer."

"Then where do we go, Eri?"

I barely heard her words, and so I gestured to Dazon. She followed me to the horse, struggling to tug the pony with her, while still carrying Grazti. I did not help her. When we could hear better, I pointed straight north.

"We can't cut through that thorny weave, not in any amount of reasonable time, Alysen. That fose-bear will find us, and all of those thorns will be insignificant to the fangs of a beast that size. We cannot go back to the clearing where the fose-bear is, nor can we return to Nar. My intention still is to take you to Nanoo Gafna, and so we will go this way."

We were so close to the Nanoo, about two miles. But it might well have been one hundred because of the thorns.

"Out of the way," she said simply. "We have to go well out of our way." She didn't meet my gaze; she stared into the eyes of the bird-creature. "Certainly we won't reach the heart of the fen until tomorrow at the earliest because we have to go around."

"Better that than ending up in the belly of that monster."

"Everyone dies," Alysen whispered.

I glared at her, then looked to Dazon. He wore his fatigue like a second skin. "Come on, girl." I got on the cob and watched Dazon fall in behind it. My stomach grumbled from hunger, and I thought about the meat I'd sliced from the curl-horn. The fose-bear so close, I wouldn't stop to cook it tonight, and so with regret I reached behind me and pulled it from the pack and tossed it on the ground, hoping it would at least feed some insects.

"You don't like me, do you, Eri?" Alysen had made no move to get on the pony.

I let out a great sigh and turned in the saddle, reaching both hands down and wiggling my fingers. "Give me that beast, Alysen. Easier for you if I carry it while we ride."

"You don't like me, do you?" Almost reluctantly, she handed me the creature, the greasy mixture she'd applied to its wounds smeared over my fingers, and I nearly dropped it. I settled it carefully between me and the cob's neck.

"Alysen, I don't really know you. We lived in the same village, but our lives were separate."

"You were never around much, Eri. Always hunting or with Bastien. Even after he died, you went off hunting on your own." She stood by the pony, still making no move to get on its back. "Why don't you like me?"

"Alysen, I don't know you well enough to like you or dislike you."

She looked over her shoulder, her eyes fixed steadily on the trail we'd made leaving the clearing with the fose-bear. "Can you tree-see, Eri? Is that beyond you?"

"Yes, I can tree-see, Alysen, but not now. There's the fose-bear to consider. We need to—"

She rocked back and forth on the balls of her feet and brought her hands up. Facing the trail, she placed her thumbs together and started mumbling singsong words. I let out a great, exasperated breath.

"Alysen!" I said her name much louder than I'd intended. How did Nanoo Gafna and Lady Ewaren deal with this child? By the Green Ones, I hoped she'd minded them better. "Alysen, I will leave without you."

She drew her hands apart, a wavering blue line appearing between her thumbs and stretching as her hands continued to move. Then she brought her hands down and in, effectively drawing a box in the air. The blue outlined it.

Standing on her toes, the words tumbled faster from her lips. A gesture, and the trees that shone in the outlined square grew transparent. She'd cast the tree-see enchantment despite my admonishment to leave. And though I opened my mouth to scold her, I said nothing. I looked through the outline and to the clearing that came into focus . . . the place where the fose-bear remained trapped.

The mist column still held the great bear, though it shook, and I imagined feeling the ground tremble. Or *was* I imagining that? I tasted the air and immediately picked up the monster's scent, stronger in its still-growing rage. I felt the fear of the small woodland animals fleeing in all directions from it.

Overhead, hawks, crows, and small owls scattered. The shaking intensified, and I thought I saw cracks appearing in the solid mist. The pillar rocked back and forth, difficult to notice, but it was moving.

I gasped as the foggy pillar that held the bear fell forward, as if hurled by a giant shove. It rolled back and forth on the ground, wildly, and the cracks became more visible. My hunting knife was in my hand, the other was clenched on the cob's reins. We were far enough from the bear—for the moment—but still I clutched the weapon.

"That's it, Alysen. There is no more time. I will leave you." I meant the words this time, and perhaps she sensed that, as she turned and finally got on the pony.

I kneed the cob and flicked the reins. The horse required

no urging, fully realizing the threat and fearing for its life. It galloped north, faster than it should have given the darkness and the tangle of undergrowth and the promise of broken ground in the distance. But I did nothing to slow it. Dazon sped up, at the cob's shoulder and easily keeping pace despite being worn down by the long day. I listened for the draft, close behind, and for the fell pony. Though I'd made a vow to keep Alysen safe, I had meant what I said about leaving her. There was no use in all of us dying just to settle her curiosity about the fose-bear or the strength of her magic.

I felt a drag upon my energy, from being awake so long and from tasting the breeze so often. A cold pain announced itself in my head and quickly settled into a punishing ache. Would the Green Ones' will see us through until dawn?

Grazti whimpered and reached to its sides, grabbing the material of my leggings in its small hands. The creature prodded me with a claw, and when it had caught my attention, its wide, round eyes looking up into mine. It raised a webbed arm and pointed northeast. Grazti jabbed a squat finger with force for emphasis.

9

THE PATH THE BIRD-CREATURE INDICATED WAS NOT QUITE THE direction I'd intended to take. For some reason, however, I was willing to accept its guidance. We'd found Grazti in these woods, so perhaps the little beast was far more familiar with them . . . and I was far too tired not to consider its help.

The way slanted upward, and after well more than an hour of fast travel—I guessed at the passing of time because time and distance were fuzzy to me now—a section of the woods parted to make way for a small, rocky ridge. The ache in my head lessened, and I was entertaining thoughts that we'd managed to elude the fose-bear. The cob and Dazon appeared less nervous, too, though foam flecked Dazon's mouth from the exertion.

We needed to stop and rest.

The dark seemed more intense here because of the shadows cast from the stone and because the clouds were thickening overhead, blotting out most of the starlight. What scant light found its way to the ground was made ghostlike by a low-lying haze.

Just staring at the haze relaxed me a little. It was shifting layers, thin ribbons of pale blue and eggshell white, twisting ever so slowly in the breeze.

There is magic in the world beyond my wyse-sense and beyond what the Nanoo master. It is greater than anything I can conjure, ancient and complex, and at the same time it is simple. The magic is nature itself, the beautiful haze that eased my mind away from thoughts of the fose-bear and the dead village, from Lady Ewaren's corpse.

For the briefest instant I pictured the foot. . . .

There would be time to mourn, I promised myself, after Alysen and Grazti were with the Nanoo and I was on my own.

Then I let the haze hold my attention as the cob slowed, and Dazon slowed, and I heard the clip-clop of all the horses become rhythmic and almost restful. The peaceful night scene was lulling all of us, even Grazti.

All of us caught by the magic of the world.

I slipped from the cob's back, taking Grazti with me, cradling the creature in my left arm and holding the reins with my right. The cob would do well to travel for just a little while without my weight on his back.

So drained.

I felt my shoulders slump, and I rolled my head to work a crick out of my neck. I managed a shuffling walk as I kept my eyes trained on the rocky ridge and the ribbons of haze. The last bit of fear for the fose-bear drained away. I knew if the monster was intent on us, it would have caught us by now.

I strained to make out features in the ridge, a futile attempt for the most part, but I could see two high-standing fangs of rock, the space between them doubly dark. Grazti stabbed its stubby finger directly at the dark spot.

I paused, then took a step in that direction, nearly stumbled and with effort regained my balance. I was so very, very tired.

"This was once a road." Alysen's words startled me.

She was right; my boot heel scraped on a relatively smooth surface. I steadied myself against the cob. In that instant Grazti gave a determined push on my arm, and then another, and the creature was out of my hold and down on the ground. It held at my ankles, alternating between looking up at me and pointing to the dark space.

"Grazti wants us to go there," Alysen said. Then she moved her hands, quick, swift shifts here and there. No loom stood before her, but her motions were those of a weaver. Her fingers plucked at the air, drawing to her the ribbons of haze. It was as if she used the tendrils to craft something, the haze seeming to pass through her fingers, added to more ribbons, sparks of light emerging within them and growing brighter.

Grazti crouched at Alysen's ankles now, wide eyes fastened on the square of light she was weaving. She finished by drawing the last ribbon to her, now hardly more than an eggshell white thread, weaving it into place, then rolling all of it into a ball and holding it above her head and away from her body.

Her magical creation was as bright as a full moon, and it allowed us to see the gap between the gate rocks. The road we stood on twisted into that gap, and we could tell it was no flattened merchant's trail we stood on but an old thing of flat stones fitted together, the stones smooth from the long years.

"All right," I said. "Let us follow this old, old road and see where this bird-beast intends to lead us."

The road climbed as we neared the ridge, but it never presented a sharp angle that would give us weary travelers difficulty. By the time it ended at the gate rocks, my eyelids were fluttering and I was yawning. It was all I could do to keep setting one foot in front of the other and pushing on. Alysen was exhausted, too, her light-globe flickering. Grazti walked on its own, close to Alysen, sometimes darting a few feet ahead, then scampering back. The bird-creature had a rolling gait like a bulldog, but at times it reared back like a horse and took several steps on its hind feet.

"Eri, I'm tired." Alysen dropped the ball of energy and wilted.

Despite my own weariness, I caught her and held her up. After a moment, she steadied herself and I reached down and picked up the ball. The light was faint, but I focused on my wyse-sense and fueled the ball with my own fading energy. It brightened, and I put my arm around Alysen's shoulders. Supporting her, I held the ball as if it were a torch, and we shuffled ahead.

I knew if we didn't rest soon, we were indeed finished.

Grazti seemed familiar with the area and paused only a moment between the stone fangs before edging beyond them. A cave stretched beyond, massive and with a ceiling. Dazon and the other horses refused to pass through the fangs, until I handed the globe back to Alysen and tugged on their reins. I didn't want to leave Dazon outside, fearing he might stray. Once Dazon was in the cave, I brought in the other horses.

It looked as if the cave had been formed by an earthquake, a tumble of stones settling against one another, the walls end-locked at sharp angles. Grazti led us straight to a sheltering corner. I settled Alysen and the light-ball there, retrieving her blanket and spreading it out. She rolled onto it and fell instantly asleep.

I tugged the horses in close, took the packs and saddles off them, and then stretched out next to Alysen, too tired to bother with my own bedroll. The light-ball, no longer feeding off my energy, sputtered out.

Blackest black surrounded us, and I dreamed of the Village Nar, populated with corpses.

10

I AWOKE WARM, THE SUN FILTERING IN THROUGH THE CAVE mouth and stretching to touch me. Over my face hung a small black paw that bore the faintest outline of a leaf from my spell last night. Grazti's feathered face came closer. The greasy balm remained, and had done its work. The bird-creature looked completely healed.

I sat up and stared. Such a badly organized camp I'd made last night! Any Moonson would feel shame. In my exhaustion I'd haphazardly dropped the packs and the saddles off the horses. I'd made no sense of anything.

Water . . .

My mouth and throat demanded it.

Grazti withdrew at my stirring and trotted to the packs.

The bird-beast looked over its feathery shoulder at me. I couldn't read the creature's expression, but it apparently could read mine. It rummaged in the pile and retrieved one of the water bottles, grabbed it in a clawed hand, and returned on two feet to me, moving awkwardly for the weight of the bottle.

Grazti stopped short and dropped the bottle, then edged it toward me.

I picked it up eagerly and drank deep, relishing the feel of the water flowing down my dry throat. I forced a limit on myself and finally stopped, catching sight of Alysen.

"Lie-a-bed," she accused.

"That may be," I returned. "But I'm not a slug-a-bed."

Alysen brought from around her back a long, thick leaf filled with bulbs scraped clean of their skin. "Murrows," she said.

I reached for the nearest, smelled it as I brought it up to my lips. I didn't hesitate. I crunched, and the sweet-sour essence of the ground fruit filled my mouth. These nut-bulbs had not come from our supplies.

"Where . . . ?"

"I found them growing in the high grass along the ridge," she answered. "Not far from this cave."

This fruit was the food of nobles, I knew from the days I'd visited with my father last year. I'd not had it since then, and I savored each bite, calling on my enhanced sense of taste so I could thoroughly enjoy it. I could easily become drunk on it. Alysen ate one, too, enjoying it nearly as much as I.

Grazti, however, had other fare in mind. The bird-beast pounced with one hand and grabbed a beetle that had been skittering across the floor. Grazti held it up for inspection, then clamped its beak on the beetle and swallowed with a satisfied purr. Suddenly, Grazti's head snapped to one side; the creature was obviously listening to something outside the cave.

I hastily swallowed my mouthful of fruit and extended my tongue. The breeze that seeped into the cave carried the faint stench of the fose-bear, and this sent a shiver down my back. But it was not a strong smell, and the hunter in me knew the monster had not come this way, rather the breeze just held a reminder of it. I detected no other menace, and so I coaxed my wyse-sense to tug some of my energy so I could taste for other things.

I didn't get the chance.

Grazti gave a harsh, raucous cry that echoed off the nearest wall. The bird-beast repeated it, as if it were a broken string of words. And it was answered with the beating of wings. Shiny black insects the size of bats displayed a jewel-like luster in the sunlight.

"Death-eaters!" Alysen shouted, dropping her fruit and dropping prone to the cave floor.

They poured in from cracks in the ceiling, scavengers known to live in the woods and to come out only after the sunset. But the cave must have been dark enough for them, and they made straight for Alysen's leaf-tray of fruit.

They landed one after another on the wall near our niche, on the floor all around the nut-bulbs, wings folded and heads turned in our direction. They had no scent; this I knew from encountering them in the woods during evening hunts with Bastien.

But had I tasted the breeze earlier, searching for danger, I would have detected them . . . at least in this number. There were dozens and dozens of them, their hard-shelled bodies as long as my hand. Their legs clicked across the stone as they hurried to the fruit and fought over it. Their mandibles opened and closed. The ones on the wall started toward our packs, and this spurred me to action.

I leapt to my feet and crunched several beneath my boot heels as I rushed to our pile of belongings. I felt, through my leggings, several of them crawling on me. I shuddered; they were filthy things and said to be dangerous not because of their bite, which I was feeling now through the material on my legs and back, but because of the diseases they carried in the faint slime that covered their bodies.

Normally they feasted on the remains of animals, but I knew that when corpses were scarce they were capable of eating anything. Since there was no half-rotted feast here, they were going for our food—and perhaps us.

"Eri!" Alysen was rolling on the cave floor, trying to knock the insects off her. There were cuts on her arms and cheek, and I couldn't tell if they were from the stone floor or from the death-eaters.

I started stomping on the ones within reach, and brushing the ones off the packs. I didn't want them to get at our food supplies, but that wasn't paramount in my mind right now. I reached over Alysen's satchel and grabbed my weapons belt. I strapped it on and pulled my long knife from its sheath, then I used it to stab at the ones on the satchels. At the same time I continued stomping on them.

"Eri!"

I'd expected her to use a wyse spell to deal with the insects swarming her—she'd been so quick to use the magic last night. But it took concentration to shape wyse-energy, and I realized she couldn't concentrate with the insects crawling over her. I made my way toward her, crunching more as I went, flailing out with the knife when one flew off the wall and went straight for me.

I saw Grazti hopping and pecking at an insect. The bird-creature drove its beak down, splitting the death-eater in two and whooping in triumph.

"Stay still, Alysen!" I used the flat of the knife blade to brush the insects off the girl, then stepped on them and pierced their shells with the knife tip. Within a few moments she was free of the death-eaters, and I'd returned to our belongings, slaying the insects still crawling there.

I heard Alysen behind me reciting arcane words, and I knew she was starting another enchantment.

"Stop," I told her. "Magic does not answer everything. Save your energy for something more threatening than insects."

Her words faded and I heard her stomping the death-eaters, too.

I felt one bite my neck, and I cringed. I reached up with my free hand and grabbed it and threw it against the nearest wall. I'd killed more than half of them by the time they fluttered to the cave ceiling and found their way into cracks I hadn't noticed the night before.

"They are supposed to be scavengers," Alysen grumbled.

"Hungry enough to go for living things," I returned as I looked over my arms and felt my neck.

I'd been bitten several times, and I suspected Alysen had also. There might be nothing to worry about; catching a disease from them was not a certain thing. Still, I would not take a chance on it. "Where you found the ground fruit, Alysen, were there other plants growing, like the kinds around the Village Nar?"

She looked at me oddly, then nodded, and brushed at the cave floor with her feet to clear the broken death-eaters off her blanket. "Why? Why think of plants and fruit where there's all . . . this to deal with?" she asked after a moment. She didn't raise her head, just kept on brushing at the insects, trying to push them into a pile. Grazti helped her, munching on one of the death-eaters as it went, making a sucking noise to get the juice out of the shell. "Why do you want to know about the plants, Eri? There's more fruit there, but not much of it is ripe."

"Not for the fruit," I returned.

Alysen raised her head then, the expression on her face a mix of surprise and pain. She swayed and fixed me with a piercing look. I took a long stride to her, and she caught at my upper arm. She only now realized the insects had truly hurt her.

"The death-eaters," I explained. "They can make you sick . . . as quick as the bite from a venomous snake might work, the insects have a poison—"

"And I am poisoned. The plants, Eri . . ."

"There might be something there to help you."

"Bastien. He taught you about plants."

"He taught me about a lot of things, Alysen." I helped her out of the cave, and sat her on a flat rock not far from the entrance. Then I retreated into the cave and brought the horses out, Grazti following and settling next to Alysen. I made one more trip into the cave, just to make sure no more death-eaters had returned, then I brought out a couple of the packs and dropped them near Alysen. I'd go back for the others after I'd looked for some herbs.

The air was sweeter away from the cave, and I breathed deep to chase away the scent of the crushed insects. I would have taken time to enjoy this place, and the feel of the wind teasing my face, were I not in a hurry to help Alysen.

I worked quickly and deliberately, on my hands and knees searching through a riot of plants that grew at the edge of the rocky ridge. The soil was rich here, and moist, but it wasn't swampy like the land we'd traveled across when we found Grazti.

Saw grass was predominant, and in it I found a row of the nut-bulbs Alysen had fed us. This had been a cultivated field at one time, else the plants would not have been growing so uniformly. All the fruit I found was not yet ripe, but I made a note to come back and pluck some of it anyway before we left, hoping it would ripen in the sun.

Ranging a few dozen yards farther away I saw smatterings of soapwort, absinthe, birthwort, and hollyhock, also growing in rows, and all of the plants nearly choked out by weeds.

I inhaled deeply over a row of meadowsweet and lavender, treats for my senses, which had been assaulted by so much death yesterday. I inhaled again, drawing as much as I could into my lungs, then I scolded myself for taking such a liberty when Alysen was in trouble.

I continued to search through the incredible variety, and at the same time I looked inward. I, too, was feeling something from the bites and scratches of the death-eaters. My face was flushed, and there was a hotness in my limbs, a fever I'd need to get rid of quickly. Meadow clary and common valerian, mallow, bear's foot, meadow rue, and feverfew. I found all those things and wondered at who could have lived here so long ago to plant a garden of aromatic and medicinal plants.

I gathered up stalks of valerian, mallow, and feverfew, careful not to ruin the plants lest some traveler need them in the future. Then I returned to Alysen. I noticed a thin sheen of sweat on her face, and her expression showed she was uncomfortable.

She didn't talk to me, though I expected her to ask questions about what I was doing. I took the handle of my ax and used it to grind the feverfew into a green paste. Setting that aside, I mixed valerian and mallow into another paste, went into the cave, and found a nut-bulb the insects hadn't fouled. I sliced it and spread the mixture onto it like one would put jam on a piece of bread. I passed it to her and took a slice with the paste for myself.

"Eat it," I said. She hesitated and I added a firm look. "Quickly, Alysen."

She complied, drawing her face together into a point and gagging.

"Yes, I know it tastes bad." Horrible, in fact, as I forced down the slice and made one more for each of us. I passed her another, and she shook her head. I did not want to argue with this girl, but I would force it down her throat if I had to.

"Alysen . . ." I said her name as a warning, and she finally accepted it, practically swallowed it whole so she wouldn't have to taste it.

Next, I took the feverfew paste and spread it on the cuts and bite marks on her neck and arms. When I'd covered them all, I used the rest on my own wounds. The process took quite some time, and the sun was high overhead when I was satisfied that I'd tended to her and myself to the best of my ability. I wasn't the skilled healer Bastien had been, but I had a rudimentary knowledge of what things helped with fevers and infections.

Already I could feel the hotness leaving me, and I could breathe easier. Alysen, too, had improved and was getting to her feet. She made a move to enter the cave. I knew she wanted the rest of her belongings.

"I'll get them," I told her.

She didn't protest.

Minutes later the horses were saddled and the packs were in place. This time I rode Dazon and let the cob carry most of the satchels. Grazti sat on the pony in front of Alysen.

"Where are we going?" Alysen was staring at the cave, then at the ridge, twisting around and looking to the edge of the forest we'd emerged from last night. "The fen isn't this way."

"But we're not terribly far." My tone was comforting. "A little retracing . . . after we pluck some more of that fruit."

"But not too much retracing," she said. I suspected she was thinking about the fose-bear.

"Perhaps no retracing," I decided after a moment, frowning that I'd so easily given up on the fruit. "We'll go around the ridge and come at the fen from the north." That would take us farther from the bear and the tangle of thorns. Certainly I could find a creek soon so the horses could drink and we could replenish our water skins.

Despite the herbs and having something to eat and drink, my head still ached. I suspected it was because I'd called on my wyse-sense so often yesterday. There is a price for employing magic, and calling upon it as many times as I had was risky. I would pay for it the rest of the day with a throbbing that centered over my right eye. Had I the right herbs, I could thwart the headache. And though several herbs grew in the field that had once been someone's garden, they weren't the correct ones for this malady.

"You think we can do that? Find the Nanoo from the north? I've only ever—"

"We'll find them." I wanted to be rid of Alysen, wanted to know she was safe with Nanoo Gafna. Then I wanted to be about my business of revenge on Lord Purvis. "We'll find them today, Alysen." I tried to think of other things, focusing on the taste of the . . . murrows, Alysen had called them, royal fruit and the smell of the lavender. I didn't need her reading my thoughts at the moment.

I noticed that Grazti had wrapped its clawed hands into the fell pony's mane and was gently tugging. I would leave the bird-creature with the Nanoo also. I didn't need to be looking out for anything save myself while I carried out my bloodoath.

My headache flared more strongly, and I closed my eyes for a moment. I vowed I would not call on my wyse-sense again until the pain vanished. I heard a whispered moan from Alysen, and I reluctantly opened my eyes again. Had the herbs not been effective? No. It was something else.

Her breath came quick. "Eri . . . I feel . . ."

Pain stabbed above my eye.

"Place of Fire Stones. Now."

Had those words been spoken aloud? They hadn't come from Alysen. I swiveled in my saddle, looking to the cave behind us, the ridge, the field of herbs and weeds, then to the edge of the woods in the distance. I saw no one.

Another jolt of pain struck over my right eye. I gasped and slapped my palm against my forehead.

"Place of Fire Stones. Now. Now. Now!"

I'd heard the words in my head, so loud this time the pain from them competed with my headache.

"Grazti," Alysen said.

The girl spoke true. The words had come from the bird-creature.

"Powerful ground there, at the place of Fire Stones," Grazti continued with its mental-speak. The bird-beast's beak clacked and its eyes flashed as if the creature had become instantly irritated.

"The . . . place . . . of . . . Fire . . . Stones?" I forced the words out, the pain growing worse. Alysen was feeling it, too, I could tell. Her lips quivered and she clenched and unclenched the reins.

"Powerful there. Place of Fire Stones. Now." Grazti tugged on the pony's mane and the bird-beast's stubby legs kicked against its sides. It trotted forward in compliance. "Now. Now." Grazti nodded its head violently and looked up at Alysen. "Now or die."

Was that a threat? Was Grazti threatening to kill Alysen and me if we didn't agree with its wishes to go to this place of Fire Stones?

"Yes, Eri. It's a threat," Alysen whispered in answer to my silent question. "I don't think we should have rescued this thing, Eri. Not at all."

I could slay the bird-creature. I could slip off Dazon and in two steps be at the fell pony, pulling Grazti off and hurling it away. I could cut off its owllike head with my knives.

Alysen screamed and clutched the sides of her head.

Or could I? Could I kill the creature before it slayed Alysen?

Had Grazti divined my intentions and struck at Alysen to keep me back?

I chewed on my lower lip, so hard I tasted blood. Bastien had taught me well, but I'd not learned enough. I was not wary enough. I'd taken this creature in, protecting it and sheltering it, thinking it a benign beast. I'd so thoroughly let my guard down to this new threat!

The pain flared again, so sharp it threatened to pitch me from Dazon.

"All right!" I spat the words. "We'll go to the Fire Stones." Whatever they were. Wherever they were. We would go there. And during the journey I would plot what to do with the bird-creature. Then I would plot my best course back to the Nanoo's fen. "We will go to the Fire Stones now."

The ache above my eye subsided just a bit.

11

IT WAS FEAR FOR ALYSEN THAT STAYED MY HAND AGAINST GRAZTI. Had the bird-creature been sitting in front of me on Dazon I would have twisted its neck in my hands and been done with it . . . but it was in front of Alysen, and every time she tried to raise a hand against it, she gasped in pain and grabbed the sides of her head.

By the Green Ones! I realized now why the woods had trapped the bird-creature and had built the thorny wall.

Parts of the woods, particularly the area that surrounds the Nanoo's fen, is thick with ancient magic and designed to protect the witches from evil influences. Grazti was heading to the fen, just as Alysen and I had headed there.

Grazti's intentions were clearly malicious, and strong enough for the old, old magic to detect the creature's presence and react. The woods had grown the thorny wall and held the bird-creature fast in its writhing vines. Grazti likely would have perished there had we not come along. I don't believe he could have broken free.

I remembered the cry I'd heard in my head as I entered the plant-weave.

Alysen must have sensed the creature as it had fought futilely against the vines; it had likely called out, looking for a soul who could hear it. Alysen was capable of reading my thoughts. No doubt she was receptive to Grazti's summons.

I knew that normal animals, fortunately, were not capable of malice or manipulation. Grazti—or whatever it was called— had skillfully manipulated Alysen; me, too. Manipulated . . . and worse!

I thought back to the cave Grazti had led us to. Just before the death-eaters swarmed us, the bird-beast had cried out.

Had Grazti called them to us?

Sensed them in the cracks in the stone and brought them down upon us?

The insects, though large and numerous, could not have bested both Alysen and me . . . but had Grazti hoped that one of us would have died there of disease so there would be only one of us to control? Or perhaps the creature had only wanted us weakened.

I still tasted the blood in my mouth from where I'd bit down on my lip.

I let Grazti and Alysen get a little ahead of me, then I extended the tip of my tongue and concentrated on my wyse-sense. I'd vowed not to do that until my headache was past . . . but I wondered if the headache was not caused by my overuse of the wyse-power yesterday, but by Grazti.

I tasted the hunger of the horses; they'd not been allowed to graze long enough this morning, and all of them were thirsty. I tasted a hint of lavender, from the plants becoming more distant behind us. And I smelled wildflowers growing nearby, though I couldn't see them through the tall tufts of grass that stretched away from us to the north. I ordered my senses to go beyond those physical things, and was rewarded by tasting Alysen's fear and pain. A moment more and I tasted evil. That confirmed what I'd already surmised—there was nothing good about the creature we'd rescued from the animated woods.

I closed my eyes, trusting Dazon to follow the fell pony. I knew the cob and the draft were directly behind Dazon, instinct or a pack mentality keeping them with us. I was grateful that they didn't need to be tethered. The provisions and clothes in the satchels and packs on their saddles might be needed . . . if we could make it past the Fire Stones and once again be on our own. I searched my memory; Bastien had never mentioned such a thing as the Fire Stones.

Would we find more of the bird-creatures there? Or, by chance, might Grazti let its guard down enough for me to strike before we ever got there? I wanted that opportunity, as I had no desire to discover the nature of the Fire Stones.

I only wanted to reach Mardel's Fen and the Nanoo.

But the answer to that possibility rang no, as each time I rode even with the fell pony and my fingers fluttered to a knife or the chain at my waist, Alysen was subjected to intense pain—and the throbbing above my eye intensified to the point I could hardly think.

I'd never traveled this far north.

We spent the whole day riding, stopping only twice to stretch our legs, eat some of our provisions, and drink, and during this entire time Grazti clung to Alysen.

The bird-creature had to sleep sometime, didn't it? I would strike against it then. No chivalry in that, but my first concern had to be Alysen. If the vile beast had slept last night I couldn't have proved it, I'd been oblivious to everything in my exhaustion, but it looked weary now, perhaps tired from the strain of managing Alysen and me.

This night I would not sleep, though I would pretend to.

This night, I would slay the creature while it rested, when it presented no threat to Alysen.

If I was fortunate, however, I would find an opportunity earlier.

I stayed alert, despite the ache in my head, watching Grazti constantly, looking for its head to bob, as if it dozed, or for the creature to be distracted by something in our surroundings. The bird-beast turned to glance at me occasionally, as if it sensed I was watching.

The land we crossed seemed oddly devoid of wildlife. The fescue grasses didn't flutter with the passage of ground squirrels, badgers, or other animals that might wander this type of terrain. The copses of trees were spaced farther and farther apart, and they were looking straggly now, especially the birches and ginkos, half dead due to lightning or drought or disease— some of the low cover looked scabrous in places. We stuck to an old trail and didn't travel close enough for me to see what caused the trees' malady. Had the circumstances been different, I would have investigated. What affects the plants, affects the land, affects the people.

"What happened here, Eri?"

Alysen hadn't spoken in quite some time, and so her words startled me. I was certain that she still ached, from whatever

Grazti was doing to control her, but she glanced at the land to the east, perhaps to take her mind off our predicament.

"What do you think happened to the trees?"

"There were more here once," I admitted. I nodded my head forward, indicating shattered trunks along a ridge, so long dead the wood was stringy and rotted.

"A fire, you think?"

Perhaps she hoped we were near this place of the Fire Stones. "Yes, perhaps a summer fire, when the grass was so dry a touch of lightning set it all off. But it happened a long while ago, Alysen. There are strong trees all around."

"Just not many of them."

"No." After a moment, I shivered. "Too few of them." The earth had died in places, I tasted that, and could not nourish the kind of forest that had once grown here.

I looked away from the trees and to Grazti, then I glanced at the sky and saw a flock of starlings heading west. I had noticed occasional lone birds, but this was the first flock in more than an hour, and it was a small one.

There should be more birds, more animal tracks . . . more everything. The stillness kept my mind off Grazti for a few moments. The hunting had been bad around our village in the past many weeks and I'd ranged quite a bit farther to the north to find the curl-horns. Except for the fose-bear, I hadn't noticed game in the marshy woods. So the decline in the animal population was not just limited to the environs of the Village Nar. Fewer animals roamed the land here, too, but why? Were they fleeing from something? Dying off from the same affliction striking the trees?

"Eri!" Alysen gasped in pain. "Stay with me!"

I'd been so caught up in the land that I'd drifted back. I made a clicking sound, thumped Dazon once in the side, and he caught up . . . but I held him back just a little, not wanting to ride even with the fell pony. I wanted Grazti to keep turning around to look at me, to keep him uneasy and distracted. Maybe I was hoping to tire him out. And as the miles crept by, he looked at me less and less often, his head bobbed more, and I saw his beak open in a yawn.

I smiled. I knew I wouldn't have to wait for nightfall.

The opportunity came shortly before sunset.

I urged Dazon a little closer, finally coming up to the fell's shoulder. I put a finger to my lips to signal Alysen to remain quiet.

She nodded her understanding.

Grazti seemed inattentive.

I leaned forward across Dazon's neck and peered around Alysen. I saw that the bird-beast's eyes were closed. Its small clawed hands still grabbed hanks of the pony's mane.

Was the creature sleeping?

My fingers reached for the handle of my longest knife to slice him.

Or should I simply yank the vile creature from the saddle and hurl it as far as I could?

I opted for the latter, replacing the knife, my fingers reaching for Grazti now. Perhaps the knife might have been the surest method, but it also presented risk to Alysen and the fell, all of them so close.

I took a deep breath and grabbed Grazti by its feathery neck, my fingers digging in and squeezing with all my strength, as I might be able to break its bones and end its evil life with one gesture. In the same motion I lifted and flung the bird-beast, so fast it hadn't time to spread its membrane wings and stop its fall. The creature landed in a patch of browning fescue, screeching both audibly and inside my head.

Pain shot hard above my right eye, and I slammed my teeth together to keep from crying out. I jumped from Dazon's back and drew both knives, racing toward Grazti and ignoring Alysen's call and the horses' whinnies. Each step was agony; felt as if spikes were being hammered into my heels.

What power did the creature have that let it inflict such suffering? Never had I known such a beast existed!

Never had I felt such pain.

I hurtled toward him, pushing off and slashing with my knives, the sun catching the blades and making them look like molten silver. The knives whistled through the air. So much force I put into the blows! It was like flying, my body parallel to the ground and streaking toward the hateful creature.

The bird-beast rose on its hind legs, shook out its head as if clearing its senses, and then glared at me, making no effort to move . . . but it had made an effort at something, as pain stabbed into my stomach! I curled and dropped to the earth, less than a foot away from it, though I didn't drop the knives.

I'd never felt such complete misery.

"Thrice-damned beast!" I cursed through gritted teeth, forcing myself to my knees.

Its eyes glimmered darkly, and I swore it had an amused expression on its feathery face. "I will kill you!" Even as I said the words, I doubted myself capable of it. It was all I could do not to writhe in the grass. I briefly thought about death, believing that might be a welcome relief to this magic-induced suffering.

I heard Alysen shouting, one of the horses whinnying shrilly and stomping on the ground, Grazti making a disconcerting cackling sound, my heart pounding loudly in my ears. I heard a sharp noise, one I'd never heard before.

The sound repeated, and then was followed by Alysen's scream and a loud thump.

Struggling to my feet, swaying in pain and sweating from the effort, I looked at Grazti and risked a glance behind me. The knives slipped from my hands and I felt my chest grow instantly tight.

"Dazon?" The word was a croak escaping my trembling lips. "Dazon!"

The warmblood I'd considered my closest companion lay on the ground, unmoving. Foam was thick around his lips. Alysen hovered over him, looking at his still form, looking up at me.

"Eri," she mouthed. It was a plea.

"Dazon!" Now I said my companion's name in anger. His chest didn't rise and fall. His eyes were fixed. He was dead, slain by Grazti's foul magic. I dropped to a crouch and spun, snatching up my knives in my sweat-slippery fingers. "Thrice-damned beast!"

Gratzi kept cackling and shaking its head, opened its beak and emitted a sharp barking sound. The pain struck above my eye with an even greater intensity, rooting me to the spot. The bird-creature edged back, staying just out of reach, gazed up into my eyes, and held them tight like they were caught in a trap.

"Fire Stones," it said. The voice dripped with malevolence. "Place of Fire Stones. Now."

My lips trembled, not from fear, though I should have been

feeling that. They trembled in rage and in grief. In the passing of a few moments, this *thing* had murdered my longtime companion, my prized gift from Bastien.

Grazti had demonstrated that I was but a puppet, and if I didn't comply with the evil creature's every demand, I would continue to lose things . . . perhaps even Alysen.

If I stayed my hand and escorted Grazti to the Fire Stones, would the little beast let us go? Or having served our purpose, would we just end up like Dazon? I thrust my knives into their sheaths and turned back toward Alysen and the horses. She watched me, her face unreadable.

The little bird-creature would not keep me in thrall much longer.

I wanted to bury Dazon, but I hadn't the tools to dig a hole deep enough. And I doubted Grazti would grant me the time anyway.

"Se hala yorma se hala roo," I whispered as I approached Dazon. It was a prayer I'd heard Bastien say over his living horses. *"Se hala neda hala roo. De-orma hala deral roo. Se hala roo."*

The prayer was longer and more involved, and I wished I had time for it, all of the words meant to bless horses on a journey. I blessed Dazon on his journey to wherever the spirits of animals dwelled beyond this world. And I prayed that when my time here was ended I would see Dazon again.

"Fire Stones. Place of Fire Stones."

"I know," I spat to Grazti. "Now." I bent and brushed Dazon's neck and I slipped off his bridle, wanting some remembrance with me.

Replacing the cob's bridle with Dazon's, I arranged packs on the back of the fell and the cob, putting most of them on the cob. I took the saddle off the draft, dropped it on the trail next to Dazon's still form, and then swatted the draft on the rump. The horse ran to the east, and I felt a stab of pain above my eye, punishment for releasing one of the horses.

I didn't know if the draft would survive. There looked to be enough grasses and wildflowers to eat. But there might also be predators, such as wolves. Still, I didn't want to keep him with us, one more horse Grazti could slay to punish me or to keep me under its little clawed thumb. I doubted the bird-beast would kill either the cob or the fell . . . at least not until we reached the Fire Stones.

12

GRAZTI DIDN'T SLEEP THAT NIGHT—NOT UNLESS IT MANAGED TO nap in the few fitful times I dozed. Alysen slept well, though, and I was grateful for it. Strong in the wyse, she'd need to stay alert for a chance to go against the beast.

"What is so special about this place of Fire Stones?" I'm not sure why I bothered speaking to the bird-beast, maybe to occupy it or distract it. Maybe just to learn anything about it or learn something about where it was leading us.

Grazti glared at me, clawed hands twitching.

"Why do you need us to take you there?"

"Faster," it said after a few moments of silence. "Long legs and horses, you are faster."

"And getting there quickly is important, isn't it?"

Its eyes narrowed and darkened, and a shiver passed down my back.

"Because you need magic for some horrid purpose, and you couldn't pull the magic from the fen."

It snarled, spittle lining the edges of its beak. "No," it

admitted. "That magic . . . that wood-magic is unreachable."

I shifted slightly, feeling an ache starting in my head. "How did you get there, Grazti, to those old woods?"

The pain lessened, thankfully. I waited for an answer but did not receive one.

"Did you find someone to take you to the woods? Just like Alysen and I are taking you to this place of Fire Stones?"

The creature's eyes widened and glimmered, and I knew it wasn't going to answer that question. Yet, I wanted to know. Perhaps I would press it again later.

"How did you know about the magic in the old woods?" I tried. "And the magic in this place of Fire Stones?"

The pain returned to the spot above my right eye, sharp, as if a piece of metal were being twisted into my head.

The bird-beast looked away from me, and I glanced at Alysen. I hated to think it might be up to Alysen to strike at Grazti. But the damnable creature continued to force intense headaches on me, making it almost impossible to use my wyse-sense, and very difficult even to think.

We started again at first light, the cob and fell pony making wuffling noises that I knew meant they were still tired, having had little rest last night and getting little chance to graze and drink.

I thought of Dazon as I absently stroked the mane of the cob. Crust was this horse's name. From a colt, Bastien had trained her and hand-fed her. He said her favorite treat was bread crusts, and so he named her after that. I didn't know why he'd called my horse Dazon, or if the word meant anything in particular. I'd never thought to ask him, and now I was sorrowful for that. Tears welled in my eyes. I was sad for so many things. In the course of but a handful of days I'd lost so many people I'd cared about, and Dazon. I had no one left, and I'd entrusted myself with the care of a girl that at the moment I could not save.

"Eri?" Alysen studied me. "What's wrong?"

"Other than this?" I gestured with a hand to indicate Grazti and the land we traveled across. Then I wiped at the tears with my fingers. "Everything's wrong, Alysen." The admonition surprised me; I'd not intended to open up to the girl.

"It's Dazon, isn't it?"

I twined my fingers in the cob's mane, closed my eyes briefly, and nodded.

"He was a friend, Alysen."

"And you don't have many of those, do you, Eri?"

I didn't answer that question.

We stopped briefly when the sun was directly overhead, as a narrow, shallow creek crawled across our path and gave us all a chance to drink our fill. The land was even drier here, the creek half as wide as its banks indicated it should be. The ground beyond it felt parched. The drought was unusual for this time of the spring, though I had to admit I'd not been this far north before and so couldn't tell if things were amiss.

I saw no concentration of trees, just lone trees here and there, tall and scraggly. A few white oaks stretched tall to the east, a couple of poplars and stringy barks grew to the north and west. The terrain was for the most part flat, but that changed deep into the afternoon when the land dropped away to form a valley.

The walls were steep, and navigating the side to reach the bottom presented a treacherous problem. I knew I would have had an easier time with Dazon, more sure-footed than Crust. Too, Dazon had been an extension of me. I'd not ridden the cob before this regrettable trip.

I had pictured valleys being verdant and beautiful; so Bastien had described the one he'd traveled through while in his early years with the Moonsons. He'd mentioned a waterfall and a wide river, mist rising above both and painting his face with a faint sheen of cool water. This place was the opposite, all rocks and hard-packed clay, with only rare tufts of grass to break the monotonous red-brown expanse. There was a dry riverbed at the bottom—the wide, deep cracks looking like an ugly pattern from a disturbed spiderweb.

"Close," Grazti announced with a hiss. "Close place of Fire Stones." The malevolent creature's eyes glimmered with anticipation.

Grazti's report sent mixed emotions dancing in my mind. I wanted this business with the bird-beast to be done. But I also worried what would happen once we reached its destination.

"Grazti, how came you to be in those woods? The ones with the grabbing vines?" I'd asked it before and was not satisfied that the creature had not answered. I knew someone had taken the creature there. But who? And what had happened to them afterward? If Grazti had come from this place called the Fire Stones, it would have been a long, onerous journey to the woods, given the beast's stubby back legs. "And how did you know to go there for magic?"

Grazti shrugged what passed for its shoulders.

"What . . . exactly . . . did you want in the woods?"

The creature paused, then looked over a shoulder at me,

eyes narrowing to needle-fine. "Obvious," it said after a moment, its voice a rasp as dry as the valley. "Power."

"And when the forest wouldn't let you through? To get its power? When we rescued you?"

"Gave up forest power," Grazti replied evenly. "Gave up hateful forest. Go place of Fire Stones. Place of Fire Stones welcome us."

"Where are you from, Grazti? This place of Fire Stones?"

"Long time caught forest with grabbing vines. Saved me you did. Long, long time caught." Grazti cackled and turned back to face the fell pony's neck, signaling the conversation's end. "Dead almost. You saved me."

Pity, I thought. What a great, great pity we had saved the bird-beast.

We reached the place of Fire Stones, as Grazti called it, near twilight of the following day. I stood straight beside Crust, craning my neck to work out a kink and trying to ease my stiff back. A trapper and a hunter, I was nevertheless not used to riding so long and for days in a row.

"This is ugly," Alysen pronounced. "Except for over there."

"Over there" was a pasture that butted up to the western edge of the stone plateau we stood on. It was such a stark contrast, a verdant piece of grassland ending at barren rock, like nature had drawn a line and permitted nothing to grow beyond that point. I wished Bastien could have seen this. I felt certain the woodsman in him would have been compelled to study it.

The cob and the fell pony quickly made their way to the middle of the pasture, and I took off their saddles and packs. Then I returned to the hardscrabble ground. I saw features here that resembled the cave Grazti had led us to, where the death-eaters had attacked. The stone was of the same kind, and the pillars that had marked that cave entrance—their twins were arranged everywhere across this acrid expanse of stone. Gray ash lay in depressions that might have been an inch deep or several feet—I hoped I would not need to find out. Dull red streaks stretched to the horizon in places, a few traveling up the bases of some of the pillars and looking like leaping flames. The closer I stared at these pillars, the more certain I became that they were columns of fire, glimmering as the stars began to wink into view.

Crust and the fell grazed in the pasture, the greenery standing unusually high for this early in the season. When the cob got her fill, she dropped on the ground and started rolling. Perhaps she was trying to assure herself that the grass really existed, wanted her whole body to testify to it. Scents of sap, crushed leaves, and wildflower blossoms reached me. For an instant, things seemed not so bad.

Grazti squatted not too far from the horses. The creature's hands and bill were in constant movement, catching insects fleeing the disturbance Crust had caused by her motions. By all signs, the bird-creature was having rich hunting. To the east, the stone sloped upward, cut halfway through with crevices. Water bubbled out of one, running down the rock face—it wasn't the waterfall I'd envisioned from Bastien's description of his valley. But the water was fresh, a ribbon that snaked across the plateau and into the pasture, forming a pool and then continuing and disappearing over a cliff.

I continued to scrutinize the land, deciding I disagreed with Alysen. This wasn't ugly at all. Stark, but the colors in the stone, even in the dusk of twilight, were attractive and distracting. There was a sense of healing and peace here, and I carefully stuck out my tongue and drew upon my wyse-sense.

I tasted the sweat of the horses and the freshness of the grass Crust rolled in. I tasted a sweetness in the air that I hadn't smelled since the day I'd caught the curl-horns. I sensed uncertainty in Alysen, and knew that feeling echoed in my own heart. I sensed a great glee, this coming from Grazti; the little beast was obviously pleased we'd reached its destination and could feast.

Deeper, I sensed a strong pulse of energy. It flowed down the slope with the springwater and spread out under the plateau. As I concentrated, my heart started to beat in time with it. I felt it flow under my feet and up into the columns, feeding the fire they appeared to be.

I felt stronger, even rested, though I hadn't slept in more than two days. The pain that had lived above my right eye melted. There was as much power in this piece of ground as there was in the woods near the Nanoo's fen. I was leeching some of that power, and I knew that Grazti intended to do the same . . . after the creature finished its insect banquet.

I heard stone shifting, grating against stone, and I saw one of the columns turn, the red flame-streaks crackling and hissing. I smelled something burning, and when I stared, I saw a single wisp of smoke rising from the closest column. Rocks burned?

"Fire Stones," Grazti said. It had finished eating and had silently slipped near me and poked my leg with a claw. "Grazti at place of Fire Stones."

"So you don't need us any longer." I put strength behind the words, and I gestured to the horses. "We will be leaving you now, Grazti." I took a step toward the pasture and stopped, every muscle in my body rigid and unmoving.

"Longer," Grazti purred. "Stay. Not go." The bird-beast crept around in front of me, far enough so it didn't have to crane its feathered neck much to look up into my face. "Never go. Never ever ever ever go."

I heard the grating sound again of stone rubbing against stone. My wyse-sense was so overly strong here that without trying I could still smell something burning and pick up the hint of smoke, still smell the sweat on the horses and hear Crust rolling in the grass and nickering happily, hear the fell drinking at the stream. I still felt the energy pulsing through the ground and into me, and I knew into Grazti as well.

I thought I saw miniature bolts of lightning flicker between its fingertips. But I must have been mistaken, as such magic did not exist in the world. Or did it? I tried to move, tried to pull the energy from the earth and into me at a faster rate. My legs tingled as if they were going numb, and I discovered I could move my hands and wrists. I breathed deep, thinking the very air might be tinged with wyse-energy.

Grazti was doing the same, and this time when I looked to its fingers I *knew* I saw miniature lightning bolts flickering. The vile creature grinned at me, a taunt, cocked its head and leaned forward, touching its claws to the stone.

"Never ever ever," Grazti hissed. "Never ever ever ever."

Then its claws sunk into the rock as if the stone were mud. Ripples of dark red radiated, interrupting the energy I'd been drinking in. Instantly, the tingling in my limbs disappeared, and I was as stiff as a statue again.

"Never ever." Grazti cackled again, this time louder and deeper, an eerie, malicious sound that was hurtful.

"Never for you!" This came from Alysen.

I could see her only out of the corner of my eye, as I couldn't even turn my head. She was between two of the columns, flames writhing up the rocks and flowing like water around her feet. Sweat beaded on her face and plastered her black hair to the sides of her head. So wet, it looked as if she'd been standing in a thunderstorm. Her eyes . . . I couldn't be certain, but I thought some of the miniature strokes of lightning flashed at the edges.

She'd been drawing on the energy, too, and Grazti had been so preoccupied with me that it had not taken her into account. I truly believed Alysen more magically potent than I, a notion nurtured when she had trapped the fose-bear. It was a notion given even more credence now. The flames flowing around her feet churned away from her, racing like a fire that had found a bed of dry, brittle twigs to gorge on. The waves of flame washed over Grazti at the same time it was working its foul magic against both of us.

Agony drove deep into my skull above my eye.

Alysen threw her hands to the sides of her head and screamed.

But she wasn't held still like me, and so she fought through the Grazti-induced pain and pushed the fire higher.

It was Grazti's turn to scream. I couldn't see the creature for the flames roiling around it, circling it like the streaks circling the stone columns. So blistering was the fire, the bird-beast could not escape. I smelled burnt flesh, but only briefly.

The crackling fire roared and whooshed, blotting out all sound and making me fear if it would engulf me.

Then suddenly I was free, my legs and arms tingling fiercely, as if every part of me had fallen asleep and protested my motion. I leapt back from the fire, the heat abating only a little. Fire crackled up all the columns now and raced along the sides of the stream. It teased the grass at the edge of the plateau.

"Alysen, stop!" I whirled to face her, seeing her eyes fixed and flashing. I dashed toward her, jumping a line of fire and darting past a column with flame tendrils that struck out whiplike. "Alysen!"

Caught by the magic and the power of this place, she stared transfixed.

"Alysen!"

She blinked then, and I shouted to her again and again. Then I was on her, shaking her shoulders, gently at first, then harshly. "Alysen, stop the fire!" I turned her so she could see the grassland, the horses rearing nervously and stamping at the ground. In a heartbeat they would bolt, and there was no place for them to escape the flames but over the cliff. "Alysen, listen to me!"

She shook her head and her arms, her skin going instantly paler than normal. Her lip trembled, and a faint line of blood sat on the corner of her mouth, as if she'd bit her tongue. She let out a breath she'd been holding. I heard it as a great sigh and felt it as a strong breeze. It blew across the flames and vanquished them.

"Eri. Help me."

I looked back to her. She crumpled, and I dropped to my knees next to her, wrapping my arms around her and holding her close. She shivered, as if freezing. The magic had demanded so much of her it had taken her heat, the inner fire that fuels the heart. I tried to give her some of mine. I took one glance away, to the spot where Grazti had stood. Ashes and charred feathers blew south across the rock.

13

I HELD THE BACK OF MY HAND AGAINST ALYSEN'S FOREHEAD. SHE was now burning with a fever, though she shivered and trembled like one caught in a winter storm. I'd not seen the wyse exact such a price for its use, but I'd also not seen it wielded in the manner Alysen had demonstrated.

My use of wyse magic had always been subtler . . . out of respect, and out of fear.

Alysen had wielded it to save our lives.

"Eri, I heard Grazti call to me. It sounded so helpless and frightened. In my head it was calling and whimpering."

"That . . . thing . . . can't hurt us anymore, Alysen. Grazti's gone."

"Now it is. Now, but not before. Grazti called to me, Eri. When we rode in the woods near the Nanoo's fen. The place with the tangling vines." She gulped in the acrid air and clung to me. "I didn't think you heard the creature. And I didn't know it was cruel—not then. I thought it was in danger. Its cries were so desperate, its voice was so strong in my head. Loud, pleading. And yet . . . so weak. Grazti was dying, Eri. I sensed it, and I wanted to help. I didn't know that any of this would happen. I saved the creature . . . and now I've killed it. I never killed anything before."

I let a silence slip between us for several moments. In it I heard some night bird cry, and I heard Crust nicker. "You thought you were doing the right thing, Alysen. Your intentions were good when you rescued Grazti. You couldn't have known that the woods had caught the bird-beast for a reason."

I wanted to tell her that of course she'd been wrong, that it had been impulsive and selfish of her to bolt from the clearing and into the enchanted brush. I wanted to shout at her that her act had cost us days and days out of the way of the Nanoo's fen, and had cost the life of my precious Dazon—and brought pain and suffering on us. But I kept quiet and stroked her hair and prayed she was too tired to read my troubled, angry thoughts.

"They wanted to control her rule," Alysen said after a few more moments. "They wanted to control her."

I cocked my head, not sure if I'd heard Alysen correctly. She was slow to continue, so worn out from using the wyse.

"They were desperate to control her, I think."

"Control who? What are you talking about?" Had the fever made Alysen delirious? One moment she was talking about Grazti, and the next . . .

"The Emperor and your father. They wanted to control the Empress. That's how all of this started. That's when everything went so horribly, horribly bad."

Where has this talk suddenly come from?

I put her at arm's length and studied her face. Her eyes were closed, and she looked so pale.

"Because of all of that, because they thought to control her, Lord Purvis came to the village, Eri. Because of the Emperor and your father . . . because of them, the Empress sent Lord Purvis for you, too."

How can she know such things? More—why would she say such things? I swallowed hard. *My father?*

"The Emperor and your father," she repeated, opening her eyes. "They made the Empress killing mad."

I shook my head. "You've a fever."

"They made the Empress furious, your father and the Emperor. The rage on her face, it reminded me of a roaring fire. I saw her."

The Empress's face? Had Alysen truly seen the Empress? No, the girl had not left the village since her arrival, save to go on a few jaunts with Nanoo Gafna. She could not have seen the Empress, and I told her so.

"The Empress and the Emperor rule this island continent, Alysen." But it was just the Empress now. "You've never seen the Empress, nor have you set foot in the great southern city. You need rest."

"I saw her, I say." She continued to breathe raggedly, and though I again and again urged her to rest, she kept talking. "The Empress always has been the real power. Everyone knows that, and her decrees and rules have been just and for the good of most of the people. But she is not without her enemies, including the one she shared her bed with."

I turned her face to look into mine. "You're dreaming things, Alysen. You've used too much magic and—"

"Your father conspired with the Emperor, Eri. For how long, I don't know. And what exactly they meddled with, I don't know. But I do know that the two of them wanted to cut the Empress's power, befuddle and charm her, I think. They wanted to make her weak, just like Grazti becoming weakened by the fen. But Grazti died, and the Empress lives. Your father and the Emperor, though . . . the Empress was the fen that ended their threat."

"You're dreaming," I repeated. *Or you've gone mad.*

"I wish this was all a dream," she shot back. Her tone was stern, but there was little strength in her words. It sounded as if talking was a struggle for her. She paused to catch her breath. "But it's real, Eri. And I should have told you before. I am so very, very sorry I said nothing before. It was cruel of me."

Alysen couldn't know these things. It wasn't possible, I told myself. And yet . . . Bastien had taught me that few things in this world are wholly impossible.

"Alysen, if it's real, how do you know all of this? What claim to this knowledge do you have?"

I told myself that in her exhaustion she'd become confused, was fabricating things about my father. Perhaps Alysen was trying to unnerve me, though for what purpose I had no clue. Maybe she was talking nonsense so she wouldn't have to think about killing Grazti and about everything else bad that had happened.

It was very possible Alysen had somehow slipped into madness . . . a backlash from using the wyse so much, slaying a creature she'd rescued, and above all, watching the people of the Village Nar being slaughtered. Her world, and mine, had collapsed in the passing of a handful of days.

"Eri, I'm not mad. Don't think such things of me." Her words sounded even more strained. She desperately needed sleep. Still, I let her talk, my curiosity winning out over my common sense. "Eri, I know all of these things—and more— because I tap into the land and watch people. Hidden things are not hidden to me. I can see and learn anything I want to. Nanoo Gafna taught me to scry."

I gasped. "Scry? That is not magic to be used lightly!" I did not try to hide the venom in my words. "It is dangerous magic! It is magic I'll never use." In truth, I didn't know how to use it.

The cob let out a whinny and I looked to the pasture. She and the pony had calmed down and were grazing again, the fire and the threat well out of their memories.

"I scry more often than I should. But once I learned the magic, I just couldn't help myself. It, scrying, became a . . ." She paused, searching for the word. "Habit. It became a habit. And because of it I learned so much. Oh, Eri, I know lords and ladies who are untrue to each other. I know about brother alchemists who require tribute from the Village Oakton to help the crops grow—and who will cause them to wither if enough isn't paid. I know about a noblewoman in S'har who took her life after her child was born dead. I've seen so many things that . . ."

The cob nickered and pawed at something on the ground in front of her. She cast her head back and let the wind catch her mane. I wished Dazon could graze in the pasture. I had a sudden image of his body, surely bloated now, being picked at by

crows. I fought against the bile rising in my throat and returned my full attention to Alysen.

"What about my father? And the Emperor? How do you
know *those* things?"

She cast her eyes down. "I know those things because every
day I'd slip away from my room and use the magic. I looked in
on various villages and cities . . . on the ruling city most often; it
is all so fascinating, Eri, the scry magic. Wonderful and horrible,
and once you start watching someone, you have to keep on. You
have to know what will happen to the people you've been looking in on. Every day, Eri. You have to watch them every day."

"My father—"

"I watched your father die, Eri, though I hadn't intended to
see such! I saw the Emperor die before him. They made it
look like he died in his sleep, the Emperor. But I saw them."

I edged away from her, my hand tipping her face up again
and finding her eyes and holding them with my stern gaze.
Her eyes didn't drift, like Bastien said a liar's did. They stayed
true and unblinking, though they were filled with a horrible
weariness.

"I should have told Nanoo Gafna about all my look-seeing,
I know, Eri. But I was afraid she'd be angry that I was using
the rare magic, and that somehow she'd unteach it to me. I intended to tell her, eventually, though perhaps not until word
of the Emperor's death reached the village. I did not tell her,
though, even when the news came just before Lord Purvis and
his men rode in. I did not tell her because my words would
have changed nothing. The Emperor would still be dead. Your
father would still be dead. And my words could not punish
their slayers, for I looked upon them through a muddy puddle.

No one would believe the magical visions of someone my age. No one that mattered."

She shook her head, and raised a corner of her lip. "And, Eri, even with the scry magic I'd used, I couldn't anticipate . . . couldn't discern the difference . . . from an evil bird-creature and a helpless one."

Anger and disbelief flooded me. Could this child truly have such magic? I knew she was powerful. But could she scry? And had she really seen everything she said? Did she see the Emperor die? My father die? I wanted to doubt her, but I couldn't. With all my breaking heart, I knew she spoke the truth.

"You are of the House of Geer, Alysen. Strong with magic, someone would believe you." I paused. "I believe you. You should have told Nanoo Gafna—before the men came." It felt as if my stomach rose into my throat in that moment.

If Alysen had told Gafna about the scry images, would the village have been spared? Would Gafna have learned that Lord Purvis was coming for me? Could my life have been given in exchange for the village? Or would Gafna have ordered the villagers to flee? Could all that bloodshed have been avoided if Alysen had said something to the Nanoo?

"You saw who killed my father, Alysen." *Why tell me now? Why not tell me back in the Village Nar when you told me about the slaying of the villagers on Lord Purvis's command?* "Did Lord Purvis kill my father?"

"No blood on his hands, Eri. He ordered it, though, ordered your father's death. I didn't hear the words, the scry magic won't let me listen. Only watch. But I saw him outside your father's room. You don't need to hear things to understand what is going on."

"And Lord Purvis came to the Village Nar for me."

"Because of your blood."

"Because they killed my father and wanted to kill me, too. Because I am strong in the wyse." *But not near so strong as you, Alysen t'Geer.* "Why didn't you tell me this before?"

She shuddered and shrugged, and I pulled her close again. She coughed and coughed, and then her body stilled and her breathing became more regular. "Eri, they want you for your bloodline. To end it—that has to be what this is all about. Your father worked against the Empress, and the Empress wants to end the chance that your family's magic could dethrone her."

"The Empress . . ."

"Wants the magic to die."

I stroked her hair, something I remembered my mother doing when I was a young girl with nightmares. "Do you truly think the Empress is behind all of this? You're certain?"

I felt her shoulders shrug again. "I did not see her in the murder rooms. But I watched her before, often with Lord Purvis."

"The Emperor . . ."

"He wanted more power, Eri, I told you. I didn't need my scrying on him to learn that. Rumors were whispered from village to village for more than a year about the Emperor and the Empress. You would have heard them yourself if you were not always hunting and working."

I nodded. "Rumors that their marriage was uneasy."

"See why I could not tell any of this to Nanoo Gafna?"

"Alysen, the Nanoo care nothing about royalty and power and people manipulating each other. But they care about nature and the magic in it."

Alysen nodded now. "And Nanoo Gafna would have been angry at the use of the scry magic."

She pushed herself away from me and shakily stood. She rubbed her arms with her hands, then drew her cloak around her. "You must promise not to tell Nanoo Gafna what I have told you, Eri. You must promise me."

I stood next to her, looking past her and to the horses. "Alysen, don't you think she—"

"Promise me, Eri. I told you of your father. I told you why he was killed. I shared my secrets. Now I'll have your promise."

I slowly and carefully regarded her. She was half my age, but probably had two or three times my power. She needed Nanoo Gafna and the other witches to help hone her skills . . . and to control them.

"I promise, Alysen. I do not like it. But I promise."

14

I FLINCHED, AND MY TONGUE PUSHED AGAINST MY FRONT TEETH. But I held my mouth closed and fought to keep from asking Alysen more questions. My mind and heart reeled, and I felt weak . . . not just from the heat and the pain I'd suffered at the bird-creature's will, but from everything that had happened. My father dead, murdered. Had he truly conspired against the Empress? I'd no clue of that when I'd visited at the side of his sickbed. My eyes snapped wide now, remembering something. My father . . . on his sickbed he'd mentioned that I should swear fealty to the Emperor, be prepared to serve him. He'd made no mention of the Empress.

Did Alysen speak true of all this? How could she scry? A mere girl? Scry magic was powerful and guarded, and the Nanoo hadn't been known to share its knowledge. Nanoo Gafna had never taught me such . . . and I'd known Gafna for a decade. This girl had been in the village not quite a year. What could—

"The Emperor wanted to rule and to gain favor with the

Dawn Priests." She moved close again and looked up into my face. I felt her breath on my neck. "You want to know why Nanoo Gafna taught me such magic. How could you understand, Moonson? You turn to weapons of the hand and not of the mind. You spent your time with Bastien, and left little for Nanoo Gafna." She thumped her fingers against the knives hanging from my belt. "I will never use such primitive things. There is too much strength in my thoughts, and too much power in the wyse."

"Magic is a gift, Alysen. One not to be abused . . . wielded as a bludgeon." I didn't want to talk about magic, though. I wanted to know about my father and his murder and—

"I *am* magic," Alysen returned. "So very much of me is magic." She edged closer, and I backed away. "When I was very, very young, Eri, those in the House of Geer and our neighbors told me I was ensorcelled by my mother. But my mother told me in secret that was only partly true. It was not Mother that my power came from, but from the Green Ones themselves."

"Alysen, the Green Ones are gods. You speak blasphemy."

She shook her head and drew her lips into a thin line. "I speak true. Sealed by the cold iron, my mother was in her youth. She suffered a laying on of the Black Force. When I was born my mother begged that I be sent away from our manor to be helped . . . to learn how to wield all the power inside of me. So I was taken to the Exile Holding. But there was no one there who could help me. I returned home and was sent away again."

"To the Village Nar and Nanoo Gafna and Lady Ewaren."

She took in several deep breaths and held me still with her

searching eyes. She edged closer again, and this time I did not back away. "What do you know of the feeding of the fields, Eri?"

"Little." Her nearness unnerved me, but I wouldn't give her the satisfaction of knowing that, so I did not move. "Little enough."

Alysen's voice took on a singsong lilt, like that of a boring recitation made before a tutor. "Just as the Dawn Priests require payment for their prayers and services, in the spring there must be payment to the Green Ones to thank them for the bounty of the earth. Thus the maids of the clans in a Holding gather so that a choice may be made for the proper messenger."

"I don't understand, Alysen."

"You don't understand because the Village Nar had no Dawn Priests," she returned. "The messenger must be a maid, indeed, never the seed of man having touched her. Fair of face and of body she must stand, well tempered, quick to offer aid . . ." Alysen paused, then her voice took on its regular tone again. "Then they bid her farewell and give her to the Green Ones."

"No longer a—"

"No. My mother . . . she was a messenger."

"Your father . . ."

"Is one of the Green Ones."

I shook my head slowly and took a long step back. I felt suddenly pricked by the thought that she was playing with me. I stared deeper into her eyes.

"Eri, Nanoo Gafna and Lady Ewaren kept me safe." She finally stepped away from me and narrowed her gaze. "And I should thank you for keeping me safe, but I cannot bring myself to say the words . . . not when the Village Nar died because of you. If only I could have done something, but the no-see had pulled me out of the world, like I was in a locked house looking out a window. But you weren't in that locked house with me."

So cruel, her words! But also true. Again I wondered if I'd been in the village if I could have spared all those people. I was stunned, angry, defensive . . . all those feelings battering at me and welling up within me at the same time. Her words were daggers stabbing at my heart, wounding me all the worse because they were true. I could scarcely breathe.

"Your fault, Eri."

My fault. Yes, I believed her in this, too.

I tried to center myself. I could not change what had happened to the Village Nar . . . but I could make something right by fulfilling my bloadoath and making Lord Purvis share the fate of Lady Ewaren and the others.

I shivered and searched for a way to make myself feel whole, though I knew that was impossible now. What was possible was getting Alysen into the hands of the Nanoo.

I so wanted to be rid of this girl and her hurtful words!

"Alysen, we cannot, either of us, wander at will from the other . . . like you did in the woods of the tangling vines. You have to stay with me if you want to stay safe. You've proven to me that Nanoo Gafna found you a willing and able student. Doubtless you have many talents you've not displayed, spells you've not shown me. But . . ."

She smiled, and I saw no pleasant line of lip in it.

I so wanted to hand her over to the Nanoo this very instant.

"Talents and other spells. Perhaps, Eri." Alysen leaned back against one of the stone pillars. "Very well. I'll not run off again." She had a hand against the red-stained stone on each side of her body. "Favor me this much, Moonson. Favor me and stand you so also against the pillar behind you."

I hesitated, trying to read her expression. "I am no Moonson. I try to live by the principles Bastien taught me. I embrace honor and do my best to live righteously. But I am no Moonson."

My tongue tip tasted the air. I caught no hint of evil or deception from her, just anger and loss. I wondered if I was a lackwit for doing what she asked.

"You say you are not a Moonson because only men born into wealthy homes can enter the knightly order?"

I didn't answer her.

There came a flow of wind down from the rock face. It was a chill breeze that felt welcoming after the fire Alysen had conjured. It wrapped pleasantly around me and brought a sense of autumn to this place of Fire Stones. The rich spiral notes that made up a bride song of a varle sounded. And just for a moment—a very quick moment—I saw color enwrapping Alysen. It was a swirling circle of color, purple and green, then shifting to pale blue and shimmering orange. As I watched, it turned sun-yellow, then gray. A moment more and it had changed to the maroon of her skirt. Her clothes softened as I watched, like they were old and most of the dye had been sucked out of them. The colors seeped into the rock behind her, causing the stone to flare with an unnatural beauty.

It was a ward of some sort, nothing I could have performed. Alysen was far deeper into the wyse and its ways than I. The ward enclosed me now, taking the color from my clothes, but not whirling about me as the colors had her. I slipped down the rock and settled cross-legged at its foot, my hands resting on my knees. A part of me said I should not permit this. Putting a ward on someone without their consent oversteps propriety. But another part was curious, and that part believed I could rise and walk away at any moment.

Perhaps I'd become so beaten down by everything that had happened that I was too tired to argue with her.

Lord Purvis and his men had gone to the Village Nar for me. Did they still look? Had I become the quarry just like the curl-horns had been mine?

An unusual restlessness settled in my heart. I could not go back to the Village Nar, not just because of the men who pursued me, but also because that part of my life was over. In my mind I saw the bloodied corpse of Lady Ewaren and smelled the death of the villagers. I tasted grief and hate, both of those emotions now coming from me.

By the Green Ones! The feelings of grief welled and churned and worked to weaken me. I stretched a hand up to touch the tear-shaped moss agate stones of my necklace, then dropped the hand back to my knees, my eyes welling with tears.

Through the haze of colors I saw Alysen settling at the foot of her own pillar.

"The Emperor is dead." Alysen's words were stiff. She'd repeated that phrase so many times to me. Her eyes were fixed on the trail behind, the one we'd followed to come to this place of Fire Stones.

"My father is dead, too, Alysen. So you say."

If she heard me or saw me, I couldn't tell. Perhaps this un-known ward she'd cast had drained her . . . she'd used so much wyse-power on this rock plateau that she likely had no energy left. I continued, slowly, giving weight to every word I spoke.

"Alysen, if my father was murdered, then poison was the weapon. Perhaps the murderer had a talent—there are as many black-hearted users of the wyse as there are white-. And there are enchantments beyond the wyse, not as powerful, but certainly useful. My father could have been struck dumb, un-able to call out a warning. There are poisons that take your voice."

When I was very, very young, my father had begun school-ing me in poisons and how to taste for them merely by setting my tongue near the substance. Then he was gone to the Em-peror and Empress, and my mother had schooled me in other things—cooking and sewing, tasks I was ill-suited for. I again studied poison with Bastien. But these were of the woods—vines and ivy, snake venom—things one encountered in na-ture, not found laced into food by enemies.

"He was poisoned, wasn't he, Alysen?"

She didn't answer for the longest time, still looking toward where we'd come. I opened my mouth to repeat the question, and she held up a hand.

"I saw him die, Eri. Do you know why I looked in on him with my scry magic? Oh, I visited a lot of places through a muddy puddle, but most often the capital city. Everything there is so beautiful. The ladies in clothes made of silk and lace, hair in spiraling curls and a red tint to their cheeks. Fine food on tables in fancy inns. Places I'd dreamed of being and can never go because I am of the House of Geer."

"Why did you look in on my father, Alysen?"

"Because you had one. Because I heard you mention him at dinner one night. Because I didn't have an earthly father and was curious what he might be doing in the fine, fancy city to the south. A handsome man, your father. I wish I hadn't seen him die." A pause: "Poison, maybe. I did not see him eat or drink, I'd not been looking in on him long. I saw men in his doorway, the man now I know as Lord Purvis, one of them. I saw him stumble and clutch his chest. And I saw him die."

I didn't stop the tears. I let them spill over my cheeks and into my mouth. So salty and sad, they tasted. I let my breath come ragged like I was a babe who'd fallen and scraped her knee.

Alysen looked puzzled. "You spent years away from him, Eri. Why grieve for a man who was your father only in name?"

"Because he was my father." No sisters, cousins, at least that I knew of. And my brother was long gone, away in some army. Did my brother know of our father's death? Was my brother safe because there was no magic about him?

"My father." I knew my father loved me in his way, I saw it in his eyes when I visited him at his sickbed. Oh, why hadn't I stayed longer on that trip? What pressing thing awaited in the Village Nar that I had to return? Why had I thrown away the letter he'd written?

"There is no heir to the throne." Alysen deftly changed the subject. "The Empress has no child, and she is at the far edge of an age that would let her have a child. A distant relative will be named to succeed her, I'd guess, in the event something untoward happened to her. Perhaps the border nobles will start courting her, hoping to wed her and father the next Emperor while she still might be fertile." Alysen was looking at me now, though her eyes seemed distant. "What do you think will happen, Eri?"

I shrugged and studied Alysen. A child, her head danced with adult concerns. She was too mature for her age, and yet too immature to suit me. "Alysen, I've never cared for royalty and their trappings."

"Like the Nanoo."

"Like Bastien."

"I don't think the Empress will consider courtship. Not now. The Emperor out of the way, I think she'll go after the Southern Border Lords and work to expand her country rather than her family—though I could be wrong. She has no heir. The Emperor always opposed a war, and so did the Dawn Priests. But the Southern Border Lords might look to their boundaries now."

"A war? Already the land is scarred . . . by something. Game animals are getting scarce. The land doesn't need a war." Again I pictured the dead Village Nar. "There doesn't need to be more killing."

The starlight softened, and I looked up. A thin layer of clouds drifted across, blotting out the larger constellations. In the silence that filled the minutes between Alysen and me, more clouds appeared, these thicker and darker, dropping down to nearly touch the stone rise and blotting out the sight of the stars altogether.

15

I TASTED THE AIR, CLOSING MY EYES AND CALLING ON MY WYSE-sense to tell me what the wind knew. Brimstone came at me first, followed again by the stench of burned flesh, Grazti's. I smelled the gentleness of the fell pony and the pleasure of Crust at having rolled in grass and drunk deeply of cool water. The cob was purely happy, not having any idea how close he'd been to danger if the grass had caught fire, and not understanding what had happened with Dazon or with Grazti. Horses are such simple animals. I found myself drinking in the cob's joy—I so desperately needed something to lift me from this melancholy.

I rose, scraping my cloak against the pillar behind me. Alysen sat still, eyes closed and lost in thought. I stretched and rolled my shoulders, forced out thoughts of the Village Nar and my dead father, and tasted deeper of Crust's rapture.

My heart finally lighter, I tasted for other things. I picked up the stone that stretched away under my feet and rose in pillars all around me. It was different stone from the cliff face that reached high and touched the low-hanging clouds. The stone spoke of ancient fires and liquid rock, when in ages past this land had been volcanic and when a mountain—the cliff all that remained of it—often had painted the ground with molten lava. The pillars were shaped by magic, by witches from an old time, I guessed. And whatever significance the pillars had to their rituals or wards was long lost.

I tasted a river deep beneath the ground, thick and slow, and rising with the land and spilling out a crevice in the cliff and satisfying Crust and the fell. I sensed that it had not always flowed below the earth, but that some great upheaval had changed the land. I had not sought these bits of knowledge, but sometimes when I tasted the air it gave me all manner of impressions.

Longer I tasted and found more water, heavy in the air and heavier in the clouds above. My tongue told me rain was coming soon, and that it would not be a gentle one. I felt the energy in the sky, and it told me a storm was stoking. Harsh weather was more certain a thing than speculations concerning the Empress and the Border Lords to the far, far south.

We needed shelter. There was no roof or creviced wall here; the pillars stood apart and did not promise cover—not against a storm, in any event. I continued to study the clouds, hearing a distant rumble that signaled it was already raining to the west.

The darkness hid much of what lay farther north. I was sure we were far enough north—though it hadn't been of our own volition—to be safe from Lord Purvis and his men. I needed Alysen away from me. Then I wouldn't worry about being safe. I would worry only about fulfilling my bloodoath.

I swung around the pillar and strode toward the horses. Crust had been rolling again, but he stood as I approached, nostrils quivering and ears pricked forward. I knew that he was sensing the coming storm, too—animals could sense such things without the need of magic. I stopped at the collection of saddles and packs, and I whistled for Crust.

The cob kept staring at the clouds, nostrils wide. I whistled again, and she looked to me, answering my call with a long whinny and running toward me, thudding hooves hitting hard against the ground. She trotted a little to my right and then picked her way in a circle to reach me. I put the saddle on her, cinched it, and added two packs to the back of it. Then I whistled for the fell pony, Spring Mist. She came immediately, and I saddled her and put Alysen's packs on her back.

I looked back to the stone pillars and cliff face. All around the dark was deepening and the shadows were inky black. Lightning flickered overhead. Again and again, thin and light, looking delicate, though heralding something that would be fierce.

"Alysen, we need to leave! We must find shelter."

She still sat against the pillar, too far away for me to see if she had her eyes closed.

"Alysen! Listen to me!"

She raised her arms above her head, gripping the pillar and inching up it. Then she looked to me and pointed at the cliff face, where the slender waterfall came down.

"You want shelter, Eri? There's a cave in there. I would've thought your wyse-sense would have shown it to you."

I edged my tongue out beyond my teeth and found the wyse magic again, this time focusing only on the cliff and finding the cave Alysen had mentioned. I cursed myself for not searching further, when I found the underground river. Inside the cave that stretched behind the narrow waterfall, I felt a dampness . . . but it wasn't wet. The river flowed through the stone, above the roof of the cave. It would accommodate the horses, too.

I took their reins and led them now.

I didn't wait for Alysen. I went straight to the waterfall, stopping only when I needed to coax Spring Mist and Crust through the water . . . and that took some doing. It was blackest black inside, the water that cascaded over the opening a ribbon of silver-gray. Alysen joined us just as thunder rocked the ground.

I heard the snap of lightning, then thunder again.

She stood just inside the opening, cloak wrapped around her, so still she could have passed for a statue. I saw her outline only because she stood next to the ribbon of water. Thrusting the nickering of the horses to the back of my mind, I stretched out my arm and tentatively touched her shoulder.

She shivered, still staring at the ribbon of water. She shivered again when lightning snapped and thunder boomed.

The brash child—daughter of a god, she claimed—trembled in fright. Her hands fell limply to her sides, and she spoke in the strange singsong voice she had earlier.

"I am Alysen, true daughter of Lady Magen of the House of Geer and one of the Green Ones. I have not given myself to the Nine Circles of the world, and yet I have true sight and straight thought. Without giving any man Liege Oath, no city or country, I am strong in the wyse."

Moisture gathered in her eyes and spilled over to make

runnels down her scratched and dusty cheeks. She raised a hand to smear the tears and dust together.

"I am no power-worker." I spoke a little louder than I'd intended. I wanted to give weight to my words and to be heard above the waterfall and the rain that had started pattering against the rocky plateau outside. "I am Yulen t'Kyros, and we do not stand in Kyros, for that was taken by floods in another season. Nor are we anywhere near the House of Geer or the Village Nar or the Nanoo's fen. We are near-lost, Alysen. And it is well more than all right for you to act like a child. You are but a child, Alysen."

I didn't have to look in her face to know her eyes were glazed with fear. "Not near-lost, Eri, completely lost. Grazti ordered us this way and that way."

"Ever north, though."

She nodded.

"So near-lost, but if we travel south, until we find something familiar . . ."

"We'll eventually find the Nanoo." Her voice was raised at the end, as if in a question. "I didn't know that Grazti was a loathsome thing. If only I'd thought to taste for evil . . . or if you'd thought to do so."

"Enemies are often hidden things, Alysen." I dropped my hand from her shoulder and let my fingers dance across the rock behind me. It was moist from the waterfall, and soothing.

"Not to you, Moonson. Your enemies are Lord Purvis and his men. They—"

"I tell you again, Alysen, I am not a Moonson. Bastien was a Moonson, and I was trained by him. But—"

"He called you Moonson, though perhaps not to your face.

I heard him tell Lady Ewaren you were as much a Moonson as the knights in the great city to the south."

"But I am not noble-born."

"No."

"And only noble-born *men* are knights."

"And only knights can be Moonsons."

"Yes, Alysen."

"I understand, Moonson."

I let out a deep breath. "Then understand this, Alysen. Since I have enemies, I will find allies." Though I would call on no ally to help me fulfill my bloodoath.

"The Nanoo are your allies."

"And we will find them, Alysen, since we are—"

"—not completely lost," she finished for me.

I felt her smile through the darkness.

The storm intensified, the rain drumming hard and the thunder playing havoc. If the sky had a mood this night, it was anger. Roused and fighting mad. Thunder roared and rumbled its arguments to the ground. Water poured down steadily, harshly *rat-a-tat-tat*ting against the stone, so harshly it sounded like hail. Everything so loud, we couldn't sleep until the night stretched toward morning.

We slept soundly then, in those early hours, even Spring Mist and Crust. The rain continued, softer now, restful and sonorous and rhythmic. For the first time in the past few days I'd found something to be thankful for—nature's lullaby and bones so tired that they didn't protest the cave floor for a bed.

The rain ended when the first rays of the morning sent the ribbon of waterfall to shimmering bright silver. I passed through it, slowly, unbuckling my weapon belt, loosening the lacing of the hide jerkin, and slipped it off. The coarse linen of my shirt followed, then I pulled off my boots. I let the waterfall rush over me, taking off the dust and the worst of the memories of the previous days. But it couldn't wash away all the heartaches.

Soon, I stood naked between the stone pillars, my clothes spread out on the rocky plateau to dry. The air was a little cool, but I didn't mind it. I looked to the north, where a faint double rainbow arced across a cloudless sky.

The horses grazed while Alysen washed herself in the fall. We ate from our dwindling provisions, careful not to take too much, and we filled our bottles with water, drinking as much as we could before refilling them to bursting, then dressing and getting on the horses.

"Have we again come into favor?" Alysen asked.

"Perhaps." I wondered if I would ever feel good again. My body was so tired and full of aches, my mind weary. I had slept well, but it would take several nights of such deep sleep to thoroughly recover—physically and emotionally. So much had happened in such a short time, like a sword falling and slitting reality.

By the Green Ones, why had all this come to pass?

And now we were faced with a journey from a land we'd not been in before, without even a suggestion of a map. I'd watched where Grazti had led us, but there were so many twists and turns to the creature's course, as if it had deliberately kept the path confusing.

"I'm sorry about your father, Eri."

I was taken aback by Alysen's words. She'd not expressed compassion for me before.

"And I'm sorry I looked in on him and saw him die. Maybe I looked in because I envied you, having a father and all."

"It is time to get matters straight, Alysen." I kneed Crust into moving. When the *clip-clop* of his hooves was echoed by the fell pony's, I continued. "Each of us has a truth to add to the whole. I am Yulen t'Kyros. My father was of the old blood and born with the talent. His was the power of taste—as mine is. In the Year of the Leopard my father was taken to the great southern city to serve as taster and cupbearer for the Empress and Emperor. My brother became a squire, and I never saw him again. After the Law of Wyse Right, my mother and I were taken to Galleen Holding, where my mother died two years later, having been stung by veesor ants while helping to bring in the harvest."

I told no bard's tale of heroics, and might well have been repeating something Alysen already knew. Too, she might not have been interested in the details of my life, only that I had an earthly father. *Had.*

"I was left alone after my mother's death, Alysen, stripped of kin and too young to make my own way in the world. No family volunteered to take me in at Galleen Holding. Lady Ewaren of the Village Nar had been known to take in young people with talents, and so they sent word to her. She agreed and gave me my own room. Bastien of the Moonsons was newly arrived at the Village Nar and lessoned me in arms. And he tried to teach me a bit about the wyse, as he had what he called a trivial talent. Nanoo Gafna helped, teaching me to center my wyse skills. Now a handful of days ago I come home from a hunt to discover Lady Ewaren of the Village Nar dead, those of her household slain, news that my father has also suffered his end, and with him, the Emperor. Lady Ewaren was tortured, no doubt in their effort to discover where I was. But she didn't know."

I paused, reached for my saddle bottle, and drank deep, though I was not thirsty. Alysen's tongue appeared between her lips and swept across them. I handed her the bottle and she drank in turn. She swallowed and took another mouthful, swallowed again, and gave me the bottle back.

"I am Alysen of the House of Geer. My clan has since before the War of the Underlings had ties with the Green Ones, as well as with some families strong in the wyse. When my mother began showing, after a Green One . . ." She stroked her chin, searching for the words and not finding ones to her liking. "There were those who saw themselves belittled as a clan to have a woman pregnant with no earthly husband. So they arranged my mother's marriage to an Arms Lord who hated magic. I had an unfortunate childhood; I was strong in the wyse and unable to use it lest I risk punishment from my . . . father. About a year ago, I could not stand it any longer, and out of sympathy—and out of trying to protect me in a dwindling Geer line—my mother sent me to Lady Ewaren." The breath hissed out between her teeth, and she shook her head.

After a few moments of silence, I spoke again. "I have no home beyond the Village Nar, either. I cannot go back to Kyros. The floods destroyed it years past."

Alysen rubbed a bruise on her hand. "Geer is closed to me. There are people in the settlement who would be the first to deliver me to some lord to be used as a kitchen girl." She stretched forward to scratch at a spot between Spring Mist's ears. "So the deep, deep woods of the Nanoo, Mardel's Fen, is where we'll find our refuge, Eri. We'll be safe from Lord Purvis and his men, from fose-bears. Safe, and free to use the wyse. Nothing to menace us."

I didn't let her see my frown. She would be safe with all of the Nanoo to watch over her. But I had a bloodoath to fulfill. My own safety was of no concern.

16

THE SUN AND THE STARS GUIDED US. BASTIEN HAD TAUGHT ME to read them well. But we were not able to travel straight in any one direction for long because of the hills and gullies. The valley that we'd traveled through to reach the place of the Fire Stones was even more treacherous as we retraced our steps. The fierce rains had washed away much of the scant earth that had covered the steep sides, leaving great patches of slate and granite, tipped at awkward angles that threatened to injure Spring Mist and Crust. So we took an easier route and could not accurately backtrack.

I took us the length of the treacherous valley, finding more gently sloping ground at the far western edge of it. Under the umbrella of an old, half-dead elm, we camped. We didn't speak much, both of us finding the silence to our liking, and we made our way up the rise the following morning. Our rations were gone, and I would have to hunt this day to feed us. It would not be an easy thing, as I could not leave Alysen, and her presence would make hunting more difficult. I prayed to the Green Ones that we could find spring berries along our path.

"South?"

"Yes, Alysen, we're traveling south."

"Beyond that, do you know where we're going, Eri? Are we still near-lost?"

I allowed myself a faint chuckle. I'd not laughed since several days before the Village Nar slaughter. The sound of my laughter made me uncomfortable. I should not be finding happiness at this juncture. "Alysen, I've not been in this territory that I can recall. Though if hunting had gotten much worse, I daresay I would have discovered this place."

I stopped, cocking my head and listening. All I could hear were the small animal sounds—birds and ground squirrels. No snapping of wood to indicate boars or curl-horns or other large beasts. Perhaps I could find us a rabbit.

"What's that?" My gaze followed Alysen's extended finger. And to the west, through a gap in a clump of birch trees, I spied a cottage.

"Let's find out. Perhaps someone there will offer us something to eat in exchange for chores." I was tired of riding, and investigating the cottage was as good an excuse as any to get off Crust and stretch my legs. Within moments, we were at the clump of birches, then beyond them.

"No one lives in that home. Not anymore, Eri."

"That looks to be so." I slid off Crust and passed the reins to Alysen. "Please stay here. Please."

I knew it was a gamble that she'd heed my words.

There was a gate around the cottage, like one might find

in a village. But there was no village in sight—though I did spy what looked like the remainder of other homes. The gate was open and the cottage stood alone, run-down, with weeds growing high out front in what once was an herb and flower garden. The front door was halfway open, hanging at an odd angle because one of the hinges had pulled loose. There'd been no fire in the fireplace for a good while, and I knew the place had been abandoned—but after a moment of sniffing, I knew it was not unoccupied. I freed the double-hooked chain from my belt, twirling the loose, heavier end.

I heard Alysen suck in a deep breath, and I cringed, fearing she would talk or make some other noise and give our presence away. With an exaggerated shake of my head, hoping that might keep her silent, I crept toward the front door, breathing shallowly and picking my steps carefully so I would not break a twig or rustle the weeds.

I stopped myself from calling on my wyse-sense. Alysen claimed I used weapons when I should use my mind. But I regarded the magic of the earth too highly to call upon it without thought. I did not need my wyse-sense to tell me what waited inside the cottage. My eyes and nose had picked up enough signs to know.

A few feet from the cottage door, I gave up on stealth and rushed forward, raising my leg and slamming my heel against the wood, splintering it and leaping inside. A squeal cut through the air, then another, this second one long and painful to my ears, as it was a squeal of pain. I slammed my chain against the pig, drawing the hooked end across its throat to kill it quickly. I respected all life, and I didn't want to cause the beast to suffer more than necessary.

"What is it?" Alysen pushed what was left of the door all the way open. "What . . . oh my!"

I knelt on the floor of the one-room cottage, remnants of crude furniture around me, slain wild pig in front of me. "Hungry?" I asked her.

Though she looked in horror at the blood and the dead animal, she nodded yes. "Very, Eri. I am very, very hungry."

I butchered the pig behind the cottage, Alysen collecting pieces of the broken furniture to burn in the fireplace. She wanted no part of watching me with the pig. As she finished her task earlier than I, I called to her to search through the overgrown garden in the front to see if there might be something there to supplement the meat. I suspected she knew nothing about gardening, as I'd never seen her work in the gardens in the Village Nar. But she surprised me and discovered early coriander, caraway, costmary, clary sage, and spring savory. Perhaps indeed she knew gardening. As she said, I was often hunting and rarely around.

Though there was much of the day left, we stayed in the old cottage, as it took hours to cook the wild pig. We contentedly stuffed ourselves with the meat, tearing what we didn't eat into strips that we wrapped with the herbs and packed for the next few days. The horses grazed on wildflowers and the herbs Alysen hadn't picked, and they drank from a rain barrel that miraculously stood intact to the side of the cottage. The room was smoky, the fireplace thick with the char of long-ago fires and begging to be cleaned, but we didn't mind the smell as we sat in front of the flames and enjoyed this scrap of civilization.

We swept up a space where we could lay out our bedrolls

with an old broom we had found. It was not near so comfortable as our rooms at Lady Ewaren's house, but it was far better than our accommodations of the previous few nights.

Shortly before midnight another storm erupted, and I brought the horses inside to crowd us. I wondered if the sky was sending me a message—that the remainder of my life would be plagued by storms of a human nature.

I left a few pieces of wood in the fireplace to give us some light and stirred the embers, as again the thick clouds blotted out the stars. Normally I slept better in darkness, but tonight I thought the glow would make both of us rest easier.

The storm was thankfully short-lived, and well before the sky started to lighten the air filled with the chorus of insects and the cries of night birds. My fingers played with the moss-agate tears of my necklace, and I thought of Bastien. If it hadn't been for his teachings, I would lack woodland skills and Alysen and I would be in a far worse situation.

We left the cottage early the following morning, and three long, soggy days passed before we reached the part of the woods that felt familiar to me. Another day, the sun high overhead, and we returned to the marshy ground where the thorny wall and the grasping vines had entwined us with Grazti. The wall was gone, no trace of it but in our memories, nor was there any sign of the depression where the bird-creature had been caught.

"Are you sure this is it?"

"Yes, Alysen, through this way we'll come to the heart of the fen. Had the woods not railed against that . . . damn bird-beast, we would have been through here well more than a week ago."

She smiled, but it was a nervous one. I could guess from her expression what she was thinking. She would be safe here with Nanoo Gafna, but it would not be the sort of life she wanted. She'd admitted to me she yearned for the fancy life of the great southern city. This would not even be as "fancy" as the Village Nar.

"Everything will be fine, Alysen." I wanted to make her feel better . . . perhaps so I would feel better about leaving her with the Nanoo. There would be no place for her at my side as I carried out my bloodoath.

My mouth was dry as I slipped from the back of Crust and led her between the trunks of twin black oaks. I'd been this way before, spying artfully curved branches and almost invisible scratches in the bark of old rock elms. Bastien had taught me that trees do not grow haphazardly. The differences in soil and rainfall, coupled with temperature, dictate what varieties grow where. Yet in this fen there was a mix that did not follow nature's rules. Longleaf pines stretched up more than a hundred feet, dropping their long needles on the ground to create a spongy carpet over the sodden earth. Piñon pines, with their tasty nuts, grew alongside them . . . a tree that should be found far, far to the west of here. Bald cypress, which craved the wet of this place, stood next to paper birch and big-tooth aspen, trees that should have been in the colder climes of the distant south. Too, there was a scattering of pin oaks, which Bastien told me favored high, dry places.

It was the Nanoo who'd grown these woods, aesthetically pleasing, scenting the air and providing nuts and a carpet and wood to build homes. They'd arranged Mardel's Fen much in the same way a lord and lady would arrange the furniture in their manor house. I was in great awe of the Nanoo; to have such power to sculpt nature was a gods-given gift.

Perhaps when I'd completed my bloodoath, I would return here and make a life for myself. I knew enough of the Nanoo's ways to be accepted. Besides, where else would I go? I had no one, and my home was a village of the dead.

I pressed on through the woods, a stern look to Alysen keeping her behind me. She knew not to run off this time—the previous episode of that had gifted us with the vile Grazti.

Gnats danced across my face, but I didn't bother raising a hand to brush them away. They were insignificant compared with everything else I'd encountered. I saw webs, and they only served to remind me of our House Lady weaver. I walked by them quickly.

Then we passed beneath a tall willow birch, and I felt the weeping leaves brush my shoulders.

Few people are welcomed into the heart of the fen, and I know I am blessed to be one of them. I continued to draw the precious, damp air into my lungs and thank the wood spirits with each step. I looked over once at Alysen, as we neared a dead black willow, its thin branches dangling down and looking like a nest of giant spiders. Her lips were moving, and I hoped it wasn't in the conjuration of some spell.

No matter, I would have her in Nanoo Gafna's hands within minutes, and then I would be about my bloodoath.

The Nanoo are a reclusive folk, eccentric and peculiar and secretive. Not many of them venture from the fen, choosing to live out their long lives on this stretch of soggy ground. Nanoo Gafna, however, had spent two days of every other week in the Village Nar for at least the past ten years. On occasion she stayed for longer. Bastien said it was because of Lady Ewaren, that their families were entwined a generation or two in the past, and that they were "faint relatives" who enjoyed each other's company. However, Lady Ewaren said Gafna came because she was overly fond of milk, and that the Village Nar was the closest source of cow's milk to the fen. I knew Gafna would not be visiting the Village Nar again.

The dead branches of the willow rustled as we walked beneath them, some playing along Crust's back and withers. The cob nickered appreciatively. Then we were beyond the big tree and walking through a row of feathery fescue that grew in water that reached above our ankles.

A moment more and we were in the heart of the fen.

I offered a silent prayer of thanks to the Green Ones that we'd finally reached our destination. Ancient, thick, twisted trees ringed an egg-shaped clearing filled with reeds and standing water. The gnarled branches looked like serpents artfully intertwined.

I looked from one tree to the next, then I told my mind not to believe my eyes. In that instant, I saw the Nanoo community. The base of each tree was actually a cottage, with hollows forming doors and windows. Smaller cottages grew farther up, and squirrels and jays flitted from home to home, telling the Nanoo of visitors. I knew the animal messengers were unnecessary—the trees had announced our presence the moment we neared the Nanoo's standing stones.

Wisteria eria eria eria. It was the breeze calling my name. I dropped Crust's reins and approached the largest of the trees, an impossibly thick walnut, kneeling in the water and feeling the mud take hold of my knees, the toes of my boots, and my leggings. Alysen came behind me, holding her skirt up to keep it dry. She did not kneel.

Eria eria eria eria. The breeze persisted, soft and melodic and curling around my head. I bowed until my forehead brushed the fescue.

Eria eria.

"Wisteria of Nar, you are welcome here, friend of the Nanoo and friend of the fen."

I raised my head and let my gaze drift over the speaker.

She faced me, nearly six feet tall, though her shoulders were rounded with age. Her skin was tanned and so deeply lined it looked like the bark of the walnut tree she'd emerged from. Her arms were long and the fingers that dangled below the sleeves of her earth brown gown were thin and curved, like the talons of a bird. Much about her was birdlike. Her neck was thrust forward, head lowered, long nose leading. She took quick steps, head bobbing like a bird's. Her hair was a thick, coarse tangle that dropped to her shoulders, appearing like the nest of a hawk.

"Wisteria, what brings you here?" Her voice was thin and musical, also like a bird's, and it reminded me in particular of the song of a thrush.

I rose, head still bowed, then I slowly tipped my chin up and met her eyes.

They were bright green, like wet emeralds, the only thing about her that did not hint of her great age. Unblinking and intense, they made me feel as if I were drowning in them—oh so pleasantly drowning. Her eyes spoke of intelligence and humor, experience, understanding, and now flashed with curiosity and concern. She looked past me and to Alysen.

"Nanoo Shellaya," I addressed her. "We are here to seek counsel with Nanoo Gafna."

Nanoo Shellaya ruled the fen, though I know she considered herself more a guardian or custodian than queen of the witches. Nanoo Gafna once told me Shellaya had begun her rule more than one hundred years ago. The Nanoo were the same race as Alysen and I, but the woods enriched them and blessed them with a longer life.

Other Nanoo joined us, all with tanned tree-bark faces, though none so deeply lined as Shellaya's. They were a tall people, long-limbed and for the most part thin. Though predominantly women lived in the fen, I saw a few men among them, all dressed in earth brown clothes, some with green sashes. They easily blended with their surroundings. No children showed themselves in the clearing, but I spied two small faces peering out a window.

"Nanoo Gafna has not returned from her visit in the Village Nar, Wisteria. A visit longer than she has ever taken before." The concern was heavy in Shellaya's thin voice. "But your presence here tells me she is not in the village."

In unison, Alysen and I dropped to our knees. I heard the girl gasp behind me.

"They got her, Eri. The demon-of-a-man got Nanoo Gafna."

Again the images from the slaughtered village struck me, and in my head I heard the bellow of the cow demanding milking and the irritating sound of swarming flies. I smelled the blood that was everywhere.

The foot . . .

The tattered garment that had been Lady Ewaren's dress.

"That demon-of-a-man Lord Purvis killed Nanoo Gafna, too." Alysen let out a sob.

I didn't try to stop the tears that cascaded down my cheeks. I had yet another friend to mourn.

17

AS NANOO SHELLAYA SHUFFLED FORWARD, THE STANDING WATER rippled outward to touch my legs. She stood in front of me, her birdlike hands on my shoulders, and I poured out the story of the Village Nar.

I was no longer the docent of Bastien, no longer the hunter he had taught, no longer the proud, determined woman who had left the Village Nar a week ago and managed to single-handedly slay a pair of large curl-horns. I was just a drained young woman who'd lost absolutely everything and had thoroughly given in to her despair. I'd forced myself to function before, watching over Alysen. But now she was safe, and the magic of this ancient place cocooned me like I was a babe.

I don't know how long I stayed on my knees, the water seeping up my leggings and into my tunic, the mud sucking at me as if I were a tree trying to take root. Eventually, however, the tears stopped. My stomach ached from crying, and despite the eternal wetness of this place, my chest and throat were achingly dry.

Nanoo Shellaya tugged me to my feet and guided me inside her cottage. Someone retrieved my satchels from Crust, and I dressed in warm, dry clothes and sat on a crude bench in front of a low table. Shellaya sat opposite me. Behind her, Alysen sat cross-legged on a braided rug, an oval wood bowl balanced on her knees, and she sifted her fingers through the seed beads that filled it.

I'd been in Nanoo Gafna's cottage before, but only hers. Nanoo Shellaya's was much larger. I was amazed that there were three rooms inside the base of this tree. We sat in what passed for her kitchen. Strings of wooden beads hung in the doorways of the other rooms—through one I saw a long, thin bed. The other room was cloaked in shadows, but the scents that spilled out hinted that it was Shellaya's conjuring room.

She pressed a mug of tea into my hands. The mug was tall and wide, ceramic glazed to a high polish and painted with yellow and orange flowers; it was not something made here. I held my nose over the brew and inhaled. The aroma was pleasing and unknown to me.

I took a sip and held the liquid on my tongue. Flowers of some sort, blended with spices. Wholly wonderful. I took a long swallow and eased back on the bench.

"Nanoo Shellaya, I am so very sorry I—"

"Never apologize for grief, Wisteria." Her voice sounded stronger in the cottage. "Grief is not a sign of weakness, but rather a measure of valor. It shows you have ties to the world and that you cared deeply for the people lost to you."

"And dear Dazon," I whispered.

"Your horse."

I nodded and drank some more.

"Finish that, Wisteria. All of it."

I did as she instructed, watching as she took the mug and shuffled from her bench to a fireplace, where a cauldron heated. The flames warmly lit the room and seemed to present no threat to the tree or the cottage's furnishings—practically everything in this place was wood. She used a birch ladle to refill the mug, then she returned to me.

"Look to the surface, Wisteria, and let your soul settle just a bit."

Surface? I stared at the tea, seeing my reflection and instantly frowning. Not one to worry about my appearance, I was nonetheless taken aback by it. My hair, though a short cap, was tangled and dusted with small burrs and strings of wildflower pollen. Dirt streaked my face. I shook my head and looked away. As I did so, I caught something out of the corner of my eye—another reflection. I returned my gaze to the tea.

Nanoo Gafna stared back at me. Or at least I thought she did.

"My sister lives," Nanoo Shellaya said. "I would have felt her death. I suspected something amiss, else she would have returned to the fen last week. But Gafna is a wanderer, and so when I searched and felt her spirit, I wrongly suspected she was wandering . . . perhaps in search of ever-sweeter milk." She smiled at that, her green eyes twinkling. "The juice of the cow has ever been my sister's greatest temptation."

I continued to stare at the miniature reflection, my hands wrapped around the mug, and now Nanoo Shellaya's wrapped around my fingers. She leaned over the table and the top of our heads touched. The image in the tea shifted slightly, pulling back so we could see where Nanoo Gafna was.

Gafna sat in a straight-backed chair, a lantern on a stool nearby casting shadows across her lined face. Her clothes were tattered, and there were scratches and bruises on her arms.

"By the Green Ones!" I hushed. I saw that her left hand was mangled, the fingers broken as Lady Ewaren's had been.

Alysen joined us at my outburst, but she could not get close enough to see what we found so interesting in the mug.

"She suffers," Nanoo Shellaya said. The merry light faded from the old woman's eyes.

"Because of me, Nanoo Shellaya. The men who hold her, and who beat her, came to the Village Nar looking for me. Had I been there instead of hunting and ranging so far, only I would have suffered. Everyone else would be all right."

The image shifted again, pulling back so Nanoo Gafna was so tiny we could no longer make out her features. She was against one wall of a large room that was filled with long tables and benches, the lantern by her the only light. It was a place of fellowship, a dining hall, perhaps. Nanoo Shellaya's hands pressed hard against mine, and in response ripples filled the surface of the tea. A heartbeat later I saw the exterior of a long house. A thick wisp of smoke trailed up from its chimney. Another heartbeat and I saw the edge of a village, a river coursing by its eastern edge, a lone hill rising to the west.

Then the image was gone and Nanoo Shellaya leaned back and curled her bird fingers around the edge of the table.

"You do not know, Wisteria, that your presence in the village would have changed things."

"They wanted me," I told her plainly. I explained about the death of the Emperor and my father, Alysen jumping in to announce that the Empress was after me to end the magic in my line, a potential threat to her.

"And why would they think you such a threat, eh, Wisteria? One woman, a huntress and a farmer from a simple village? What threat could you be?"

"No threat if I am dead," I answered quickly.

"A threat indeed, then. You are a powerful woman. But you are a threat they created by their failure."

"And by their success," I added. "They succeeded in killing everyone and destroying everything I held dear."

"Save Gafna." Nanoo Shellaya tugged the mug away from me and held it close, looking straight down and mumbling words I could not understand.

Alysen watched her closely, with more reserve than I'd ever seen her show. Her mouth moved, too, and I realized she knew what Shellaya was saying.

"So they hold Nanoo Gafna, thinking she will tell them where to find me." I was furious this Lord Purvis would hold my old friend, furious she'd been beaten. "They still may hold her, the murderers."

"Demon-of-a-man," Alysen hissed.

Nanoo Shellaya did not raise her gaze from the tea. "You are mistaken, Wisteria. They do not keep my sister Gafna in their lair for that reason. She is Nanoo, and if this Lord Purvis has any sense about him, he knows he cannot break her."

I raised an eyebrow.

"They keep my sister, perhaps not because she will tell them where to find you, but because you will come for her, Wisteria. She could very well be the lure, and you are the fish they hope to catch."

Shellaya got up and returned to the cauldron, dumped the tea in it, and stirred. "Will you stay the night, Wisteria." She did not pose it as a question. Again ladling warm tea into the mug, she brought it to the table and handed it to me. "Drink all of it. You'll need your strength." She added to this small biscuits and honey. Then she exited the cottage, leaving Alysen and me alone.

Alysen waited a few minutes before sitting where Nanoo Shellaya had been. "Eri . . ."

I stared into the tea, seeing nothing but my pitiful reflection this time. I took a long swallow and reached for one of the biscuits, pouring a little honey over it before taking a bite. It was good and sweet and filling. I closed my eyes and savored it.

"Eri—"

"I hear you."

"Eri . . ." She took a deep breath and paused.

"What, Alysen?"

"You're going after Nanoo Gafna, aren't you?"

"I have no choice." I chewed the biscuit, and Alysen left me alone until I'd finished. Then she took a biscuit and poured honey over it. She started nibbling at it. "Alysen, Nanoo Gafna is a friend, and an innocent. She was merely a visitor in the village when—"

"The Nanoo are never merely anything, Eri." She worked on the biscuit and regarded me, once more striking me as older than her years. Perhaps because she was god-sired, she looked at things through older eyes.

"It doesn't matter what they are, Alysen. Gafna is my friend, and I'll not have her share the fate of Lady Ewaren and the others."

"What makes you think they won't kill her when they've caught you?"

I didn't answer her for a few minutes, fixing my stare on the flames that curled around the cauldron.

"Well, Eri?"

"What makes you think they'll catch me?"

"What makes you think they won't?" She took another biscuit and went outside.

I finished my tea and biscuit, then stretched out in front of the fire. Nanoo Shellaya was right. I would need my strength, and I would need to be well rested. I suspected this would be the last long sleep I would have in some time.

The sky was lightening when I left the cottage, but the moon remained, a pale silver-white sliver that reminded me of the necklace Nanoo Gafna always wore. I had not seen it on her in the image in the tea.

I saddled Crust and put one satchel on his back. I'd left the other in Nanoo Shellaya's cottage, setting the ivory ribbons on the table for Alysen. I ran my fingers through my short hair—clean now and free of burrs. The ribbons were a frivolity I would never use, and Alysen seemed to favor fancy things.

I noticed that the pony had been saddled, and I turned back to Nanoo Shellaya's home and saw Alysen in the doorway.

"You're not coming with me, Alysen. I know you're fond of Nanoo Gafna and that you're more powerful in the wyse than I am, but—"

"I'm not going," Alysen said. There was a pout to her lips, and so I knew I'd hurt her feelings.

"The Nanoo here will take good care of you."

"I don't need to be taken care of, Eri. I can well manage for myself. As you said, I am more powerful in the wyse than you." She put her shoulders back, emphasizing that proud point. "Perhaps I should go so that I can take care of *you*." She smiled slightly, then the pout returned. "But, no, I'm not going." She slipped inside the house, where the shadows swallowed her.

"But I am."

I hadn't heard her, so silently she'd moved through the fen and gotten on the fell pony. Nanoo Shellaya seemed too tall for the pony, but she was so slight that she didn't present much of a burden. She was dressed in a long brown robe, nearly the color of her skin, with a cloak slightly darker. A backpack that looked like a spiderweb, or rather one that had been artfully woven from dried vines, was hooked to the saddle. It was too small to contain more than an extra robe and a small amount of food.

"Nanoo Shellaya, you can't—"

"No one tells me what I cannot do, Wisteria of Nar."

"I . . ." I found myself at an utter loss for words. The leader of the Nanoo intended to join me, intended to leave her people in Mardel's Fen and travel south to find Gafna. I should be honored by her presence, but in truth I did not want to be burdened by it . . . for that's what it would be. She was ancient by the standards of man, and Gafna once told me she'd not seen Shellaya—nor the others of advanced age— leave the fen in decades.

I should be honored she wanted to come with me. But I did not want to trade watching over a child for watching out for a very old woman.

"These men—Lord Purvis and his men—are murderers, Nanoo Shellaya. They are dangerous and—"

"You need not worry for my safety, Wisteria of Nar. I can well look after myself. And if by chance I should come to harm . . . well, I have spent enough years on this earth that it will not miss me overmuch if I leave it. Nanoo Rane will watch over the fen."

I opened my mouth to offer another protest, but realized it was futile. I had exchanged watching out for a willful child for watching out for a willful aged witch. My shoulders sagged and I shook my head.

"You need me, Wisteria of Nar." Nanoo Shellaya made a clucking sound and flicked the reins, and the fell pony complied and started walking. "But I'll not tarry for you. Best hurry."

The other Nanoo waved to her, some of them leaning out the doors and windows of their tree-homes, others standing in the center of the community. The one named Nanoo Rane followed the pony for several yards, until Shellaya passed beyond the veil of the dead black willow.

"You heard Nanoo Shellaya, Eri. Best hurry." This came from Alysen, who'd returned to the cottage doorway. She waved and offered me a faint smile.

I got on Crust and gently kneed her. I did not return Alysen's gestures.

18

WE DIDN'T SPEAK UNTIL WE LEFT THE FEN.

I imagined she thought about Nanoo Gafna. I thought about Gafna, too—and about Lady Ewaren, all the people of the Village Nar, my father, Dazon . . . But more than all of those whom I'd lost, I thought about Lord Purvis. My hands tightened on the reins, so tight my knuckles turned white and my fingers tingled with an uncomfortable numbness.

I could not see a future for myself, perhaps because my mind was flooded with grief and thoughts of vengeance. Little more than a week ago I'd had a future mapped out. I knew Lady Ewaren intended for me to eventually take her place as House Lady of the Village Nar. Lady Ewaren was not of far advanced years, but she had no children of her own, and she'd told the village elders that I was to follow her. I knew all the village operations, and I knew how to fight, though my skills had not saved the village. I'd been studying the young people of Nar, deciding whom to teach my skills of hunting and defense. I would have my own docents.

That future was lost to me. And now all I could see were broken bodies. All I could taste was the bloodoath I'd made.

Shellaya interrupted my dark musings.

"My sister Gafna talked often of you, Wisteria of Nar." We were on a merchant trail, one to the east of the fen and Nar. We'd decided not to pass through the village of the dead and so took a slightly longer way south. "My sister Gafna said kind things only . . . though she mentioned on more than one occasion that she thought you should spend more time in the garden than on the hunt."

I didn't reply, knowing full well that the Nanoo did not approve of hunting, and I did not want to get in an argument about eating habits. Shellaya had not asked me any questions, and I'd earlier told her everything I felt necessary. My words were unnecessary at the moment. Hers, however, I listened to intently. I learned more about her with each utterance.

I rode even with her so she would not have to raise her thin voice. She talked about the fen and the planting season, herbs used for healing, her voice getting stronger rather than weaker from her discourse. An hour or so later she spoke again about Gafna.

"My sister said you are strong in the wyse, Wisteria of Nar, and that you are slow to use it." She paused and pulled the hood of her cloak over her head so that it shadowed all of her face and her bird-nest hair.

I looked ahead on the road and saw three horses and riders. There were no wagons, and the horses were pale and tall with long, braided manes and tails, meaning it unlikely their riders were merchants—and certainly not common villagers. A minor noble and his retainers, I decided, when I noticed that the man in the lead had a sword hanging from his belt.

The Nanoo are distinctive with their heavily lined dark skin, musical voices, and unusual mannerisms. And I suspected Nanoo Shellaya didn't want to draw attention to herself, so she rolled her shoulders so that her sleeves fell down past her fingertips. She nudged the pony to travel on the far-western edge of the road.

I directed Crust to follow her closely.

"But being slow to use the wyse is not a fault, Wisteria of Nar. It shows restraint and is evidence that you hold magic in esteem. My sister Gafna especially likes that about you."

"Please, just call me Wisteria," I said. "Eri, actually. Lady Ewaren and Bastien called me Eri. Gafna calls me that, too, sometimes." That was the first I'd spoken since leaving the fen. "And I'm no longer of Nar, Nanoo Shellaya. Nar is lost to me. Lost to everyone."

"Eri." She nodded. "Then just Shellaya. I am past the age of needing titles . . . Eri."

"Someone will burn all of Nar, you know. A relative of one of the dead, I believe. No one will live in a place like that . . . too much blood on the ground. Too many horrid memories in the air. It is a place of ghosts now."

The three riders traveled single-file, keeping to the east side of the road, the one with the sword staying in the lead and obviously watching us. As we neared them, I saw they were well dressed and clean, their faces shaved, their boots showing minimal dust. There were no packs on the horses, and so I knew they were not going far, perhaps to the Village Grauthen, a little north and to the east of the fen.

I nodded politely as we passed the trio and I resisted the temptation to use my wyse-sense to discover more about them. I admonished myself for being overly suspicious, and I kept myself from turning to look over my shoulder to see if they were watching us. Bastien had called me a trusting soul, and though I might well have been, I was now a distrustful one.

We rode without stopping until midafternoon.

I was surprised at Nanoo Shellaya's resiliency. There were no horses, or even mules or donkeys in Mardel's Fen, and yet she rode the pony without complaint as if she was born to it. When we stopped, she slid off the pony easily, and led it to a pond ringed by low ferns and shaded by oaks and black walnut trees. She still walked stoop-shouldered, but she did not evidence the awkward gait of someone who was unaccustomed to riding and had ridden for hours without rest.

"We will look in on my sister Gafna," she told me. Shellaya dropped the pony's reins and knelt at the water's edge, cupping her hands and drinking.

I joined her, after I gave a brief rub to Crust's neck. "She is in one of two villages, Nan . . . Shellaya. Either Dewspring or Elspeth's Knot. They're within a few miles of each other, and both sit on the river and are in the shadow of the great hill we saw on the surface of the tea. I have not been in either village since I was a child, and so the building we saw is unfamiliar to me."

She motioned for me to kneel by her.

"Scry magic is not so difficult a thing as you believe, Eri."

Had she poked into my mind? How could she know what I thought of the old spells of the Nanoo?

"It is rare magic," I returned. "Dangerous, I've heard."

"Rare?" She shook her head, the hood falling away. "Not rare at all, Eri. It requires a gift of the wyse, to be certain. But it also demands a strong desire to see a particular something, an itching curiosity, if you will."

"I desire to see Nanoo Gafna," I stated. Then I gasped. In the water in front of Shellaya and me was Gafna's lined visage.

She looked more tired and worn than I'd ever seen her, worse even then when I'd watched her in the tea. The water clearer than the tea, mirrorlike in the sun, I could make out more details. There were large, dark bruises on her face, and I knew she'd been beaten, one of her eyes blackened from a punch. Her hair was a horrid tangle, a section of it matted with something. Blood, I believed.

"My sister does indeed suffer, Eri."

I wondered if Gafna was a sister to her by blood or if all Nanoo considered one another brothers and sisters in the wood and the wyse.

"Dying . . ."

"Not yet, Eri. They still need her for something."

"To lure me."

Shellaya shrugged, her gaze locked on the weary eyes of Gafna. "They'll not let her die until she is wholly useful to them, and then useful no more." She pushed up the sleeves of her robe, and her birdlike fingers hovered over the image, as if she could touch Gafna's lined skin and ease away the bruises.

"Shellaya, can you pull the image back, so we can see the building again?"

Still she kept her gaze on Gafna. "I could, but why don't you do that, Eri? This is your vision, after all."

I leaned away from the water, startled, and in that instant the image of Gafna winked out. Shellaya shook her head and made a soft *tsk-tsk*ing sound.

"My vision?" My words were a whisper. "I conjured that?"

Shellaya nodded.

"But I don't know how. Nanoo Gafna never taught me how to scry. Alysen said Gafna taught her. No one taught me." I barely stopped myself from telling Shellaya that Alysen used the scrying magic often and had looked in on the great city . . . and saw my father die. But I'd promised to stay silent on that matter.

"Some magics do not require teaching, Eri. Some magics come from the heart and are nurtured by the wyse."

"I've never used such magic before." I looked at the water, again trying to see Gafna in it and seeing only the sunlight and my own face staring back.

"But you have, Eri. In my home."

I shook my head.

"In the tea. Remember?"

I turned my head and looked at her. "The tea?" I mouthed.

"That was your scry, Eri. Not mine. Oh, I could have called Gaftna's image, probably should have days ago. I just hadn't realized my sister was in trouble. Gafna was known to wander, as I told you. Always, always wandering."

"My image? I did that?" I looked back to the water and saw my reflection. "How?"

Nanoo Shellaya didn't reply, but out of the corner of my eye I saw her rock back against her heels.

"Shellaya, I don't know how to do this."

Again no reply. I let out an exasperated sigh and thought of

Gafna. At the same time I focused on my wyse-sense. A heartbeat later Gafna's image superimposed itself over my reflection, and then my reflection faded away.

"By the Green Ones! I can scry."

"See? Not rare magic at all," Shellaya whispered. She edged forward again, bird fingers once more hovering over Gafna's battered face. "Not rare. But dangerous—you are correct there, Eri." She traced the outline of Gafna's head. Gafna's eyes opened wide and seemed to stare back at us. "Finish the magic, Eri. Find out where she is."

I wanted to say "I don't know how," but apparently I did know . . . or I was learning. I imagined Gafna getting smaller, so I could see all of her. The image wavered and I was afraid I was going to lose it. Again I focused on the wyse, feeling the arcane energy of the world and finding it stronger in the water than in the ground beneath me. Was that possible? That there was more magic in water than in earth or in the air? I shook my head to shake off my questions and concentrated on the wyse. I directed it to circle the image of Gafna, like a hawk circles prey on the ground, making the colors more intense and the details clearer. The lines on her face seemed deeper and the bruises looked more painful.

"Smaller." I urged the magic to pull back from Gafna, and I was surprised that it did just what I wanted. Once more I saw Gafna seated on the chair, but this time I noticed that her ankles were tied to it, and that her hands were tied together in her lap. I tentatively opened my mouth, wondering if I could taste the scene.

Suddenly my senses were flooded. I picked up the scent of the dirt and grass under my knees, the black walnut that rose behind me, its bark damp from a recent rain and smelling wonderfully heady. I picked up a pine that rose between two large oaks, its fragrance as delicate as an expensive perfume oil. There was the sweetness of wildflowers—red and white trillium and bluebells—the soft musky odor of Shellaya, and the foul smell that swirled around Gafna. I was surprised my senses extended inside the vision.

Gafna smelled of old sweat and dried blood and was sitting in her own waste. She'd not been released from the chair in long, long hours. My eyes started to water, and I tasted a smoky acridness. I caught sight of a large fireplace in the middle of the room and saw a hint of orange from embers— the smoke smell so strong I couldn't tell precisely what they'd cooked . . . some sort of meat. A bony hound lay stretched out on a rug, his legs twitching in some dream.

I detected the smell of the dog, and of a man wearing clothes that had not been washed in some time—not sweaty, but suffused with the odors of the fireplace smoke and dirt. Too, I could smell the old wood of the tables, chairs, and benches that filled most of the large room. I willed my vision to distance itself farther still from Gafna. Near the door, the man sat, head slumped forward, his lower lip quivering as he snored.

I looked once more at Gafna, wanting so much to speak to her. She seemed to stare straight at me, unblinking, her expression strong.

"She sees you, Eri. Gafna is so strong in the wyse that she knows someone watches her. Strong enough to know we watch her from this very pond."

"Can she hear us?"

Out of the corner of my eye I saw Shellaya shake her head. "The magic does not work that way."

Neither could I hear anything in the room where Gafna sat, though I knew I could have heard the man snoring if I stood in the building. I could have heard the sounds of the village outside.

I could hear other things, of course—Shellaya's breathing, the faint clicking sound the walnut branches made in the wind, the song of a jay perched high above me, my own frustrated sigh.

"Smaller." I concentrated harder and felt a shiver, like I'd been caught in a chill breeze. The wyse exacted a price for overuse, and I suspected I was pushing the magic too much. Still, I persisted. I was rewarded a moment later when I saw the outside of the building.

It was the village's lodge house, well cared for on the outside as evidenced by the recently painted trim and shutters. The door was painted, too, a dark green that matched the cloaks of the two Moonsons who stood at attention outside the door.

A shiver raced down my spine, and not from using the wyse.

"So wrong," I whispered. "Moonsons should not be doing this. They are noble and honorable men."

Bastien would not have allowed Gafna to be so treated and so confined. Neither, I believed, should any Moonson. What righteous man would stand by and not help a battered woman?

A worse thought occurred to me, and I shuddered.

Had a Moonson beat Nanoo Gafna? Was one of them responsible for her deplorable condition?

"More, Eri. Find out the village where my sister is held."

The image drifted back from the Moonson guards, the wyse magic fueled by my growing anger. I saw muddy streets and wooden buildings, people—some worn-looking and some men burdened with sacks and pieces of timber. I imagined myself a bird gliding above it all, and the vision shifted to accommodate my wishes.

The streets spiraled out from the lodge house like the spokes of a wheel. The river formed the eastern boundary, the village perched on a cutback. The high hill loomed to the west.

"It is the village of Elspeth's Knot," I told Shellaya.

I looked to my left, but the elder Nanoo was not there. I looked behind me.

Shellaya sat astride the fell pony, beckoning me with a bird-like finger to hurry.

19

WE REACHED THE EDGE OF ELSPETH'S KNOT LATE THE FOLLOW-
ing afternoon. The village was easily twice the size of Nar.
From the number of homes and shops, I guessed that more
than two hundred people lived and worked there. A considerable number of sheep were confined in several pens to the
west of the village. I remembered that the village was known
for its wool, and that their most noted craftsmen had the ability to dye the weave, making the wool a very desirable com-
modity in cities.

I saw a ramshackle building beyond the sheep pens, and
near it cattle were kept, along with a large gray goat with an
overlong beard. By the smell, which reached me here even
without the use of the wyse, I could tell the building was a
slaughterhouse. Nanoo Shellaya was wrinkling her nose in
disgust at the thought of killing beasts for food. I, however,
touched my stomach and wished for meat to fill it.

She got my attention and nodded toward the river to the
east.

Birch trees with stark white bark contrasted sharply with the blue-brown water. Two docks stuck out on to the river, and a fishing boat and two small rowboats were tied there, gently bumping against the pilings.

"We will wait by the trees," she said. She led the pony to a clump of birch and tied the reins to a low branch. She turned to look at me, a puzzled expression on her face.

I, too, was puzzled. Why was she clinging to the river rather than going into the town? I knew the Nanoo were a wise and mystic people, and I could not fathom all of their intentions. Why did she want to wait?

I stood at the north border of Elspeth's Knot, looking down a straight street lined on the east side by several merchants— a potter's, a cobbler's, a narrow building with a crooked roof that by its sign proclaimed it a chandlery. I could read, but there were few words on any of the signs I spotted. I saw pictures of shoes, a mug of ale, cups and plates, barrels, a horse head, and more. I knew that the majority of common folks could not read, and so looked to pictures for information about what businesses offered.

On the west side, residences made of wood and stone sat in a precise line, all of them small, save for one midway down, which rose three levels. A sign out front had a painting of a bed on it, and so I figured it must be a boardinghouse or perhaps an inn. To sleep on a bed, I mused, with a quilt and a pillow and walls to hold back the wind. Again I was missing my room in Lady Ewaren's house. I was missing, desperately, the comforts of civilization.

At the end of the street was the hub, or center, of the village.

My eyes locked on to the green door of the lodge house—the one I'd seen in my scry vision. Nanoo Gafna was in there. I could sense her presence, as without trying I tasted the wyse that spiraled outward from that place. Gafna was nearly as strong in the wyse as Shellaya. Two Moonsons stood outside, though from their builds I could tell they were not the same men I had scryed yesterday.

The wind gusted from the east and I looked in that direction. Shellaya clearly had been responsible for the breeze, an effort to get my attention. She motioned for me, and I led Crust to her. I dropped the reins, knowing the horse would not leave.

"We will wait here, Eri."

I opened my mouth to ask why, but didn't get the chance.

"We will wait until darkness, here by the river. In the dark we will take back my sister Gafna. It will be a more suitable time. We would have a better chance at success."

"Wait?"

She nodded and drew the cloak around her and sat at the base of the largest birch. She tugged the hood down over her face, knowing villagers could see us here and not wanting them to know that she was a Nanoo. Save Gafna's wanderings, the witches rarely ventured from Mardel's Fen, and her presence could draw the whole village out to ogle and ask questions.

"Shellaya, I do not want to wait. Gafna is hurt, we saw that in the scry vision. I want to get her out of there."

She shook her head. "There are too many people bustling around, Eri. After their evening meal, that is the time. Gafna is suffering, yes, and my heart grieves for that. I would take her pain if I could. But now is not yet the time to do something about it. Especially if this is a trap set to snare you."

"Let them try to catch me, Shellaya." I balled my fists and set them against my hips. A once-docent of Bastien, I'd not take orders from this woman. She was wise, the leader of the Nanoo of Mardel's Fen, and I respected her. But she likely had not set foot in a village in decades and was not so familiar with the ways of men. Later was not the time, I knew. Later the lodge house, no doubt, would be filled with men drinking into the darkest hours, maybe beating Nanoo Gafna again, maybe killing her. Now, with people milling around, would be the best opportunity. Guards would not be as likely to do violence against a woman in daylight and in the open.

Besides, if Gafna was the lure, and I the prize, it didn't matter what time of day I went after the bait. They would be waiting for me.

I strode past Shellaya and onto the smallest dock, leaning over the edge and looking at the water. I knew how to scry now, and I called upon the magic again, after a few moments of concentration seeing Gafna's bruised face and swollen eyelids.

This magic came too easy for me! After this was done, after Gafna was back with the Nanoo, I vowed not to use it again. Dangerous and easy, and I'd managed well in my life before I knew how to use it.

Gafna; I focused on her and brushed away thoughts of magic. Her head was slumped forward, and I feared the worst, but I watched carefully and saw her chest rise and fall. Nothing appeared as distinct as before, and it took me a moment to realize that this was because the surfaces of the tea and the pond I'd looked in were smooth. The river had a current, though a sluggish one, and the images in it were distorted.

Damn this scry magic and my need to use it!

I focused on the wyse and the image, gazed on the entire room and found one Moonson inside, sitting across from a cold fireplace and eating berries out of a wooden bowl. I did not recognize him, nor had I ever seen the ones outside the lodge house. This did not surprise me, as I'd not been to a Moonson function in a few years, and I'd never attended the largest gatherings with Bastien.

Now was the time.

Only three Moonsons there, and by the braids and medals, the one with the broader shoulders outside the door was of some rank. If I chose the correct words, he might listen to me and release Nanoo Gafna. He could not be a Moonson without having honor in his heart. He might tell me why the Moonsons condoned the treatment of Gafna. And perhaps I could make him divulge the location of Lord Purvis. I had hoped he was in this village, but I knew that highly unlikely. There would be soldiers visible on the streets, and enough horses that the small stable could not contain them. I would have heard them snort.

Lord Purvis might be camped south of the village, and to ease my curiosity I used the scry magic to look there.

Nothing.

I let the magical image shift so that it took in the edges of Elspeth's Knot. I might find some trace of him or his men there, more Moonsons.

There were no big horses that would be required to carry armored men, only the three Moonsons—the one I'd noticed

with my magic, and the two I'd seen outside the green door—
though there were likely more . . . along with Lord Purvis's
soldiers or guards. Maybe they were in the boardinghouse I
had spotted. Maybe the horses were being kept at a nearby
farm I hadn't scryed upon.

It didn't matter where they were. There were few men to
keep me from Nanoo Gafna.

The fingers of both of my hands dropped to the handles of
my knives. I would free her, then I would see to my bloodoath.

I would see it fulfilled soon.

One of the Moonsons would tell me where Purvis was. I
would explain that I was once a docent of Bastien and that
honor demanded I face Lord Purvis. He would understand.

"My sister Gafna has not worsened," Shellaya said. She
made her clucking sound and distracted me. The image of the
city vanished from the river.

"Shellaya, we are in sight of the village from right here.
Anyone coming to the river or stepping to the end of the street
can see us."

"Two women sitting by the river are of no concern to anyone. If the curious come to visit us, a no-see will keep us out
of trouble."

Like a no-see kept Alysen safe when everyone died around her.

I could not see Shellaya's face, shadowed by the hood, but I
was certain her eyes were fixed on mine.

"I don't understand you," I confessed, breaking an uneasy
silence that had settled between us. "I don't understand
why . . ." I wanted to say "I don't understand why you sit here
so calmly when Gafna is so near, why you want to wait while

she suffers." But I stopped myself and recalled her visage when it had been free of the hood. Shellaya was a very old woman and a Nanoo, not a choice combination for a rescue mission in the heart of a village in full sun.

"I will retrieve Nanoo Gafna. I will reason with the Moonsons and bring her out of Elspeth's Knot without bloodshed. I know the Moonsons, and they will listen to me. They are honorable men. I need you to stay with the horses. Please." But would they listen? And how honorable were these Moonsons if they rode with Lord Purvis? If Alysen's words were true, the Moonsons, perhaps these very Moonsons, were at the Village Nar when everyone died.

"I tell you again, Eri, we will wait. The darkness is a better time."

I wanted Gafna out of there now.

I shook my head. "Now," I told Shellaya. "I'll not wait for darkness and attempt something skulky. I'll not let Gafna stay in that man's hole."

"Headstrong." The word was a whisper breathed out from beneath the hood. Slightly louder: "Impetuous. More like a Moonson than a Nanoo, you are."

"I was a docent of Bastien," I said. Then I pointed to the horses and to her. "Crust and Spring Mist are in your care." I let out a long breath, turned, and headed down the nearest spoke-street toward the lodge house.

The street was hard-packed earth, but I kicked up a layer of dust as I went. I felt large pebbles press against my soles. There was a street like this in Nar, and it had felt more comfortable beneath my feet.

"Take care, Eri." I heard Gafna's words as a whisper against my ear.

"The Moonsons will be reasonable. They should not hold Nanoo Gafna. And if this is all some horrid trap, I will spring it now."

20

MOONSONS CERTAINLY SHOULD NOT BE GUARDING A BATTERED woman—there was no gallantry in that. There was no honor, only shame. Bastien would not have taken such an assignment, I knew. Bastien stood as the epitome of a Moonson, and he had taught me about chivalry and bravery and what is right and good in the world.

Those lessons ended this past winter with Bastien's death.

They had begun a little more than a decade ago in the Village Nar.

I remembered that first lesson as if it had happened only minutes past. The recollection loomed that precise and rushed at me unbidden now.

THE SWORD FELT SO HEAVY IN MY GRIP THAT MY WRIST AND ARM ached and my fingers tingled with an uncomfortable numbness. I bit down hard on my bottom lip, tasting blood and somehow finding strength in that little painful gesture. It took all of my effort to keep the sword pommel at waist level, and the blade pointed up and toward my adversary, just like Bastien had showed me.

I didn't quite come up to Bastien's shoulders, and I was so slight that first year of my lessons, having spent so much of my time weaving and reading and doing little strenuous activity.

I was in front of Bastien now, feet spread and shoulders back. I was here because I'd spied on him, curious about the man who'd saved the Emperor's life at the risk of his own, the man at the center of so many wondrous tales that swept nightly around the Village Nar. I'd spied on him for more than a few days, in fact. I realized he'd known from the start that I watched him. And I wondered why it had taken so many days for him to confront me.

I suspected he had waited because in those first days he had also spied on me.

"Strength is not measured by the broadness of one's chest, the size of one's arms, or the muscles in them," Bastien said. "A man twice your size and age, girl, might not have the strength to pick up that old, heavy blade of mine . . . and hold it for as long as needed in a fight."

"Then what is it measured by, Bastien? Strength. What makes someone strong?" I bit down on my lip again, harder. I hoped the pain would take my mind off my aching arms and would help me keep a grip on the sword. I did not want to lower the blade in his presence.

Bastien drew his favorite sword, one presented to him by the Emperor in a royal ceremony he often talked about. The blade gleamed flawlessly in the morning sunlight—no nicks along its edges, as were numerous on the one in my hand . . .

the one growing ever heavier. The pommel of his fine, fine sword was brass, shaped to look like the trunk of a tree, the crosspiece a twisting limb that thinned and split and drew back to form something like a basket hilt. A small bird's nest sat in it, which you couldn't see unless you were close. Tiny white sapphires were set in the weave as eggs. A most beautiful weapon! But from the first time I saw it, I felt conflicted. I marveled at its form and envied Bastien for having it, and yet I cursed the beautiful weapon. Why should something meant to deal death be so stunning?

"What is strength, girl? Where does it come from?" Bastien advanced, bringing the beautiful sword up. Somehow I managed to lift my weapon higher and parry his. "Strength is measured by the heart, Eri. But it is born in the mind. Muscles? They help. But without the mind and the heart, even the burliest man is a weakling."

It was the first time he had called me anything other than "girl," and the first time anyone had called me Eri. That was all he called me after that day. Lady Ewaren adopted the name, and Gafna used it occasionally.

"I don't understand, sir, strength coming from my mind."

And I truly didn't understand. I wanted the muscles he spoke of, the ones so evident on him even beneath the sleeves of his jerkin.

He brought his fine, fancy sword up again, and again I parried it. My arms and shoulders and my back screamed in protest. Was I mad? A girl trying to become a warrior? Should I be wielding weaving needles rather than this old, pitted blade?

No! I wanted this, though for what reason I couldn't have said that day.

This time I took a swing, clumsy, but I still managed to keep the sword in my sweaty grip. I used both hands on the pommel now. What scant muscles I had felt on fire, and the leather-wrapped pommel of the sword was a branding iron against my palms.

"You want to quit, Eri?"

I shook my head, my narrowed lips shouting my defiance. My breathing betrayed me, though, ragged and desperate and telling him that I should indeed quit. I sucked in great gulps of air, and I'm certain he knew I could barely hold the sword.

Once more he swung against me, and once more I parried. Despite the weight of the sword and the agony that pulsed through my arms, the defensive act was slightly easier this time.

"I can do this," I hissed through clenched teeth. I wanted to be more than a weaver of lace and yarn. But just what more I wanted, I didn't yet know. "I'm strong, Bastien."

When I spoke that—"I'm strong"—something changed in me. Maybe it was the wyse talent that I'd been developing that birthed the change. Or maybe Bastien's words about the mind and the heart being a person's true strength sank in. Whatever sparked my metamorphosis from girl to Bastien's docent grew and grew that day.

And as it grew, the sword became lighter. I could hold it in one hand.

I felt something pulling together inside of me, like a storm collecting the pieces of itself on the horizon. A bracing chill traveled from my toes up my legs and settled in my chest. Then it moved down my arms and into my fingers. The cold was pure and wonderful, and I wrapped my mind tightly around the sensation, not wanting to lose it.

My vision narrowed, and I saw only Bastien and his fine, fancy sword, the thin blade shining mirror-bright. I saw only him, and yet I was aware of everything around me.

Absolutely everything.

I knew where the stables stood off to my right and where the horses grazed in the meadow.

I felt the shadows cast by the buildings of the Village Nar, even though none touched me.

I sensed Lady Ewaren watching us out the window of her dining hall, weaving set aside for the moment.

I realized Willum was watching, too, and his wife.

I smelled bread baking, the tops of the loaves brushed with butter. I smelled the earth that had been turned over in the garden.

I knew I should be hearing things—the horses making their satisfied wuffling sounds as they grazed, birds, the sound of a hoe breaking the earth—for I knew people gardened this morning. I should be hearing all the usual and wonderful sounds of this place.

But I heard only Bastien's breath, and mine, and when I concentrated, I could also hear my heart. It beat slow and steady, and it became drum music my feet danced to.

My vision became more acute, as if I looked at Bastien through an alchemist's enlarging lens. The small lines on his face were suddenly more sharply defined, the color of his eyes became more intense, and I swore I could see myself reflected in the pupils. The hue of his lips, the flush in his cheeks, the white of his knuckles showing between the tree limbs of the basket hilt—everything became more vivid.

I danced forward, forgetting that the sword was heavy and that my arm and shoulder and back burned as if on fire. I brought the old blade up, knocking aside his mirror-blade, and I caught the surprise that took over his expression. I could not match him of, course. My one slashing gesture awoke him, though, and he began to dance with me in earnest.

His swings and parries were more elegant and practiced than mine, and the blades striking each other filled my narrowed vision. It was all I could do to keep up with him.

But I did keep up.

Somehow I brought the sword up and down as I stepped in close, slashing and parrying. It became instinct. Certainly I'd watched Bastien practice, but I'd not before this day tried any swordplay myself—it was not for one of my sex and class.

Bastien spoke to me, though I didn't hear the words. I still heard only our breath and my heart. His eyes sparkled, and I took that to mean he was pleased with me.

We continued to spar for what seemed like the thinnest amount of time, but what Bastien told me later was nearly an hour. I tried to copy his moves, succeeding only a few times.

But finding a measure of success!

Most of the time I concentrated only on bringing my sword up to meet his. Finally, when he continued to speak and I continued not to hear, he stepped back and lowered his weapon, signaling an end to this first lesson.

I replaced the old blade in the scabbard at my waist. And as

I flexed my fingers, all the fire and aches came crashing at me like a violent wave.

The fingers of my right hand went numb and I shook my arm, trying to restore the feeling. I rolled my right shoulder, then reached up with my left hand to massage it.

"Sore now? It'll be worse tomorrow, Eri," Bastien said. "But I've some ointment that will help."

I didn't say anything. What could I say? Sore? Yes, I was certainly that. But soreness was the least of what I was feeling. Elation, astonishment, pride, and more emotions I was too excited to put names to—I was feeling all of those things. I wanted the chill to pass through me again, to feel strong and to think I could be something beyond a girl who wove lace in a small village.

The ointment helped, and in the passing of a handful of days I used all the ointment Bastien had. I didn't stop the fighting lessons, though I had to fit them in between a myriad other tasks—working in the garden, helping clean Lady Ewaren's manor, brushing the horses, and weaving sessions, too. But all my chores were handled quickly so I would have time to spend with Bastien.

And within a year the chores were shaved so I could spend more and more time with the former Moonson. I formally became his docent, Lady Ewaren encouraging me to learn skills such as hunting, which I'd previously thought were taught only to young men.

We continued to concentrate on the sword, but he also taught me how to use the chain, which I favored, and knives. I wasn't noble-born, and so carrying a sword could get me in trouble. Laws throughout the kingdom specified who could carry what sorts of weapon. Knives were permissible to everyone. And there was no mention of the chain; few used it as a weapon.

So I did not carry the sword, save when I sparred with Bastien, and on a few occasions in the woods . . . once when there'd been tales of a fose-bear prowling.

A FEW YEARS LATER BASTIEN ANNOUNCED THAT I WAS HIS BEST student—he told everyone in the village during a harvest-night festival.

Best student? I told him I was his only student in the Village Nar.

He laughed warmly and said he'd named docents before, in his younger years when he'd commanded a unit in the great southern city. All the young men, they could not match my fire, he said. And he said they could not match my skills.

I proudly took his word for it, as I'd not known his previous docents. Nor, for another year more, did I meet any other Moonsons.

I REMEMBERED CLEARLY THE DAY THAT NINE MOONSONS CAME to visit Bastien, right after the first spring planting.

Bastien and I had brought down four wild pigs the day before, one of them so large we had to make a second trip just for it. They were roasting over pits now, sending a tantalizing scent into the air and into every window in the Village Nar. The pigs would cook slowly, but would be ready by the evening meal— enough to feed the entire village and then some. Willum, Gerald, and Bertrum—Bertrum the Glum, they called him—took shifts turning the pigs and stoking the fires beneath them, catching the grease and setting it aside for later use.

The Moonsons arrived shortly before noon, eight of them in gleaming chain armor, one in plate, and all of them riding big, dark warhorses. They followed the proper protocols, seeking out Lady Ewaren and asking permission to stable their mounts and to join in the evening's festivities. It was a good thing the one pig was so massive, I recalled telling Bastien, as men that burly must eat quite a lot.

They spent the afternoon with Bastien, in his barracks most of the time, but they wandered beyond the wall, and I followed them. Even away from the Village Nar they walked straight and with their shoulders squared, heads up and eyes alert. They took their helmets off when they sat on the large, flat stones beyond the cow pen and a row of apple trees.

They were all clean-shaven, their hair trimmed short. One of them had a small silver hoop in his right ear. It wouldn't be until later in the evening that I saw a tiny silver oak leaf dangled from it.

Bastien stood in the center of them, and addressed them as if he still commanded Moonsons. But he didn't have their straight posture, his wounds from saving the Emperor dropping his left shoulder a little and giving him a slight limp. His voice was strong and perfect, though, and it cut across the space between the gathered Moonsons and where I hid in the tall grass by the apple trees.

The Moonson with the earring spoke of a commander who had recently died of age and injuries and that a great ceremony would be held to honor him. They wanted Bastien to speak at it, but he declined.

"I am a Moonson no longer," I remembered him saying. "In my heart, yes, but only there." He told them he had a docent he would not leave, and going to such a ceremony would take him days and days away from the Village Nar. "I'll not leave my charge at this stage in the training."

"Bring him with you," the Moonson with the earring returned. I later learned his name—Celerad t'Lurves. "Though coming from this village, he clearly is not noble-born and cannot join the order. Still, it might do him good to spend time with active Moonsons. Add to his education."

"Her education," Bastien said. "My docent is Wisteria of Nar, an impetuous girl whose skill with . . . knives and a chain is equal to mine. She'd not be welcomed at your Moonson burial ceremony."

Celerad t'Lurves nodded his agreement and pressed Bastien for information about me. Neither he nor the Moonsons were particularly interested in me—they were more curious why Bastien would spend his time with a common girl.

Why Bastien would spend his time teaching anyone, for that matter.

He was retired from the Moonsons and living in a pleasant village. Why not spend the rest of his days gardening and hunting deer? Why not read those precious books the Emperor had given him? He finally had time for reading now.

They talked for an hour or two more, until the sun edged toward the horizon and a bell signaled time for the meal. At dinner, they told stories of battles they'd joined to protect one noble's property or another, or to defend a village against bandits. All their words were about glorious deeds and honor, and

I became ever more prideful that Bastien was my instructor, guardian, and friend.

Later that night, around the village fires, there were more tales of heroics, and one of the Moonsons sang a ballad about the founding of their order.

It was a beautiful song. But I could not remember one word of it.

21

I WALKED DOWN THE SPOKE-STREET, EYES ON THE MOONSONS TO either side of the lodge-house door. I took in the other people out this day, a mix of poor and middle-class, mostly workers. Their clothes smelled of old sweat and smoke, and the men looked beaten down by their work. There were few bright expressions. However, I saw a woman holding a baby in the crook of one arm and tugging a toddler along with her free hand. They smelled of soap and honey, and the corners of her mouth were wrinkled from smiling. Her eyes spotted the knives and the chain hanging from my belt, and she gave me a disapproving glare.

The Moonsons watched as I approached. Though they stood rigid and their heads were forward, their eyes moved, betraying their interest in me. The taller one dropped his hand to the pommel of his sword as a precaution.

Did they know of me? Recognize me, perhaps from word of my description?

Was I indeed walking into the trap Nanoo Shellaya had

mentioned? I think a part of me hoped so, as I'd been through much and wanted a conclusion to my misery. Those I'd cared about had been slain, and my home was lost to me. Dazon lost. All I had was in a satchel on Crust, the weapons tied to my belt . . . and my bloodoath.

"The oak is sturdy, but not as strong as a righteous man," I said as I neared them. It was a Moonson greeting Bastien had taught me after the visit of the nine. "Do you travel to the west, oak brother?"

The taller one nodded, his face a mask. "West I travel in spirit," he answered, his voice mellifluous. "Ever west where the oak was born and where our order grew strong in the tree's shadow."

"West is where warriors gather," I returned.

"West is where the world begins and ends in honor," he finished.

I kept my face a mask, too, not showing the surprise I felt that he so formally answered my greeting. Clearly, I was no Moonson, and I'd expected him to protest my use of Moonson ritual greeting. Still, I kept my back straight and shoulders squared, my chin tipped slightly up . . . the posture all the Moonsons displayed.

About to introduce myself, I swallowed my words. I would tell them my name only if they asked. No need to reveal more than absolutely necessary and invite trouble.

"Moonsons, you hold a woman inside this lodge house, and I request her release." I took a deep breath before continuing, and I watched their expressions even more closely. The taller one's eyes were a dark, shifting gray, the color of the early morning fog that used to settle in the lowest part of the Village Nar's pasture.

The eyes were unblinking. "I ask she come with me now."

The Moonsons did not answer my request.

I set my hands against my hips. "I said, you've a woman inside who should be no one's captive." I raised my voice a little and gave an edge to my words. At the same time, I reached out with my wyse-sense, wanting to make sure no more men were coming this way. Doubt crept into me. Should I have listened to Nanoo Shellaya? Should this have waited until evening?

Or did the time of my attempt matter nothing? I was one woman, not an army, and asking for Gafna's release was the only way to affect it. Force was not the answer.

"You know our greeting, lady," the shorter Moonson said. His eyes were so dark brown they could have passed for black, and his chin was scarred from some battle. "And you carry yourself well and sure. What do you know of the Moonsons?"

"That they are brave and honorable men." I nearly added, "who should not be guarding a battered, aging Nanoo." He did not say anything else, and so I tried again. "The woman who is held inside—"

"Is a prisoner of Lord Purvis of Elderlake," the scarred man interrupted. "We watch her for him, waiting for his return."

A mix of emotions coursed through me. Relief that Lord Purvis was not here; I'd suspected as much from the lack of horses and soldiers, but I hadn't been certain. Anger that he was not here—as I had my bloodoath to fulfill. Curiosity was the strongest, and the taste of it rested strongly and bitterly on my tongue. Why wasn't Lord Purvis here? What was he doing?

"I have not heard of this Lord Purvis," I said.

"He commands the Empress's army, and he is recruiting men now in Derilynn and Tichal."

Those were villages to the east, on the other side of the river and near the coast. They were better than a day's ride from Elspeth's Knot.

"And we need tell you no more, Lady . . . ?"

There, he'd asked for my name. "Wisteria t'Kyros, formerly of the Village Nar." The last I cursed myself for supplying.

The taller man's eyebrows rose. "Lady Wisteria t'Kyros, know you that the woman held within is the prisoner of Lord Purvis, as we've explained."

"What is she charged with?"

The scarred man pursed his lips. "Charges have not yet been posted, Lady Wisteria t'Kyros."

"Then why—"

"You can ask Lord Purvis about her crimes when he returns," the taller finished.

"And when will he return?"

"He did not say."

I kept my wyse-sense searching, wanting to make sure no more Moonsons—no more people—were approaching. I grew bold and took a risk with my words.

"Since when do the Moonsons answer to someone like Lord Purvis? If he is the Empress's man and commands her soldiers, he is not a Moonson. You are above that, above taking orders from someone outside your order."

Neither man answered this. They were not like the men I'd met in Bastien's company. Perhaps not all Moonsons were so honorable.

"Are you a friend of the woman, Lady t'Kyros? Or some re-lation?" the scarred man asked.

"Friend." After a moment, I added, "A very dear friend."

"We will let you see her, Wisteria t'Kyros, out of courtesy to you. But she is not to be freed unless Lord Purvis says so. And you will go in unarmed."

Relief flooded me—they would keep their posts and not come inside with me! They were trusting me and keeping to their assignment. I quickly unbuckled my weapons belt and set it against the lodge house, at the side of the taller Moonson. I took off my cloak and draped it on my arm, turned, to let them see I carried no other weapons, then I took a step back and waited.

The scarred Moonson opened the door and stuck his head inside. "Braxton, this woman has come to see the Nanoo. She may have a few minutes with her." He turned to me. "We grant you this courtesy, Lady Wisteria t'Kyros, because you have a familiarity with the Moonsons."

"I was a docent of Bastien t'Ikkes," I said as I brushed by him. Perhaps that, too, was something I need not have said.

They closed the door behind me, and the man inside the lodge house sat straight, taking his feet down from the chair opposite the one his bulk threatened. He wasn't a Moonson, likely a local from the looks of him, thickset and wearing common clothes that strained at the lacings. He had an ax strapped to his belt, similar to a woodsman's. I paid him no more attention and strode directly to Gafna.

My heart seized with each step I took, and I forced down the wyse that brought so much information to me . . . the scent of her suffering, which threatened to push me deeper into despair. The odor of her dried blood was heavy, as was her anger. I'd not known a Nanoo to be so angered before, but I would have been surprised had she not been furious with her captors and the men who had slayed the villagers of Nar.

She looked up as I neared, her wide, tired eyes searching my face and finding compassion and my own heartbreak. I knelt in front of her and started working on the cords that tied her feet to the chair legs. I saw her hands, also tied, the fingers of the left one ugly and twisted, broken as Lady Ewaren's had been.

"Oh, Gafna!"

"Stop." The villager Braxton was on his feet and walking toward me. A ponderous man, I heard the protesting creak of the plank floor beneath his heavy-soled boots. "Commander t'Djale said you were to visit, nothing else. She's to remain tied."

I dropped my hands to my sides and inched back, satisfied I'd at least loosened the cords. "My apologies." I thought to argue with him, saying the Nanoo's cords were still too tight, that she shouldn't be so confined. But I knew my words would not free her. Nor would words comfort her. My presence helped, though. Through my wyse-sense I felt her relax, and I sensed some of her anger dissipate.

"I'll be watching you, so do nothing foolish." His tone was insouciant, and that bothered me. "She's a prisoner, you understand."

"I can see that. And obviously a very powerful one, else she'd not be tied like this. She must present a terrible threat to you, this frail-looking woman." Again, I knew I'd said things I shouldn't. Bastien had tried to teach me to hold my tongue, to only speak neutrally to strangers, but that was one of his lessons I had trouble following.

My own anger welled stronger, as Nanoo Gafna's continued to quiet. Her eyes—I'd never taken my gaze from them—were softer. Her face still had ugly bruises splayed across it, and one of her eyelids was swollen and dark purple. I was amazed she could hold it open.

Why did they beat you, Nanoo Gafna?

I thought the words again, forcefully—*Why did they beat you, Nanoo Gafna?*—hoping she could pull them from my mind. I narrowed my eyes to needle-fine slits, and drew my lips tight. My anger continued to grow with every heartbeat that I looked upon this kind woman. I clenched my fists, the nails digging into my palms so hard I winced. My stomach roiled.

Lord Purvis, the demon-of-a-man—I borrowed Alysen's term for him—ordered this, I knew. All of this, just to find me. There were easier ways to catch me, like waiting in the Village Nar, like posting notices in every village from the fen to the great southern city.

"He didn't need to beat you, Gafna. I would have come to confront him. I would not have run. It is not in my nature to run."

"Alysen." She had trouble getting that one word out.

"She is safe. I made certain of that. The no-see you gave her worked. She is in Mardel's Fen."

She closed her eyes briefly, and when she opened them, they were filled with pain—great agony—but not for her own sufferings. They were filled with pain for the people of the Village Nar.

"Nanoo, Alysen and I . . ." Tears ran down my face, and again I tasted the salt of nightmares. "Alysen and I, we were the only survivors, Nanoo Gafna. Alysen because of you, the no-see you cast. And I because I'd chosen to hunt and not tell anyone where I ranged. My fault. Everything that happened is because I ranged from the village."

She shed tears now, too, clear snakes cutting their course through the dirt and dried blood that covered her cheeks. "Not your fault." The words were hollow-sounding and dry. She needed water. "Nothing is your fault, Eri."

"Had I been there, Nanoo Gafna . . ."

She shook her head, the tangle of hair brushing over her shoulders.

"Show me, Nanoo. What happened. Please." I knew that Alysen's words of the attack should have been enough for me, but I knew Gafna could make it all real. I wanted to see Lord Purvis, and Gafna could show him to me. "Please, before the Moonsons declare my visit over."

She let out a breath, the sound like a hot breeze blowing across parched ground. She closed her eyes and drew her chin down to her chest, and I heard the big villager step closer, perhaps curious.

I closed my own eyes, thankful to have the battered image of Nanoo Gafna eased from my sight.

"Show me," I whispered.

And Nanoo Gafna did just that.

22

I SAW THE VILLAGE NAR THROUGH GAFNA'S EYES.

Lady Ewaren walked near the garden, nodding to Gafna and Willum, making a clicking sound to get her favorite horse's attention. Gafna turned, following Lady Ewaren's progress through the village. I felt a concern rising in the witch that was evidenced by Gafna's uneven breaths and her hand rubbing against her forehead. Things in the distance were blurred, and I realized that was because Gafna's vision was not so sharp as mine.

A moment more and I was hearing through the Nanoo's ears, and drawing in all the scents of the place. I'd left hours before on my hunting expedition, and now through the shared vision I heard Lady Ewaren ask Gafna if she'd seen me.

Gafna replied no.

A shiver danced down my arms at the odd sensation of being in another's body, as if in a dream. It felt as if I responded to Lady Ewaren, but it was Gafna who spoke.

"Something is wrong, House Lady." The words were

Gafna's, but my lips moved in time with them. "I had a vision last night, as I slept before your hearth. It was full of foreboding, and I should have heeded its message. But I am getting older, House Lady, and lately have not been giving my visions enough credence."

Lady Ewaren smiled, and her eyes sparkled like the sun reflected on water.

"It is a beautiful day, Nanoo Gafna."

Gafna shook her head. "I should have sought counsel from my vision, House Lady. I feel a storm coming. In the air . . . something untoward races so swiftly our way. I feel . . ."

My lips stopped and Gafna's line of sight was now the road that led into the village from the south. I heard horses, their hooves pounding so hard it reminded me of thunder.

The storm Gafna mentioned?

The approaching horses were snorting, being ridden hard, and ours in the pen by the stables raised their heads and whinnied nervously.

A glance to the stables, and I saw fingers in front of my face—Gafna's fingers—motioning to Willum. He started putting the horses in the stables.

"Something is wrong, House Lady. Terribly wrong. This storm is on us." Gafna put more force into the words this time. I felt my face draw forward into a point, Gafna's face. Consternation and worry.

The thundering continued.

"Eri?" Lady Ewaren persisted. "Where is Wisteria?"

Gafna shook her head again. "Not here, House Lady, thank the Green Ones. Hunting most likely, as she did yestermorn so very early."

"Alysen?"

Gafna whirled, spying Alysen in the door of the manor. "Alysen is in danger, House Lady. Unlike Wisteria, she has not escaped the coming lightning."

"See to her, Nanoo. I'll deal with the riders, whoever they may be. Keep Alysen safe." Then I watched Lady Ewaren rush away from Nanoo Gafna, asking the very air questions—what could possibly threaten this village?

I saw Alysen, Gafna's fingers wiggling in some gesture at the girl that at first looked as if she knitted invisible strands. A moment more and Alysen faded, becoming translucent, like a reflection in a pool, then gone altogether.

The no-see spell. Nanoo Gafna knew something horrible indeed was descending on the village. How did she know?

I tried to ask, but no words came out. I was Nanoo Gafna in the vision and, at my request to her, was forced to see only what she saw. I could not know what she knew. Nor could I ask her questions. That was not the nature of this magic.

Gafna spun away from where Alysen remained hidden, just as the riders came into the village, horses thundering in through the south gate, past the stables, stopping in front of the manor, the lead horse inches from Lady Ewaren.

There were more than two dozen riders. No, more than three dozen, I saw, when Gafna turned her head to take in those holding back by the cattle pen. Most of them were soldiers, all of them in what must have been the colors of Lord Purvis. There were Moonsons with them, too, four Moonsons . . . none of those four was one of those guarding this lodge house in Elspeth's Knot.

"Lady Ewaren." The voice was rich and compelling, and it

came from the man who got off the lead horse. His armor was plate, not the chain the others wore, and braids draped the shoulders of his tabard. He stepped in front of Lady Ewaren, too close to be polite. "I search for someone you shelter in your village, Lady Ewaren. I would have her brought before me . . . now."

So many things happened in the next few moments.

Soldiers dismounted and drew their weapons. They held by their horses, waiting, eyes trained on their commander.

The Moonsons looked to one another and began talking among themselves. Their voices were too quiet for Nanoo Gafna—and thereby too quiet for me—to hear.

"Who do you seek?" Lady Ewaren asked. "Who is so important that it requires so many armed and armored men?"

Most of the commander's face was hidden by his full helm, but his lips were visible, and they crept upward in an ugly sneer. I imagined that all of him looked ugly. "Her father . . . call him most magical, Lady Ewaren. And that magic is strong in her. The wyse, some call it. Where is she?"

I felt Gafna gasp and saw through her eyes as the man, who could only be Lord Purvis, grabbed the front of Lady Ewaren's gown with one hand and her hair with the other. He yanked her head back.

"Where is she, Lady Ewaren?"

Our House Lady did not answer at first.

I—Gafna—glanced up and saw a soldier pull Willum from the stables and run him through with a sword.

"Lightning." Then Gafna hushed. The blade had struck that fast, shimmering silver in the sun like a bolt of lightning. "The storm."

I blinked furiously.

"Where is she, Lady Ewaren?"

I barely heard the House Lady's answer: "I don't know."

Another soldier sliced the throat of the cattleman.

"Lightning," Gafna repeated. "The storm destroys us."

Another soldier loosed throwstars at a cow, flicking the silver stars away from him as if he were flicking away gnats. The cow bellowed in surprise and pain.

Gafna's stare came back to Lady Ewaren.

The commander gestured with his head and two soldiers grabbed Lady Ewaren's arms.

"I don't know," she said again.

"Hunting." This came from Willum's wife. "Hunting, damn you all!" She sobbed and rocked forward over her husband, his blood smeared on her smock. "Why kill my Willum? Why? The one you want is hunting!"

She screamed other words, but Gafna shut them out and returned her attention to Lady Ewaren. They had her on the ground; one of her slippers had fallen off.

"Hunting where, House Lady? And with whom? With how many?"

Lady Ewaren shook her head, her hair coming loose and getting dirty and tangled. "Alone, and I don't know where. I tell you again and again and again—I do not know where." She tried to catch her breath. "But if I knew . . . if I did know . . . I would not tell you."

Gafna dropped to her knees, mouthing over and over old Nanoo words, the start of another spell I had no knowledge of. Another no-see? Her gaze angled to the ground, and I could see her fingers stretching forward and touching the earth.

"Her fingers," the commander said.

"Yes, Lord Purvis?"

The rage rose in me, threatening to choke me. The rage was so strong it pulled my mind back into the lodge house. Lord Purvis; I'd seen him through Gafna's eyes, or rather saw his form. Encased in expensive armor, broad-shouldered and proud-looking. His armor and cloak, the braid and gold medals he wore—all were as much wealth as the Village Nar possessed. All of that wealth on one vile, vile man.

I'd seen his eyes through the slits in the helmet, dark and powerful and unblinking. I would remember those eyes. Until my last day I would remember them. I forced myself back into Gafna's vision.

"The fingers of her left hand, Gisles. Break them. One by one. Perhaps the pain will cause the House Lady's tongue to wag a little more freely."

Why? Why couldn't I take action rather than merely observe? Why couldn't some part of me reach through Gafna's magic and stop them from hurting—killing—Lady Ewaren? I was physically sick with grief over what was going on in the vision and over what I could not do. I knew what I would soon see, and my anguish hit me in the stomach as strongly as would a mailed fist.

Through Gafna's ears I heard Purvis turn and click his heels, clap his hands. Footsteps indicated that men rushed toward him. Still, all I could see were Gafna's fingers and the ground. I heard Gafna's words, whispered, still not understanding the magic, if there was any, behind her odd speech.

"Into the houses, Gisles, Tate, Margal, Heroth. Kill them all. Let none escape. I'll have no witnesses. Not a single witness.

Understand?" A pause. "Now her right hand. One finger at a time. Then kill her."

If there is such a thing as hell, it became the Village Nar. Screams so hurtfully loud filled my ears and blocked out all else. So terribly, terribly loud I knew Gafna could not concentrate. She balled her fingers into fists and struggled to her feet. She took a few steps toward Lady Ewaren, who also was screaming. A soldier was ripping the Lady's green dress and was lowering himself over her.

Gafna turned away and ran.

I knew it was all the Nanoo could do, what everyone else was trying to do—flee from this company of hateful men who'd come to the Village Nar in pursuit of me. And all because of my father's blood, the heritage that had given me the taste of magic. Because my father had sided with the Emperor, and the Empress had discovered it.

Because of my blood, the blood of the village was spilled. So very, very much blood, I knew the ground could not drink it all in. My heart hammered so wildly I feared it would burst through my chest . . . Gafna's heart, her chest. It was her feet pounding across the village grounds, faster than I'd thought her aging legs could carry her.

The screams continued, worsened. I saw people running past me, mouths open, screaming.

Nothing but screams and blood and madness.

I felt madness touch Gafna's mind. Then I felt a twinge of hope. She was running across the pasture now, chest tight and hot from her efforts, legs burning and mind reeling with what she'd seen and what she kept hearing.

"Oh, Lady Ewaren." It was Gafna speaking. I wondered

how I could hear the words over the cries of terror. The words were dry and spoken with great effort, and after the passing of a few labored heartbeats I knew they'd come from Gafna sitting in front of me. The vision was fading, and the lodge house and Gafna started to come into focus around me.

I looked at two scenes at the same time, both hazy and shifting and alternately interposing themselves over the other.

I felt myself being lifted, Gafna being lifted. A soldier on horseback had grabbed the back of her tunic and tossed her over his horse in front of him like she was a sack of vegetables. Through the Nanoo's eyes I saw the horse's side and leg and directly below I saw the pasture passing by. I felt the jarring sensation of the horse galloping, and the coarse feel of the man's hand on the back of Gafna's neck.

The screams were coming softer now, because the soldier was riding past the apple orchard and the flat rocks and was circling the Village Nar. Softer also because most of the people were dead. Fewer left to scream.

"Lord Purvis!" the soldier hollered. "I've caught a witch. A fast witch!"

I couldn't see Lord Purvis, but I saw rivulets of blood running down a slope.

And then the Village Nar became indistinct, then winked out altogether, and I saw Gafna sitting in front of me. The stench of the lodge house hit me like I'd run into a stone wall.

"I could not save the House Lady," she said. "Oh, Eri, I could not save her."

"But maybe I can save you," I returned. "Take my strength, Nanoo Gafna." I spoke so softly even I had difficulty hearing my words. I knew Braxton behind me could not have overheard—and he was so close, I could smell the dried sweat that clung to his clothes. But Gafna? I was trusting that with her wyse-sense and the fact that she might be prying into my thoughts, she could effectively hear what I told her.

"Hurry. You have to hurry, Nanoo." I didn't know how much longer I would have with her before the Moonson guards demanded I leave.

She hesitated.

"Take my strength."

My eyes begged her and she slumped forward, an act that looked convincing, giving her disheveled and bruised appearance. Her forehead touched mine, and she mumbled softly. To the man behind me, I suspect she sounded like she moaned in pain. I couldn't understand what she said, not all of it, but I knew it was a spell. And I knew what it would do.

I shivered, feeling the warmth drain from me. It was an enchantment far beyond me, but not beyond a witch of Gafna's stature. I'd never attempted to learn any healing magic, seeing no need for it in my earlier years.

As her spell progressed, I weakened, and Nanoo Gafna gained strength. My helping her was necessary, for I feared if she didn't take some of my energy, she would not even be able to stand.

And she would have to stand, because I could not let her remain here.

Within heartbeats she was breathing stronger, wrinkling her nose at the smell of herself. She could have taken even more of my energy—my eyes encouraged her to do just that. But she leaned back, closed her eyes, and a measure of relief washed over her face.

"I think you've visited long enough." The man called Braxton tapped my shoulder. "Time to leave."

Bastien had taught me how to control my temper, as a warrior fights better when his emotions do not flare, when he thinks efficiently and acts rationally. I've prided myself on my ability to do that. But with everything that had transpired . . . well, I believe I'd left a lot of that control back in the dead Village Nar.

In one fluid movement I rose and jabbed both of my elbows back with as much strength as I could summon, even though Gafna had drained some of it. I connected with the man's stomach and was rewarded with the great *whoosh* of his foul breath against the back of my neck. I leapt to the side as he bent over, grasping his stomach and sputtering in anger and shock. The scents of him only added to the misery of this place.

I held my breath, clenched my hands together in a single fist, and brought that fist down hard on the center of his back.

He dropped to his knees, the impact sending a tremor through the wood planks. He reached for the hand ax on his belt and opened his mouth wide to holler for the Moonsons.

I couldn't let him call for help. I struck him again with my joined fists, on the side of his head, on the side of his neck, and then my hands flew apart and I grabbed him. Unconscious, he was falling. I caught him—barely, as he was heavier than even I'd guessed—and I lowered him to the floor. I couldn't afford to have him strike the floor and make so much noise that the Moonsons outside would hear.

My hands ached from the impact against the man. I clenched and unclenched my fists and shook out my arms.

Despite the years I'd trained with Bastien—and despite all the times I'd trained alone—I'd never truly fought a man. I'd sparred with Bastien and others, even with Willum. But it had all been *practice*. I'd never purposely hurt someone, but I knew now that my training had served me well.

I could more than hurt someone if I had to. I could have killed this man.

A quick glance to the door showed me the Moonsons hadn't heard the brief scuffle. I looked back to Gafna—she was staring at the fallen man.

There were only two windows in the room, these on the wall opposite the fireplace. For the size of the building, I'd expected more, but I suppose two were sufficient to let in air during the warm months, and, shuttered—as they were now—to keep out the cold in the winter. Shuttered now to keep people passing by from seeing the old Nanoo soldiers had beaten.

I rolled the man over and took his hand ax. I searched him and found a small, sharp knife he probably used for cutting food. I used the knife on Gafna's cords, being especially careful slicing at the ones that held her wrists.

"That man . . ."

"He'll live, Nanoo Gafna. But he'll have some measure of pain to show for it."

"Thank you, Eri."

"Your hand," I whispered. "They broke your fingers like they broke Lady Ewaren's fingers."

"Cruel men, yes," Gafna said. I detected a little more strength in her voice.

"I'm taking you out of here."

She nodded, but her eyebrows rose in the obvious question of how.

"I'm not sure how this is going to work," I answered. "But we are getting out of here."

23

SOMEONE WOULD SEE US CLIMBING OUT OF A WINDOW—
certainly that was not the proper way to withdraw from the
lodge house. I didn't want to risk an alarm being sounded, and
so left the windows shuttered. The door, then, but the Moonson guards would not give us permission simply to walk outside and leave.

I gave a last glance to the man sprawled on the floor. He was
breathing regularly, and I hoped I'd not hurt him too severely.
At the same time, I hoped he wouldn't wake up for a while.

I gently tugged Nanoo Gafna the length of the lodge house,
careful to touch only her right wrist and to thread our way
through the tables so the broken fingers of her left hand
brushed nothing. She managed only a shuffling gait—so many
hours, days, likely, that she'd been tied to that chair. That she
could move at all was a testament to her fierce will—and to
the bit of my energy I'd given her.

"Quiet," I whispered, though in truth I didn't need to make
such a warning.

I pointed to the wall behind where the door would open. She understood that I wanted her to stand there. She would be hidden.

My palms began to sweat, revealing my nervousness. I took shallow breaths and waited until the Nanoo stood against the wall. My heart hurt for her, seeing her shattered hand and fragile body. She looked like a stranger compared with the witch I knew who'd regularly walked miles and miles to come to the Village Nar in pursuit of fellowship and milk.

I touched the door, fingers trembling, feeling the roughness of the wood. I thanked the Green Ones that the Moonsons had let me come in here alone. But I'd left my weapons outside . . . and likely they'd not known a woman with my fighting mettle. So they had extended me the courtesy of coming in here in part, I suspect, because they felt pity for the Nanoo and so allowed her my company.

I did not intend to be so courteous in return.

I opened my mouth, searched for the wyse coursing in my blood and in the air around me, and I registered the Moonsons' presence . . . inches away on the other side of the wood. There was no wyse about either of them, only the faintest trace of magic that is present in all things. Comparatively few people in this world are gifted to call upon the wyse. If only these Moonsons and everyone else knew . . .

Knew what I had learned from my father at an early age.

The Moonsons were talking, and I tasted their curiosity, the flavor sharply sweet. They wondered about me, about why I knew Moonson ritual. One Moonson's curiosity was so strong it burned my tongue. He questioned all of this . . . me, Gafna, what he was doing here. Had he known Bastien?

I tasted their fatigue, too, their legs aching from standing in one place so long. These Moonsons were not used to such duty, but I tasted no complaints in that regard.

Were they the only Moonsons in the village? No, as they couldn't stand there all throughout the day and night, they would need relief. So perhaps there were six or eight of them, the rest of them with Lord Purvis in a nearby village.

Two here at a time, plus a resident of Elspeth's Knot to watch over Gafna and feed her occasionally. I'd thought it would have been easier to take Gafna with them while they recruited. But Lord Purvis had ordered her beaten too harshly for that.

Again the words of my bloodoath went through my mind, sounding loud and adding to my fury.

My fingers drummed against the door, and I stepped back, holding the hand ax behind me.

The taller Moonson didn't open the door much, just enough for his head to poke inside. "Visit over?" His tone was pleasant enough.

I nodded. Before he could open the door wider for me to leave, I said, "There's a problem with your man. He's fallen." I took another step back, pivoting as I did so I put myself squarely in front of Nanoo Gafna. I tightened my grip on the hand ax, the wood slick from my sweat.

"What's this?" The Moonson came into the lodge house, squinting, as it was shadowy in here, a sharp contrast to the bright of day outside. He spotted the downed villager, who was snoring now, then noticed Nanoo Gafna was not in the chair, the cords lying on the floor. "What treachery, lady—"

My free hand shot forward, fingers closing on the thick cloth of his tabard and pulling him inside. I brought the hand ax high and slammed the end of the handle down hard on the side of his face, which his helmet did not quite cover. The one blow was not enough, and so I tugged harder on his tabard, pulling him down, even as my knee came up and struck him in the chest. The mail links were heavy, and it felt as though I'd connected with a big hardwood tree. But it was enough to knock the wind out of him.

I yanked him inside, just as his fellow loomed in the doorway, sword drawn and lips pulled up in an angry sneer.

"A docent of Bastien you claimed to be!"

I nodded. "No lie that, Moonson." I caught my breath and bent my knees for balance. I tasted his hesitancy.

"Lady, we granted you a favor because we believed you. And you repay our kindness with—"

"Treachery, yes."

His hesitation faded, and he drew his sword back.

I drove my heel into the back of the downed Moonson, who struggled to rise, then I ducked beneath the swing of the other's sword.

"But treachery for a good cause." My senses enhanced from using the wyse, I heard the blade whistle shrilly and felt the air above my head stir. I tasted the defeat of the man I stood on, as the pain and injuries I'd inflicted on him welled up and pushed him into unconsciousness. I tasted the ire and confusion of the Moonson I faced.

"I've no desire to hurt you, lady, but—"

"Nor do I want to hurt you."

We stood facing each other, hearts racing, eyes locked. There was something else in the air . . . pride and hope? Yes, that was coming from Nanoo Gafna.

Her hope drove me. When the Moonson pulled his blade back again, he let out a keening yell, signaling anyone nearby that there was trouble. I leapt forward, head down, slamming into his chest as I brought the ax handle hard against his temple. Forcing him to his back as we fell onto the street outside, I struck him again and again, my free hand pressing down against his throat.

When he stopped struggling, I jumped to my feet, tasting too many things—meat cooking somewhere, cow's hide being tanned, and—subtler because of its distance—the rippling fear of animals in the slaughterhouse.

The overall reek of the village was the strongest, layers of sweat and dirt that clung to people who were more numerous than they were in Nar.

Grease from cookstoves.

The dander of the sheep and from dogs kept as pets. The glee of children playing in one of the spoke-streets. The fatigue of laborers. The love of mothers, and the perfume of flowers growing in window boxes.

All of those things I thrust to the back of my mind. Too, I forced the wyse away from me. The magic was a boon most of the time, but in my nervousness I'd allowed it to overwhelm me. I needed to concentrate.

"Wisteria."

Nanoo Gafna had said my name three times before I shook off all the tastes and responded to her.

"I'm all right." I rolled the Moonson into the lodge house,

dropped the hand ax, stepped back outside, and shut the door behind us, still not bothering to check his condition. In truth, I feared I'd killed him, and I did not want to know for certain. Bad enough that I'd truly fought men—three of them—rather than spar for practice. Then I grabbed my weapons belt and draped it across my shoulder.

I saw two men walking down the spoke-street to my left; one of them carried a heavy-looking sack on his shoulder, the other held a long garden hoe. Both looked at me, but did nothing, perhaps not realizing anything was amiss. I heard a horse and rider, a second horse pulling a cart. Other sounds drifted our way—the conversations of people approaching, someone singing. No whistles or pounding feet. I knew we'd been lucky. But I also knew luck was a fickle thing and that soon someone would discover Lord Purvis's prisoner missing. Or one of the men inside the lodge house would wake and sound an alarm that would be answered.

"This way." I led Gafna down a street that stretched east from the lodge house, on a side where the building had no windows. There were residences here, mostly, the homes closest to the lodge house the oldest and in the worst repair. A hole in one roof; I looked closer and decided the house was abandoned. Warped boards on the front steps led to a door that hung crooked on its hinges. For a heartbeat I thought about taking Nanoo Gafna inside. But it was too close to the lodge house, and I suspected the Moonsons would search it.

I resisted the temptation to use my wyse-sense again. I desperately wanted to search for any other Moonsons or for villagers who might be aiding them. But that might cost me precious time. Instead, I tried to increase our pace, discovering that wasn't possible. A shuffling, stumbling gait was all Gafna could manage. I could carry her; I was strong enough and she was that slight. Such would draw undue attention to us, though, and so we kept to the north side of the street, where the shadows of the buildings seemed to stretch farther. We stayed close to the homes when possible.

An elderly woman carrying a covered basket opened her door and looked at us curiously. Smiling at her, I pressed on, my hand around Gafna's right wrist. The elderly woman said something to us, but I couldn't make it out. I put all my effort into getting us down this street and to the edge of Elspeth's Knot.

"No. By the Green Ones, no." Down a side street to the south, two blocks away, I spotted a Moonson. Near the wall of a long stone building, he seemed to be talking to two villagers. "Please, please don't see us. By the Green Ones, please."

We were nearly past that intersection when Gafna's legs buckled. She fell forward and I barely managed to catch her before her broken hand hit the ground. But I bumped her hand in the process, and she cried out.

My head snapped toward the Moonson. He looked straight at us, and before I had Gafna on her feet he started jogging toward us. My weapons belt slipped off my shoulder as I picked up Gafna and cradled her to my chest. It was only one Moonson—I'd just bested two of them and a villager. I could defeat this one also. But we were in the open now, and there were people on the street behind us, the elderly woman coming out of her house and calling to us. In my haste, I'd brushed Nanoo Gafna's hand again. This time she was prepared and was silent, though I saw the pain in her eyes.

She cupped her left hand with her right and I ran, dirt from the dry street kicking up behind me, people hollering, a whistle being sounded. My mind worked as I ran even faster.

Where to take us. What to do.

Could I appeal to the villagers to help Nanoo Gafna and me? Might they side with me against Moonsons?

I turned north, down the first side street I came to, moments later heading east again, down another spoke, where the buildings were newer and spaced farther apart. I heard more whistles behind me, shouts, feet pounding. I focused only on the witch in my arms and the street ahead, not wanting to trip—which would signal doom for both of us. The river wrapped around the edge of the village; I spied its blue-brown ribbon through a gap in a clump of birches.

Within heartbeats I'd reach it . . . but what then?

We were south of where I'd left Nanoo Shellaya. Alone, I'd jump in the river and swim to safety. But Gafna could not swim anywhere. We'd be caught at the river.

"I should have listened to Nanoo Shellaya." The words came out through clamped teeth. "Me, the fool."

Then we were past the end of the street, my feet thudding over grass, and I ducked beneath the low branches of the first line of birches. I tromped into the shallows and turned north, hunching my back like a turtle and trying to protect Nanoo Gafna from weeping branches that hung over the river. I tried my best to be quiet, but I knew the sounds of my sloshing carried. Still I could hear the whistles and shouts.

"Nanoo Gafna, are you all right?" I'd jarred her more than a little bit with my dash from Elspeth's Knot to the river. "How are—" I tripped, a submerged root catching my foot. Somehow

I kept hold of Gafna. I rolled as I fell, so my back struck the river bottom. My ankle twisted sharply and I felt the bone snap. I went below the surface, and swallowed silt-filled water.

Gafna kept her head above the surface and extricated herself from my grasp. Though I'd suppressed my wyse-sense, I felt her pain; it throbbed that strongly in her mangled hand.

I pushed off the bottom with my arms, sputtering and coughing and dragging air into my lungs. I stood and leaned on Gafna, my broken ankle throbbing. I listened, still hearing whistles and shouts, the thumping of feet against the ground, the rustle of willow birches.

"I should've listened to your sister," I told her.

"You intended well, Wisteria," she replied.

"My intentions caused you more pain and now will see us—" My voice caught as three Moonsoons rushed onto the riverbank, holding back the birch branches and staring at the water.

"The woman and the witch, Commander Grellor, I saw them come this way."

"Aye, Cragston, I saw them, too, heard them jump in the river." He stepped to the very edge, the points of his hard leather boots touching the water. He'd go no farther, I knew, wearing the long, heavy suit of chain mail and carrying a fine, large shield. But he'd order his men in after us. "But I don't see them."

Commander Grellor cupped his hand across his eyes and looked north and south along the river, and then scanned the bank on the other side.

"They couldn't have drowned. Not this fast," the one called Cragston said. "And they couldn't have escaped us!"

I watched Commander Grellor look right at me—through me—then slam his gauntleted fist against his shield.

"What?" I mouthed. *Can't see us? He looks right at me!*

The sun was not at such an angle to cause the trees to shadow us. We were in the open, dripping wet, supporting each other. How could the Moonsons not see—

A no-see spell, like Gafna had used on Alysen in the Village Nar! Only this time she'd put the spell on both of us. But how? Gafna suffered, weak despite the strength I'd given her. How could she . . .

Stand quiet, I heard in my mind. The voice was Nanoo Shellaya's. I turned my head, looking over my shoulder to the north. The old witch stood under the lacy veil of a massive weeping willow, Crust and Spring Mist with her. Gafna must have heard the words, too, for I felt her stiffen.

"Spread out," Commander Grellor ordered. "Cragston, take some of these men and follow the river south. Melore, to the north. I'll organize parties to search the streets and buildings."

"Lord Purvis will not be happy that we've lost the Nanoo," Cragston said.

"Then make sure we don't lose her—don't lose either one of them." Commander Grellor whirled away from the bank and strode down the nearest street.

I hadn't realized I'd been holding my breath. When I let it out, I gagged, some of the river water still in my lungs. Praise the Green Ones none of the men heard me. They were chattering among themselves, Cragston gathering some of the villagers and sloshing south through the shallows. My throat tightened, fearful the ones heading north would find us merely by running into us. But this group stayed on the bank, though one of them paused every few steps and looked across the water. They should have noticed Nanoo Shellaya, even though the veil of leaves fell around her like a cloak. One man parted the leaves of every willow he came to and looked closely. He should have spotted her.

Stand quiet, Nanoo Shellaya's request came again.

My ankle burned, though I stood in cool river water. I barely touched the ball of my foot to the riverbed, trying to ease my weight off Gafna. I succeeded in my plan, and received a stab of pain as my reward. I sucked my bottom lip into my mouth, biting it and tasting blood, hoping the new pain might keep my mind off my ankle.

I did not succeed this time. The pain was intense. Still, I kept quiet.

We stood in the river, as motionless as possible for nearly an hour. Nanoo Gafna leeched some of my strength so she could stay on her feet.

The pain in my ankle intensified as I grew weaker, but there was nothing else to do for it. I'd chosen to go after Gafna with little planning and despite Nanoo Shellaya's wishes.

Neither—thank the Green Ones—had Nanoo Shellaya obeyed my request. I'd asked her to stay with Crust and Spring Mist north of Elspeth's Knot, by the docks. But had she listened to me, Gafna would be in the Moonson's clutches again, and who knows what fate I'd be meeting. Shellaya must have scryed on us and knew we needed help—because of my foolishness.

As I stood in the silt-filled water and wrapped my mind around the pain, I tried to think how I could have done things differently. Chosen a different road away from the lodge house, maybe. Or we could have hidden in the abandoned house I'd spotted. My good foot was falling numb by the time the two Moonsons and their assembled villagers moved completely out of sight.

Gafna and I stumbled toward Shellaya, passing under the willow veil. I expected the old Nanoo to scold me. But she smiled warmly and embraced her injured sister. It was difficult to tell under the umbrella shadow of the tree, but it looked like Shellaya's rich brown skin was noticeably paler.

The no-see she'd cast on Gafna and me—and on herself and the horses—had taken a great toll.

24

THE PAIN!

I hobbled to the base of the willow, sliding down against it, the heels of my boots touching the edge of the river. I tipped my head up and closed my eyes, and I let the tastes come to me.

My pain, that was the strongest tang, and it made my eyes water. Gafna's agony registered, too, and even though she was in worse shape than me, her pain did not taste as strong.

Curiosity and concern came next—from both Nanoos, curiosity from Crust. No doubt the horse wondered why she stood in the shallows of a river under the branches of a tree. But Crust was good-tempered, and Bastien had trained her well. She stood uncomplaining, the pony at her side.

The scents of the village reached us even here—all the emotions of the people on the east edge, still the joy of children. The river's odor was the most pleasing, and the tree that rose above me smelled sweet. So I concentrated on that, as I strengthened the wyse within me.

I barely noticed Shellaya help Gafna to the bank, settling

her next to me. I was preoccupied, searching to make sure the men were not returning. I suspected they would go as far north as the docks and take a boat out onto the river. And I hoped the rest of the men would search in the village, where I had no intention of returning.

"The no-see will last some time, Wisteria." Nanoo Shellaya must have read my worry. "We are safe here. And we'll not leave until it is dark. As I told you, the evening is a better time." Did I detect a glimmer in her eyes?

I kept up my vigil while Shellaya tended to Gafna. The Nanoo were known for their healing magic, and I could taste the wyse-energy flowing from Shellaya. The elder Nanoo could not completely mend Gafna, however, and so she relied on a narrow, fallen limb to help. Shellaya snapped it, and using a supple weeping branch as twine, splinted and wrapped Gafna's left wrist and hand to keep the shattered fingers immobile. When Shellaya finished, she helped Gafna bathe in the river, then in my pack found a change of clothes that fit her.

Nanoo Gafna was in far improved spirits when she stretched out on the bank and quickly fell asleep.

Then Shellaya turned her attention to me.

"Thank you for saving my sister, Wisteria of Nar." She smiled at me. "Eri."

"Nanoo Gafna's my friend. I did what I could, and—"

"Chose well enough with your timing. Take care, though, that your impetuous nature does not bring you to ruin." She knelt at my feet, the river sloshing around her. Then she tugged off my left boot, and I dug my fingers into the dirt. "It is broken."

I nodded. "Nanoo Shellaya, you and Gafna must leave here at

sunset. Take Crust and the pony and go home to Mardel's Fen."

"We'll go nowhere without you, Eri." She touched her fingers to my ankle, and once more I tasted the energy that flowed from her. But this time it flowed into me. "You'll be well enough to travel soon."

Her wyse healing instantly quenched the fire in my ankle, and I could feel the bone mending, the sore muscles around it relaxing, the throbbing in my leg subsiding.

"Nanoo—"

"Shellaya, Eri. Remember, I've no need of titles anymore. At least not here."

"How is it you can mend my ankle, when—"

"When I cannot mend the small bones of Gafna's hand?"

Her pale face took on a sad expression. "So many bones there, Eri, and some already healing on their own, but not healing correctly." She massaged my ankle now, still directing wyse-energy into it. Her shoulders were more stooped than usual, and I knew she'd spent so much of herself that she was terribly, terribly worn out.

"I will be able to mend her, Eri. But not today. Today she is well enough, and that will serve until tomorrow."

I wanted to tell her that I should have listened to her, and not gone to the lodge house when I did. That I should have waited until evening. Her wisdom was far greater than mine, and I erred in going against her counsel.

I tipped my head back and felt the slight breeze tease my face. "So we will all leave this place, Shellaya, when the sun sets," I said. "And . . ." I paused, tasting the sweat, determination, and frustration of men in the village behind us. A fishing boat sailed past, one Moonson and three villagers on it, the men scanning the river and both banks. When they were out of sight, I continued. "You and Gafna can go back home. Alysen will be so pleased to see Gafna. Take the horses, and—"

"And what of you, Eri?"

I suspected she knew precisely what I intended to do, but I would say the words. "I've a bloodoath to fulfill, Shellaya. The man responsible for Gafna's capture and suffering is also responsible for the death of the Village Nar. I promised the spirit of my House Lady that—"

She leaned forward and touched my forehead. "Sleep, Eri, for just a little while. You'll need your strength to pursue your vengeance."

I awoke just as the last of the sun's rays turned the river molten gold. It looked like a fortune in coins that shimmered as far as I could see to the north and south. The air was cool and set goose bumps racing along my arms. And the leaves rustling all around us provided peaceful music. I could have sat in the tree's embrace, relishing nature, for a long, long while. I reluctantly got up and approached the Nanoos, Gafna on Crust and Shellaya on Spring Mist.

Shellaya passed me my pack and a bottle of water. The pack was much lighter, having only a spare tunic in it now and the pouch of coins, along with two bars of oatmeal soap and the small box my mother had given me. I slung the pack over my shoulder.

"Where will you search for Lord Purvis?" This came from Gafna, who cradled her left hand in front of her.

"To the east, if what the Moonsons said is true, that he

recruits men in villages there." I looked to Shellaya. "I will scry to try to find him."

"And then?" Gafna asked.

"When I've fulfilled my oath, I will return to Mardel's Fen." I studied the lined faces of both women. Shellaya's skin was its rich, dark brown again. "My home is dead. I've nowhere else to go."

"You are always welcome with us," the witches said practically in unison.

"Go with the Green Ones," Shellaya added. Then she made a clicking sound and flicked the reins, the pony moving out from under the veil of willow leaves. Gafna kneed Crust to follow.

I watched until they disappeared from view, then I turned and started south. On the other side of Elspeth's Knot the river narrowed. I would cross it there, and then I would find the demon-of-a-man.

25

TWO HORSES SLEPT IN A PEN ATTACHED TO THE OUTER WALL OF the village stables, and a soft glow spilled through a high window and brushed their withers. When I tasted the air I detected hay and manure and horses and more horses.

The scent of a man, just coming to work, was faint and fresh. A village this size likely would have someone at the stables all the time because horses are so valuable and particularly since the Moonsons must be keeping theirs here. But just the one young man, I used the wyse to make sure, and the emotions that swirled and that I tasted were nothing to concern me . . . contentment from the animals, happiness; boredom from the man, and just a touch of resentment and ire. Perhaps something untoward had happened in his life before he had come to work tonight and the ill emotions lingered.

I wondered what emotions someone would taste regarding me.

Flattened against the side of the stables, I sat my satchel down next to a post, and pushed the tastes away. I wanted no distractions, and I would need my wyse for something else. I listened to the night sounds—horses wuffling and nickering, one tamping its hoof against the hard-packed stable floor, and in the distance, music and laughter, likely coming from a tavern.

What I intended to do this night was not right. But I would try to make amends for it, and I would try to forgive myself later.

I slipped between the rails of the attached pen and made a low clicking sound. I wanted to wake up the two horses before I approached them. Otherwise, they would spook and the man would come out to investigate.

My eyes picked through the darkness, and I saw their eyes open and their ears prick forward. Nostrils quivering, they regarded me curiously. I continued the clicking sound and held my hands out to my sides. That one was a pony, likely a tall halflinger. So I stretched my wyse-sense toward the other horse, a vanner mare, I guessed, because of its profile. Bastien had taught me much about horses, and if I recalled my lessons correctly, the vanner was a strong but small draft horse used often by merchants and families who lived out of their wagons. It had a long mane and a feathery tail, and I imagined that it looked quite beautiful in full light. I clicked with a rhythm now and shifted my weight back and forth on the balls of my feet. Bastien had worked with the horses in the Village Nar this way, calming them and thereby making them more receptive.

The nostrils flared wider and I stopped, slowly drawing my arms close. I cast my gaze to the ground and waited. A slight breeze teased the hair on the back of my neck and brought me the dank, fusty odors of this pen and the streets nearby. I didn't need magic to pick up these scents, or to hear the mare coming closer. She snorted, took a few more steps, and stopped. I resumed the clicking and waited.

I probably could have managed all of this faster, just taking a coil of rope and looping it around one of the horse's necks, jumping on that horse, and riding away. But that would generate more noise than I wanted. I had time, and the darkness, and enough patience to do this properly.

She nickered and I raised my head at an angle, slowly, my eyes finding hers and then looking quickly away. Bastien said this showed the horse respect and served as an invitation.

It took a few moments, but the vanner accepted that invitation, clopping closer, tossing her head back, opening her eyes wider and tipping her ears up. I reached out a hand and touched her muzzle, then scratched it gently and made a sound as close to a nicker as I could manage.

Moments later, I found a bit and bridle hanging on a pen post. I put this on her and stroked her silky mane, whispered my name to her, and led her out of the gate.

"Stay," I urged, as I dropped her reins and hurried to where I'd left my satchel. I thrust my fingers inside it, my hand slightly sweaty. I didn't want to admit it to myself, but I was nervous. I wanted to be out of Elspeth's Knot and heading toward Derilynn and Tichal. I wanted to be about the business of completing my bloodoath so I could ease my spirit and bring closure for Lady Ewaren.

My fingers closed on the coin pouch, and I measured out half of the coins.

The coins had been Bastien's, and I could only guess how

many to use to buy the horse. We never used coins in the Village Nar, always bartering for goods instead . . . even with passing merchants and other villages, we traded. I sat the coins near the stable door, hoping the man would find them in the morning and consider them payment for the horse—and not keep them for himself. I thought it likely the latter would happen, as it would be more coins than he'd probably see in a year or perhaps his lifetime. But I had to try to pay for what I was taking.

In trying, I was assuaging some of the guilt I felt for stealing someone's mount. I prayed to the Green Ones this mare was not as precious to someone as Dazon had been to me. Perhaps when all of this was over I could return the horse to Elspeth's Knot. I promised myself that I would at least try.

"Time to leave," I whispered to the mare. I led her into an alley, then found a serpentlike way to get out of the village.

By the time we reached a path that ran parallel to the river and to the south, the moon was full and silvery, setting the dark water to sparkling and making it easy to find our way. I didn't get on the mare until I'd passed the southern edge of Elspeth's Knot, then I grabbed her mane and jumped up, nudging her to a fast trot, and resting my satchel between her neck and me. I was not used to riding without a saddle, but then I told myself I was not used to a lot of things—such as being on my own in pursuit of vengeance.

I could have traveled to the villages of Derilynn and Tichal without a horse. But this would be much faster, and it would be better for my newly healed ankle. I turned the mare east when the river narrowed and I knew it was shallow enough to cross. The mare balked at first, and I finally had to get off and lead her across. On the other side I hoisted myself up again, and urged her to take as fast a pace as the uneven terrain allowed.

I would stop when the moon climbed high into the sky, miles and miles from Elspeth's Knot. I didn't know if the Moonsons still searched for Nanoo Gafna and me, and I hoped they had no expert trackers in that village. Nanoo Shellaya's no-see might have been a powerful magical cloak, but I doubted it was magical enough to hide boot prints.

The miles melted, and my leggings and boots were dry by the time I tugged the mare to a copse of trees at the edge of some farmer's property. I tied her reins to a thin trunk, not trusting that she'd stay with me. Then I curled on the ground, trying to make a pillow of my satchel and wrapping my cloak tight around me. I couldn't sleep, though, something hard in the satchel settling uncomfortably against my cheek. I reached inside and retrieved the wooden box my mother had given me, and then I sat with my back against a tree and ran my fingers around the carved wood. I couldn't see it; everything was too dark. The stars winked down, but they could not touch me where I sat.

It was better not seeing. Practically everything I'd seen lately I wished I could purge from my memory—blood-soaked Nar, Lady Ewaren's corpse, Grazti's leering visage, the bruises on Nanoo Gafna's face.

"Alone." I breathed the word. I was glad for the solitude. I truly hadn't been alone since I'd discovered my slaughtered friends. I'd either been with Alysen or Shellaya or Gafna. I'd been responsible for someone, and that had kept me physically and mentally preoccupied. Now I was responsible only for myself, and for the promise I'd sworn.

Truly alone. My home was lost to me, forever. I'd never return to the Village Nar; too many ghosts to haunt me. And try as I might to recall happy times there, my mind pictured only the bodies and the blood and Lady Ewaren's torn dress.

Trained by Bastien to survive in the woods and to be the equal of any man in a fight, still I felt completely hollow and terribly, terribly frightened.

No home.

I'd told the Nanoos I'd likely come to Mardel's Fen when I carried out my oath. But now I wasn't so sure of that plan. Living in the fen would remind me of just why I was there.

Because I had no home.

Perhaps I should consider a new start in a place I'd not been before. There were islands to the east with rich farmland and herds of sheep and goats, and I knew I could find work there. Not past marrying age, I could find a husband if I tried. I'd had no suitor in the Village Nar; the community was small and the young men interested in women who cooked and wove and wore dresses trimmed with ribbons. But I thought I would like to find someone and make a home for myself.

Everyone should have a home.

Lady Ewaren had said those exact words when she'd accepted me into her manor house, and repeated them when Alysen joined us.

I had no home.

By the Green Ones, I was hollow.

I knocked the back of my head against the tree. Again and again in despair and frustration. When the pain registered I stopped and tried to picture Lady Ewaren's face, like I'd seen it in Nanoo Gafna's vision . . . before the storm came to Nar.

A beautiful and kind woman, mentor and friend and dead by Lord Purvis because he had looked for me.

"I will find you, or you will find me, demon-of-a-man," I swore. "And either way you'll pray to your dark gods for mercy."

I squeezed my hands tight on the box. The wood was smooth on the edges, like I'd remembered my mother's face being, and the carving on top was intricate and done with small tools. I rubbed my thumbs against the rounded corners and forced away thoughts of Lord Purvis and my shattered home. My shattered future.

Who'd fashioned the box?

Not my father . . . his skills hadn't taken him in that direction. My mother? Perhaps she had made it. Perhaps . . . something depressed on the lid. I felt a fingertip sink in, then the lid swiveled open.

I nearly dropped the box in my surprise, and I felt my heart beat faster. I held my breath and curled my fingers over the lip, making sure the lid couldn't somehow slide shut. I opened my mouth and extended my tongue, then sucked it back in and clamped my teeth shut. I'd not use my enhanced senses to discover the contents!

I sat motionless for several minutes, hardly breathing, my mind poised in anticipation. So many years I'd tried to open it, and resisted breaking the box only because of Bastien's words. I wanted desperately to look inside, and yet not to look. So many years I'd waited and wondered, like a child held back from a birthday box, forced to dream about the contents.

I'd shaken it more times than I could count, never hearing anything rattle inside and speculating that nothing at all nested in the box and that the puzzling box itself was my mother's gift.

I held my breath now and peered inside, seeing nothing because of the darkness. I probed with a finger, feeling silk. A handkerchief? An edging of lace, and some threadwork. I used two fingers now, pulling up the silk and exploring further. A ring, warming to my touch and telling me the metal it was made of was gold or silver, something precious.

The handkerchief had kept the ring from rattling in the box, and had also kept quiet the other tiny keepsakes. My fingertips found an egg-shaped stone, polished smooth and no longer than my thumbnail.

"Three," I whispered. "I was three years old."

My mother had walked with me every day when I was very young, often stopping at a creek so I could dangle my toes in the water and watch the small fish swim near to investigate. I'd found the stone then, pearly white and looking like a bird's egg that had dropped out of a nest and into the water. That's what I'd thought it was, and I gently scooped it up and asked my mother if I could climb the tree and find the nest and put it back. It took quite a bit of convincing on her part to get me to realize it was just a rock that time and the current had smoothed. So I took it home.

One more home that was lost to me.

My heart had opened when the box had, pouring out old memories and deepening my melancholy. I kept my fingers on the stone for long minutes, feeling its slickness and the tears spilling down my cheeks. I'd cried more in the past many days than I had in the past many years.

I had no one left.

My mother and father gone, Bastien, Lady Ewaren, the pieces of my life taken from me. Would I see them when I died? Did spirits swirl with the Green Ones? I needed to believe that. I needed to believe in something good and something beyond this disappointing world. I wanted a hole to appear in the sky that I could fly through and leave all this ugliness behind. If there was nothing beyond the world . . . what was any of this for?

I felt the other treasures, a tiny buckle, rough to the touch. Another bit of sadness—it was from the collar of a small dog I'd treasured in my earliest years. My closest companion, he fell sick one winter and died during the night. My father cut the buckle off the collar and saved it for me.

I'd looked for the egg-stone and the buckle before moving to the Village Nar.

The ring? It hadn't been mine.

Five buttons, my fingers also discovered. I didn't recall anything special about buttons. These were the size and shape of almonds, and there were "eyes" on the back of each so they could be sewn to a garment. In fact, a few threads still clung to one of the buttons. The buttons, too, warmed to my touch, meaning they were made of stone or metal . . . metal, I decided after a moment.

The last item I found crumbled almost instantly, coating my fingers with a musty powder I brought to my nose to sniff.

A butterfly wing I'd ruined. I fought a smile. After my dog had died, I'd tried to make a pet of more than a few creatures, telling my mother I didn't want another dog because it would only remind me of the first. And there'd be no dog better than the first. I wanted something else. The butterfly was one of my shorter-lived companions, beautiful in life with glistening orange and yellow wings. I'd insisted on keeping it when it died.

Now I'd ruined that particular treasure.

I closed the box and replaced it in my pack, wondering if I'd find a way to open it again. Then I brushed away the butterfly dust on my tunic and tried futilely to brush away the memories. I rested my head on the satchel, moving it so the box inside did not bother me.

The buttons? What were they from?

I shook my head to clear my thoughts of the treasures in the puzzle box. Then I touched a hand to my waist, where my weapons belt should have been. I needed a knife, and I vowed to get one tomorrow.

I finally fell asleep. I had intended to allow myself a brief rest, just so I could count myself alert and rested for the coming morning. But I slept a little longer than I'd planned; when I untied the mare and looked to the sky, I saw it lightening, the purple-blue shade looking like watery paint smeared together and telling me dawn was not far away.

I pressed the vanner, promising her feed in Derilynn, as I believed I had enough coins for that and knives and a belt. I could not face Lord Purvis without weapons. My fingers tightened on the reins. Glancing down, I saw that my knuckles looked bloodless.

"You will die by my hand, demon-of-a-man."

26

DERILYNN LOOMED AHEAD, A VILLAGE THE SIZE OF NAR, BUT more spread-out and ringing a lake that provided its liveli-hood. I'd visited this place so long ago—with my mother—that all I could recall was the dark blue water of the lake and the bright white swans that sometimes swam on it. She'd told me what caused the water's color, something about the miner-als on the bottom, but I couldn't recall for certain. I did recall, however, that my mother had been very smart.

They would have knives here because of the fishing trade, and so I kneed the mare to a faster pace. The Moonsons had said Lord Purvis was either here or at Tichal. I knew after just glancing at this village that I would not find him here.

I'd crested a rise to reach this village, and from the very top of the hillock I could see all of the small community. A pen held two horses, a cow, and several goats and sheep. There were no war horses, so it was obvious Lord Purvis had moved on.

But I could get information about him here, and acquire the knives that were occupying my thoughts. After I found a treat of oats for the vanner, I would scry on the surface of that dazzling dark blue lake and learn the precise location of my quarry. Perhaps I should have scryed upon Lord Purvis earlier, but I remained hesitant to use what Nanoo Shellaya admitted was dangerous magic.

Within moments I stood in the heart of the fishing village. I left the vanner mare with a herder at the pen, giving him a coin to groom the horse and feed her sweet oats.

"I will return soon," I said. "I've some business here, and then I'll be riding on."

He grinned warmly at me, twirling the coin between his fingers before thrusting it in a shirt pocket. I suspected coins were as much a rarity here as they'd been in the Village Nar.

I saw no shops, unlike in Elspeth's Knot, and so I asked people who came out to meet me about a metalworker. To my surprise there was none, but they pointed me to a giant of a man who sold an assortment of goods out of his cottage, things he acquired from merchants in trade for the wool from his sheep. They said he had knives and hatchets.

"I don't take coins. Never taken a single one. Never will." He looked me up and down, wrinkling his nose, no doubt at the smell of me and appearance of my clothes.

The women I'd spotted in this village wore long skirts or dresses and had hair that fell at least to their shoulders. I was a peculiarity.

"I trade for wares, just like everyone else around here. Things I can use or trade for something I can." He continued to eye me, making it clear he disapproved of my appearance, though he spoke to me in a civil tone. "Can't spend coins here or anywhere else I care to go. Can't eat them."

I left his cottage, coming back a few minutes later with the wooden box from my satchel and studying its lid. I couldn't find the spot that depressed to open it until in frustration I closed my eyes. Perhaps that was the trick to the puzzle— finding something when you weren't looking for it.

In the light that spilled through his window I saw that the silk handkerchief was a warm shade of ivory, no doubt darkened by the years. The lace was curled and off-white, snagged in two places, and the decorative threads spelled out my mother's name—Aelaren.

He tapped his foot impatiently as I peeled back the corner of the silk and looked at the egg-shaped stone, the buckle, the dust that had been the butterfly's wings, the buttons—made of silver and still stirring no memories—and the ring. It was a thick band, also silver, etched on the outside with an ivy vine. It had been inscribed, but the metal had so worn on the inside that I could not read it.

I pulled out the ring and felt it warm to my fingers. Too big to have been my mother's, I guessed it had belonged to her father or someone else important to her. I passed it to the man.

He tossed it in his palm, as if judging its weight, and then he turned it over and over. "Old, worn," he pronounced.

"It's silver," I said. "It has value."

"It'd be like taking coins. Not much good to me." Still, he didn't give the ring back. After a moment, he tried it on a finger, finding it a reasonable fit. He held his hand toward the window and studied it. "I'll give you a long knife for it." After another moment he added, "And a sheath."

"Two knives." I knew how to barter.

He shook his head.

The air whistled out between my teeth, and I plucked the five silver buttons from the puzzle box. Tiny blue gems were set in the centers, and I knew cut stones, even as small as these, were treasures. I handed him two.

"These for the second knife, sheath, and that belt."

He shook his head again, and I scooped the buttons off his palm. "Just the one knife, then."

I took the blade and turned to leave.

"Wait."

I didn't let him see my smile. I knew objects like these buttons were not likely to come his way ever again. I hated to part with anything in the puzzle box, but I needed weapons, and his were well made and the edges gleamed with a sharpness that would be useful.

"For the second knife, the sheath, and the belt. I'll take those baubles."

Minutes later I was at the edge of the lake, several yards from a half dozen fishermen who took turns casting nets, letting them sink, then after an interval retrieving them. Another man searched along the shore and in the tall grass beyond it for turtles. Tall and broad-shouldered, he had an unruly shock of hair that flared away from his head when he turned to look at me.

I moved a little farther away, took off my boots, and waded into the lake. The dark water did not seem as intense or quite as beautiful as I remembered from my childhood, but then I think the world had captivated me more easily then. The water felt warmer than I expected for this time of the spring, and the sand at the bottom felt good against my soles. My face reflected ghostlike back at me, and I tried to smooth out the ripples with my hands.

I pictured Lord Purvis as I had seen him in Nanoo Gafna's vision. Lips pulled up in a sneer, ordering his men to break Lady Ewaren's fingers, then ordering her death. The image came quickly to me, as it had been difficult to keep him out of my head. I pictured his armor, his swagger, the utter vileness of him.

The hate boiled up inside me, my heart stoking my anger.

I felt warmth against my palms and realized I'd squeezed my fingers so tight into fists that my fingernails had sliced into my skin. Drops of blood fell onto the water, onto an image of the man I'd sworn to kill. Stubble dotted his chin, heavy enough to look like the purposeful start of a beard. All of his face filled my vision, and I had to concentrate to pull the image back so I could learn his location. Seeing him in this scry would do me nothing if I could not also see where he was.

He stood between the trunks of two red maples, a breeze rustling the branches above him, the leaves casting dancing shadows across the top of his helmet. He didn't move, and I had to stare closely to make sure he breathed.

"More," I urged the magic. "I need to see more." I pulled back further and saw a horse, the one he had ridden with the storm into the Village Nar. It posed, impressive and gorgeous, at least sixteen hands high, with a well-groomed mane and tail. It was the most impressive-looking horse I'd ever seen. The horse's nostrils quivered, and its ears were forward, listening and smelling to discern the information carried on the wind.

Simple animals learned more from the world than educated men could because they, like the Nanoo, me, and blessed others, knew the secret.

The horse raised its head, and then I saw Lord Purvis turn. I swore that hateful man looked straight at me, the corner of his lip raising in what had become a familiar expression.

"That is the danger with a scry, young woman. Sometimes they can watch you back."

I whirled and saw the tall man who'd been hunting turtles.

"Be careful using that magic."

"You are a Nanoo?" I mouthed. A heartbeat later I answered the question by looking more closely. My eyes registered the tree-bark lines on his face and his dark complexion—not so many lines, though, as the Nanoo in Mardel's Fen, nor so rich a color of skin. Reed thin, the broad shoulders made him look only gaunter. Unhealthy, I'd thought at first, catching sight of bony wrists and pronounced cheekbones. But his eyes were bright and lively and did not hint at any illness.

He sat cross-legged on the shore and I stepped away from the fading image on the lake and joined him. He nested a net bag between his knees. It was half filled with hurril bulbs, an early spring fruit that grew close to the ground. He'd been collecting the bulbs, not searching for turtles as I'd thought.

He offered me one, and I quickly accepted. I hadn't eaten since right before Nanoo Shellaya and I had reached Elspeth's Knot. The pulpy fruit tasted slightly bitter, but it slid down my throat easily. He handed me another.

"Thank you . . ."

"Tillard," he replied.

"I am Wisteria." I gave him no surname, neither did I mention Nar. Titles had become unimportant to me. Too, he'd given me only Tillard.

"Yes, I am Nanoo."

My face betrayed my puzzlement, and I saw the smile in his eyes.

"Most Nanoo live in Mardel's Fen, but obviously not all of us." He reached into his net bag and pulled out two more bulbs, passing one to me. He polished his against his tunic before taking a bite. He chewed slowly, relishing the taste, then continued. "I lived in Mardel's Fen my first two decades, born to a couple who already had three children."

From my few visits to the fen, and from tales Gafna had told me, I knew most of the Nanoo were women who lived alone, and the couples in the fen rarely had more than two children. The Nanoo purposely kept their numbers down so the size of the community remained relatively constant.

"You left of your own accord, Tillard?"

He nodded and took another bite. I finished my third piece of fruit and licked my lips to get the last bit of juice. Though mildly astringent, the fruit quenched my thirst and went a long way toward ending my hunger.

"I was loved, of course, in the fen. The Nanoo cherish and cling to each other. But I was not so strong in the wyse as my older brothers and sister . . . and that was my own fault, my mind always wandered." He paused and leaned back on his hands, head turned up to the morning sun. "As did I wander from the fen. Itchy feet, I guess."

I wondered if his skin was paler than other Nanoo's and his lines less pronounced because he'd been away from the village for . . . how many years? I placed him between thirty and forty, but he immediately ended my speculation.

"After leaving the fen I traveled for a little more than a year before settling in this village. I like the lake and the people, and they like me well enough, I think, though a stubborn few are a suspicious lot. I've been here three years now. Surprised myself that I haven't moved on. Perhaps my feet no longer itch quite so much."

That would make him . . .

"Twenty-four winters I have seen, Wisteria. Not yet twenty-five, but that birthday will come soon."

Like other Nanoo, he had a way of prying into my thoughts. And like other Nanoo, age was very difficult to guess.

"I'm not prying," he said. "Well, not on purpose. Your mind is so strong you practically shout the questions to me. I could teach you to hide your thoughts, give you more control, but there are other matters to spend your efforts on at the moment."

"Such as scry magic." I licked my fingers and turned to face the lake. "Dangerous magic, perhaps. But necessary . . . at the moment." Then I told him of Nar and Nanoo Gafna, her capture and rescue and the vision she'd showed me of Lord Purvis. I hadn't intended to reveal so much, but something about him, his imploring eyes and gentle expression, coaxed it out of me. I found him so easy to confide in; perhaps that was his wyse talent, to pull thoughts from people.

"A bloodoath . . . I've not heard of such before. And the Moonsons, I know so very little about them. This Lord Purvis, though, I saw him days past, when he came to the village—"

"Recruiting young men for his army," I finished.

He nodded.

We heard a whoop and halfway around the lake watched one of the men tug in his nets and hold up a large catfish with a big white belly. His fellows congratulated him and helped him string the fish and float it so it would not die before he was ready to call his morning's efforts done and clean it. A pair of gulls hovered over the men. We weren't far from the sea, and they'd come inland in search of food.

"Seven he talked away from this village, much to their parents' and the elders' dismay. Little more than boys, really; Hallory was the youngest, at thirteen, and their presence will be missed. Promised them adventure and esteem and plied them with tales of serving the Empress." He shook his head. "Easy to see through his words, but not if you're young and dreaming."

"Several days ago?"

"Yes, more than a few days past. There were many men already with him, their horses amazing animals, coats so shiny and manes and tails braided. Put our two horses to shame, they did. All of the men wore some fashion of armor, matching cloaks and shields, looking like they were readying for battle. The ornamentation attracted our young men. And he promised them armor, swords, and horses, too, when they went back in triumph to the great city."

I raised an eyebrow.

"Yes, by the Green Ones, your Lord Purvis seems intent on some mission. You could see the fire in his eyes. His thoughts did not shout to me. Indeed, I could not tell at all what he seemed to be concentrating on."

He turned to watch another fisherman haul in his net, nothing in it so large as the catfish. "I did not like the man. And I can tell you truly that I've encountered none other in my life who I could admit to not liking."

He still watched the fishermen, and I watched him. He

looked older than his years, but then I didn't know that much about the Nanoo. I had no real idea of Gafna's age. Their skin, which looked like tree bark, disguised that.

"He searches for me, I believe." More words poured from my lips, about how Lord Purvis came to the Village Nar looking for me, how my father died and the Emperor . . . both of them slain. "Lord Purvis, the Empress, they want magic to die."

"No. Not precisely." He returned his attention to me. "Not all magic, in any event. Those around Lord Purvis shouted to me. They were not interested in magic or the wyse, though some had it pulsing in their bodies. Those men do not know the secret, Wisteria." When Tillard said my name, it sounded musical. His voice was even and strong, and I found myself enjoying listening to him. "But it is hardly a secret in Derilynn." He waved his hand to indicate the lake and the village.

I closed my eyes and opened my mouth, searching for the wyse in this place and finding it as thick as tree syrup. Perhaps the wyse was stronger in water than on the land. I felt heady, as if I'd finished a bottle of sweet wine by myself. I drank the magic in and felt it blend with my own inner magic. I don't know how many minutes I did this, as time ceased to exist for me. But when I finally opened my eyes and shook my head to clear my senses, I saw him grinning at me.

"The villagers—" I began.

"Some of them are as strong in the wyse as the Nanoo in Mardel's Fen. But they're quiet about it. And some of them know nothing of magic and would think those of us who embrace it to be—"

"Witches."

"And worse."

"No wonder you like it here, Tillard."

We both grew quiet for a time, listening to the pair of gulls and the fishermen, watching the one with the great catfish pull it and the rest of his morning's haul to the village's cleaning house.

"I think I would like to stay, Tillard, for a while. But I've the matter of my bloodoath. I put it off too long, taking care of Alysen and seeing to Nanoo Gafna."

"I remember her," he said. "And Shellaya, of course. I remember all of them. Perhaps one day I will go back for a visit and let them see how pale and skinny one of their brothers has become." A pause. "They would welcome me, of course, perhaps try to get me to come home . . . my parents and brothers and sister especially. But it would never be the same as before. I consider that home lost to me."

I had no reply to that, wondering if he pulled my thoughts of Nar and having no home myself from my mind. "I need the scry magic to find Lord Purvis."

"He saw you in return, you know. I watched your water vision. He looked right at you."

I shrugged.

"He has the wyse about him, Wisteria." Again my musical name. "Else he'd not return your stare."

"And so he knows where I am?"

"Maybe. Likely, if he is strong enough."

"Then I must find him now." I stood and brushed the dirt from the back of my leggings. I slowly waded back into the water. "I must go to him. I can't allow Derilynn to suffer as Nar did. I must go to him, not him come to me."

Tillard moved so quietly that I didn't know he'd joined me in the lake until he rested a long-fingered hand on my shoulder. "What makes you think he searches for you, Wisteria? What makes you such a threat to a man as powerful as a warlord?"

Once more I shrugged. Then even as I pictured Lord Purvis's sneering visage and called it up on the water, I told Tillard of what Alysen had said. "If I'd been in the Village Nar, he might have contented himself with slaying only me."

"What makes you think he was looking for you?" Again the question.

"I told you, Tillard. The girl Alysen . . ." I sucked in a breath. Lord Purvis returned my stare from the image. I forced the vision to pull back from him, seeing the twin maples on either side of him, his magnificent horse, more horses in the woods behind him, more men. The man closest to him looked vaguely familiar, and it took a few moments to picture him without the wrinkles at the corners of his eyes and the streaks of gray in his hair.

Celerad t'Lurres, one of the nine Moonsons who'd visited Bastien years ago in Nar. He was wearing the Moonson colors, as were a half dozen others partially obscured by the trees.

It was an odd mix of trees: maples and cypress, stringybarks and stick-thin pines. There were ferns with broad, thick leaves that demanded a warmer climate than their low-growing evergreen neighbors, which thrived in the cold.

"Mardel's Fen," I said. "The demon-of-a-man is in the fen. If he can see me, as you say, he'd know not to look for me in the fen."

"So he was not looking for you after all, Wisteria," Tillard said.

"No." Suddenly my throat went tight and my knees gave out. I felt the Nanoo catch me as I fell. "Tillard, Lord Purvis looks for Alysen t'Geer."

27

I REGAINED MY COMPOSURE AND RUSHED FROM THE LAKE, GRAB-
bing up my boots and satchel as I went. Rocks and chunks of
hard-packed earth dug into the soles of my feet, and I stopped
to put on my boots only because I feared I might step on
something sharp and in reflex twist my ankle. I'd be of little
use to Alysen if I broke my ankle again.

Tillard reached me as I struggled into my boots. I leaned
against him to make the task easier.

"Fool I am." I cursed myself, adding more foul words that
made the Nanoo blush, all strung together and all aimed at
me. "I didn't look beyond, didn't think. Fool I am."

Oh, I'd listened to what Alysen t'Geer had told me when I
came upon her that day in the Village Nar and discovered my
slaughtered friends. She said Lord Purvis had come looking
for me.

And when I'd seen the attack—the storm come to the Village Nar—through Nanoo Gafna's vision, I thought I'd heard
the same tale. Lord Purvis claimed that he looked for a

woman . . . or had he said girl? . . . strong in the wyse. One with a most magical father.

I shut my eyes and sucked in a deep breath. His words—"a most magical father." They implied the father still lived, and I knew my father was dead. Not just because of Alysen's words did I know it, but by an emptiness I felt, a severed connection, the same sensation I'd felt shortly after my mother's death. And I should have been aware of my father's passing before Alysen told me. But I'd not thought of my father in some time, and my mind had been elsewhere, worried about finding game to feed the village.

A most magical father.

One of the Green Ones.

There could be no more magical father than one of our gods. Lord Purvis had made no mention that the father was dead.

He'd said "a most magical father."

"Your thoughts still shout to me, Wisteria." Tillard ran at my side, the net bag of bulbs over his shoulder and thumping against his back. "But perception is my gift."

"Then you know about Alysen."

"But not why your demon-man would hunt her."

Indeed, how could one impetuous girl present a threat to the man in charge of the Empress's army? I reached the pen where I'd left the vanner mare. Her head was thrust deep into a bucket of oats.

"Have you a saddle I may trade for?" I called to the man in the pen. He looked up from feeding the sheep and shook his head.

"Only one saddle, and it's for—"

"My horse," Tillard said. "Give it to her, Aren, and bring Sky, please."

I looked to the Nanoo.

"Winter Sky," he said. "It's what I named him when he was gifted to me a little more than three years past. In my travels I helped a merchant and his family, and the horse was payment. Not so sleek as yours, and quite some years older, I'd judge by his teeth. But he will carry me well enough to go with you."

I shook my head vehemently. I considered the man saddling the vanner, which protested slightly. A draft, the mare was used to pulling carts and wagons, not a saddle. I hoisted myself up and hooked my satchel to the front of the saddle, and I turned her north with a flick of the reins, leaned forward, stretching toward her ear.

"Hurry, girl. Like the wind is—"

"Wait!" Tillard put a bit and bridle on a dark gray horse with pale blue eyes the watery color of a winter sky. "I said I'm going with you."

I kneed the vanner and slapped the side of her neck. The horse took off at a gallop.

"Wait! Please wait, Wisteria!"

I didn't slow, even though I heard him behind me trying to catch up. I didn't answer him, either, when he called that he wanted to help me, and that this was his concern, too.

"I am Nanoo!" he shouted. "The people in the fen are mine!"

And the Nanoo were in jeopardy because Alysen was under their protection and because Lord Purvis sought her. And Alysen was in the fen because I had taken her there. Practically forced her on the Nanoo.

Why? Why in the name of the Green Ones did Lord Purvis seek her?

I mulled over the possibilities as I demanded the vanner gallop now.

"Wisteria, slow down!"

I didn't know what to say to him, and so I kept silent. I blamed myself . . . not in the way I had when I had thought Lord Purvis looked for me, but just as strongly as I'd counted myself guilty before.

It was my fault that I hadn't looked deeper, hadn't realized there could be another answer beyond Lord Purvis coming to Nar because of me and slaughtering everyone I knew. I had believed Alysen. My father killed, Lord Purvis and his ilk wanted the bloodline ended. They wanted me dead, I'd thought. Alysen had said the Empress demanded me drummed.

Had Alysen believed what she'd told me? Had she truly blamed me? Or had she known the truth, that they wanted her? Could she not live with that truth and so pushed the fault to me?

Why did Purvis want Alysen t'Geer?

"Why?" I shouted the word over and over and over. Alysen was stronger in the wyse than I, perhaps stronger than the Nanoo because of her father. How did Purvis know about her? Why would—

The scry magic.

I pulled back on the reins in my realization, not intending to slow the horse, but doing so by accident. It gave Tillard the opportunity to catch up. His horse was larger, but older and slower, and froth flecked at its lips from the exertion. Tillard talked to me, the words a babble I rudely paid no attention to.

In truth I didn't know what he said, I was so caught up in the puzzle pieces I assembled.

Nanoo Gafna's vision!

I closed my eyes and recalled the images, "the storm," she'd called it when the men on horseback thundered into the Village Nar. I remembered Lord Purvis ordering Lady Ewaren's fingers broken, ordering her death, then the deaths of everyone, swords flashing like lightning. Purvis said there could be no witnesses.

Alysen was a witness! *The* witness.

She'd scryed on him again and again . . . and she scryed on who knew how many others. But she'd scryed on *him.*

She'd told me she'd seen him with the Empress and outside my father's room. She'd told me she scryed so often, compelled to use the magic, drawn to it like a tree-cat to nip. She was addicted to the spell. How many times had she watched him? And in return, how many times had he watched her? Had she seen more than she'd told me? Nanoo Shellaya had said one strong in the wyse could look back, and could discern your location . . . just as you could discern his. Nanoo Tillard had said the same.

So Lord Purvis must have discovered that Alysen had scryed on him from the Village Nar . . . and if she'd seen him kill the Emperor or my father, seen him commit other crimes—

"He would want her dead," Tillard finished. "Again your thoughts are clear, Wisteria. If this girl called Alysen witnessed his crimes, he might fear her and want her eliminated to keep his ugly secrets safe. And if she kept scrying on him, even while she was in the fen—"

"Lord Purvis would know to find her with the Nanoo." I nodded, once more urging the vanner mare to a trot. "He thinks he has to kill her. Not just because of what she's seen him do, but because of what she might witness in the future."

This time I kept a pace Tillard and his old horse could manage. I might well need Tillard's help, though two people against Lord Purvis and his many armored men would stand no better chance than one. Too, a large part of me suspected that no matter how fast I could reach the fen, it would be too late. Lord Purvis rode days ahead of us.

The demon-of-a-man would fail or succeed before we could do anything against him.

"Tillard, Lord Purvis did not find Alysen in Nar." I knew that was because of Nanoo Gafna's no-see. "And he did not find her by questioning Gafna, by having her tortured. Though why Gafna did not tell me he asked about Alysen rather than myself is a mystery."

Tillard let out an uneasy laugh. "The Nanoo are wise, Wisteria, most of them. But Gafna is . . ." His voice trailed off, words failing to express what he meant.

"Mad? Touched?" Perhaps, I thought. Certainly odd. Maybe Gafna didn't know he wanted Alysen specifically. "He should have plied her with cow's milk instead to gain her precious information."

Tillard cocked his head and bounced his heels against his horse's sides, urging it to a little better speed. "We are days away from Mardel's Fen, Wisteria."

I knew that.

The worry boiled in my stomach. Lord Purvis would be in

the heart of the fen well before we reached the edge of the marshy ground. And he was going there because Alysen had without a doubt scryed on him again.

Again and again.

The tree-cat drawn to the nip.

Lord Purvis had watched her as she'd watched him, and divined her location. She might as well have burned a pyre atop a mountain, so bright a beacon she'd made to lead him to her.

"My fault. My fault." I ground my teeth together and squeezed my hands so tight I once more drew blood from my palms. "My fault."

My mind had been too narrow to see all the possibilities. And my mind was also too narrow to plan anything other than killing Lord Purvis.

Tillard and I rode until his horse was too tired to go another step and we worried he might become lame. My mare was past exhaustion, too. The day remained bright until sunset, when thin clouds bled into the darkening blue sky, then became thicker and gray, scudding along and threatening rain. The air smelled full of water and was laced with the scents of hundreds of wildflowers and long, thick grass.

A small part of me praised the Green Ones for nature's perfume and for the stars that shone down through gaps in the clouds, tiny diamonds on a goddess's velvety dress. I thought looking at the stars might calm me, as I stretched on my back in the night-cool meadow and pretended I was resting on the feathery bed in Lady Ewaren's manor, quilt pulled up to my chin. But vengeance and worry and guilt burned unchecked inside me, and my stomach roiled uncomfortably and kept me from sleep.

We didn't talk, though Tillard spoke softly to the horses before lying beside me. There was nothing to be said beyond the words we'd already spoken about Lord Purvis, Alysen, and the Nanoo.

Nothing new to be learned without scrying again. I'd thought about doing that.

A stream twisted through the meadow only yards away. It gurgled pleasantly and accompanied crickets and tree frogs, which sounded like chirping birds. But I didn't want Lord Purvis to see me and to know we headed his way, and so I resisted the scry magic.

I would fight him, with Tillard. Though what two people could do against his force of armed men was, perhaps, nothing.

I finally fell asleep, fingers resting on the handles of the knives at my waist, head churning with horrid thoughts and biting memories as the rain started pattering down.

28

WHEN WE STOPPED THE SECOND TIME THE FOLLOWING MORNING, allowing the horses to graze and drink from a farm pond, Tillard gathered mushrooms and gave me the largest ones.

"I don't eat much," he explained.

"I can well see that, Nanoo Til—"

He shook his head.

"No titles," I said, recalling that Shellaya had asked I call her just by that name.

"No titles."

Could he still read my thoughts, which whirled around Alysen, Lord Purvis, and Lady Ewaren? His face didn't reveal him, and his eyes did not meet mine. Was I still shouting my private musings?

"I should eat more, I know," he said. "My friends in Derilynn constantly scold me, and some of the ladies there bring me cherry and blueberry pies in the summer. They know I don't eat meat."

I finished my share of the mushrooms and wondered just

where he'd found them. Before I could ask, he handed me his portion.

"I'll gather more, Wisteria. You will need to keep your strength." He left me to my deliberations and searched on the other side of the pond, where he could keep an eye on the horses, and when he looked up, on me.

I ate the rest of the mushrooms, finding them less pleasing than the bulb fruit he'd given me in Derilynn yesterday. In fact, I'd never cared for mushrooms or any morels, but I could not be choosy. I was thankful he'd provided for us. He certainly would not have eaten what I would have chosen—a rabbit or a pig.

Judging by the landmarks we'd passed, it would be late this day before we reached Mardel's Fen. And that was if we pushed the horses beyond the point of fatigue. I looked to them, his horse standing still, eyes closed, sleeping, my vanner drinking, flicking flies with her silky tail. I hated forcing the older animal at this punishing pace, but I had no choice.

More than once I'd considered leaving Tillard during the past night, as the vanner could manage a faster pace, and for longer. It had rained in the early morning hours, and I knew the water would wash away my tracks. I doubted he had the skills to follow me . . . but he knew where the heart of the fen hid in the woods, and wisdom suggested that I keep his company. He knew the enchanted grove of the Nanoo far better than I did.

He returned, shirt hem held out in front of him like a basket, filled with more mushrooms and with raspberries that were not wholly ripe. I quickly plucked out the fruit, eating until all the berries were gone, then feeling guilty about it.

"I did not pick them for me," he said.

So he was reading my—

"I often keep to myself in Derilynn. It is difficult for me not to listen."

"The wyse is strong with you."

He shrugged and picked at the mushrooms cupped in his shirt. "Stronger in my brothers and sister."

I closed my eyes and tried to clear my thoughts, intending to use my wyse-sense now. I opened my mouth and tasted the breeze, and shoved to the back of my mind all the things I expected to taste—the tiredness of the horses, the wonderful scents of this place, cows we could not see that grazed beyond a thick line of old poplars.

I searched for the presence of men and horses, not ones now nearby but ones that had passed this way some time ago. I didn't find what I looked for, meaning Lord Purvis and his men had come another way to the fen . . . probably used the road that stretched by the Village Nar and that Nanoo Shellaya and I had avoided because I had not wanted to smell the blood and run into ghosts.

I tasted other things, however, anxiety the strongest and pounding like a loud heartbeat inside my head. Tillard worried over the Nanoo, over Alysen, whom he'd not met, and mostly over me. What else I tasted bothered me, as I did not believe it proper or possible for a man to care about a woman he knew little about.

I opened my eyes and saw him looking at me. I glanced away and got to my feet.

"We've dallied overlong." I stretched and rolled my head, working a nagging kink out of my neck.

"I am not worried about my people in Mardel's Fen." In a few strides he was past me and ruffling the mane of his horse, hoisting himself on its back and folding his fingers around the reins. "They are among the most magical people of this world, Wisteria. And they are more numerous than the men you saw riding with Lord Purvis in your scry vision."

"The demon-of-a-man," I hissed.

"It is those men who I think I worry over. The Nanoo have been known to deal quite harshly with uninvited visitors."

His tone was flippant, but I didn't believe him. The set of his eyes, and the way his lips worked when he didn't talk, gave him away.

I was right when I'd tasted his worry.

Was I also right about the other feelings I'd tasted?

29

IT WAS WELL AFTER SUNSET WHEN WE NEARED MARDEL'S FEN. Though only a few miles from the southern edge of it, even with all the starlight in this night's cloudless sky, we were too far to see the first of the dense trees. But I didn't need to see the trees to know that something horrific had happened.

The redolence of the woods slammed into me, and I pulled back on the reins to get the vanner to stop. The mare whinnied and dug at the ground with a hoof, drew her ears forward. Tillard's horse didn't seem to be as bothered, but it was older and its senses had no doubt been dulled by the years.

"Fire. I can smell it." Tillard slid off Winter Sky. He started to tug the horse, as he alternately looked ahead and at the ground so he wouldn't stumble.

I stayed on the vanner for a few moments, watching Tillard and finally sticking my tongue out so the breeze could swirl around it. I'd been using my wyse-sense so often lately, ever since Lord Purvis had destroyed my home, that it came effortlessly to me. I'd never had to use it so often before—never wanted to. Alysen was right; I relied on my skills and weapons more than I relied on the magic of the world. I dropped my right hand to the knife handle, keeping the left on the reins.

"Tillard, wait a moment. There is no fire. Not now. But there was."

He paused but didn't stop. After a moment, he walked faster, this time not looking down and not worrying about the uneven ground. I tasted his uneasiness and fear, his horse's fear, which was not as thick. I tasted no other emotions; I was too far from the Nanoo community to pick up their thoughts. But I picked up many more things, so many it took me a few minutes to sort through them all.

Tillard disappeared into the shadows ahead, but I tracked him by his fear.

The scent of the burned trees was so sharp and painful, it felt like needles jabbing at my tongue. They'd fought hard against the blaze, the trees, being damp from the very essence of the fen, being filled with sap and life. Some of them yet clung to life, though the taste of that life was so faint and sour that I knew they were dying.

Ferns, low-growing evergreens, fescue grass, and reeds also had been caught in the fire, as had small animals. The fire had been set; lightning had played no part. And Tillard and I well knew that Lord Purvis and his men were responsible. I got off the mare and dropped her reins, letting her follow or not. I'd not force her to enter this place.

I continued to taste the grove as I edged deeper into it. The char of wood set my head to aching fiercely, and so I tried to work that particular odor out of my mouth. Charred flesh from animals, and from a man, the lump of which I made out draped over a log . . . I worked those things away, too. The fire had burned so hot it had singed his hands off, and the pink of his insides glistened through a rent in his belly. No trace of armor, no sword; I figured him to be a Nanoo.

I just needed to see if there were more of them.

Again I tasted Tillard's fear, my own rising with it. I'd wanted to believe the Nanoo could not be threatened in their domain because of the magic they commanded. But already I'd found one dead. And several yards later I found another. Near this corpse the trees were twisted, branches looking like snakes, the char on them scales. Some of the branches were low to the ground, as if the tree bent over to grasp something—like the weave had grabbed Grazti many days ago.

So the fen itself—or in concert with some of the Nanoo—had tried to snare the trespassers, like Grazti had been snared.

The taste of fear grew stronger, settling like a piece of spoiled meat in my mouth and making my eyes water. The fear lingered in the gaps between burned trunks and was thick. It felt like I swam through mud, fighting for each step.

The fear was from everything and everyone. The woods itself, frightened by the fire, which must have been aided by magic or alchemy. Still the fear—concern—pulsing from Tillard; fear from myself over the fate of Alysen and the Nanoo.

Fear from the two Nanoo who had died here.

And from the men with Lord Purvis, unaccustomed to fighting trees and walls of thorny growths. The sentiments were so thick now I had trouble breathing, the mud of emotions becoming denser as I took another step and then another.

Ahead, something sparkled on the forest floor, diamonds on a goddess's dress. It took me a moment to realize that starlight reflected up from the water that stood in this part of the fen.

I was nearing the heart, where the Nanoo lived. By the Green Ones, I truly thought about turning away and getting on the vanner, riding far from here and using the three silver buttons to start a new life.

I'd seen so many horrible, horrible things in less than the passing of a month. Could I take seeing one more corpse? And what if that body belonged to Alysen, Shellaya, or Gafna?

What if I lost the last few people I knew in this world?

"Wisteria! Wisteria!" Tillard's voice cut through the wall of fear. How long he'd been calling to me, I couldn't say. Time had lost itself in the decimated grove, and the emotions I found my way through had slowed my course. "Wisteria!"

My gaze was fixed on the stars reflecting in the standing water. The one beautiful aspect of this ominous stretch of ground captured and held my attention. I couldn't look away from them. If I did, I might see more bodies and taste more fear. Taste the anger, which welled inside me again. I might lose myself to every bad thing.

"Wisteria!" Tillard was at my shoulder, shaking me. I didn't want to look away from the stars, but he turned me to face him. "Come on, they're all in Rial."

I raised an eyebrow.

"Rial, Wisteria. Come on." He took my hand and led me through the burned tangle.

Suddenly we were sloshing through water and I looked down to see the reflected stars scattering away from my feet like fireflies dancing. The water was stagnant in patches, and the taste was strong and disagreeable, but preferable to the harsh flavor of charred trees and bodies.

"Where are we going?" I barely heard the words I spoke to Tillard, my head and heart pounded so loudly. All the scents and emotions—despair I detected now, too, hoplessness . . . I didn't try to discover where those feelings came from.

"Rial, I say again. The Nanoo are waiting for us."

Rial. So the center of the fen had a name.

I felt numb, and I let him lead me. The water was deeper here, seeping in the tops of my knee-high boots. Tillard took us around the body of a dark war horse, its bloated side rising above the water. I couldn't see what it had died of; not enough of it was visible. But the starlight shown bright enough that I could see the maggots and flies deliriously feasting.

I saw two more dead horses and three dead men, the men run through by branches and suspended above the fen floor, haloed by clouds of flying insects. Their chain mail had not been enough to protect them from the enchanted grove. Somehow the branch tips were sharp enough and the branches themselves strong enough to punch through the links.

Despite the night and the thick black slashes that were the burned trees, I could make out Lord Purvis's emblem on one of the tabards. The stench from the men and the horses dumbfounded me, and Tillard dropped my hand and stepped in front of me, took my shoulders in his hands and gently shook me.

"Close it out, Wisteria. Your gift is to taste the world, and tastes here are foul and poisonous. They are tainting you, and if you don't close it out, you'll be lost to the poison."

His words were a whisper, and he repeated his lecture, shaking my shoulders a little more firmly, then cupping my chin and tipping my head up, locking his eyes with mine. His gift was to read thoughts "shouted" by others, and so I suspected he was hearing my thoughts about the death and decay, the burned woods, and the gloom that covered Mardel's Fen like a heavy wool blanket.

"Wisteria!"

I did what he demanded, pushed away all the things I'd asked my wyse-sense to bring me. Had I a clue this would be so atrocious and debilitating, I would have looked only with my eyes and not with my magic.

"I'm all right, Tillard." He held my chin for a moment more just to be certain, then he released me and continued slogging toward Rial, looking over his shoulder to make sure I followed closely.

I felt something slimy and yielding bump against my knee, and I glanced down. Dead fish floated around our legs, their white bellies blistered as if they'd been boiled. The heat from the fire could have been intense enough to cook them. The sight of them sickened me, and I raised my gaze to the back of Tillard's head, putting more effort into pushing away the awful presence that had subsumed the fen.

I idly wondered about Winter Sky. The horse wasn't with him, and we hadn't passed it. Tillard didn't appear worried and hadn't mentioned the horse, which seemed to mean something to him. I opened my mouth to ask Tillard about Winter Sky when beyond a charred cypress I saw the horse standing in water that reached halfway up its legs.

The trees around the horse were green, and moss draped

down from some of the branches, gently teasing its gray back. It appeared that the fire had stopped abruptly, a line drawn in the fen.

Tillard stroked the side of Winter Sky's neck and made a cooing sound. The horse wuffled, and Tillard took the reins in his right hand and motioned to me with his left. This time he didn't look over his shoulder, just pressed in deeper.

We were soon rewarded with scattered greetings. Tillard bowed to each Nanoo, and as I came forward, Alysen rushed out of Nanoo Shellaya's cottage and squeezed me fiercely around the waist.

I could see over her head, and glancing from one tree to the next I spotted soft lights coming from slits that served as doors and windows. Not so many Nanoo came out this time to see me, and I wanted to ask how many had died by Lord Purvis's men and how many slept in the dark in their beds.

"Eri!" Alysen squeezed me tighter then released me, stepped back, and tipped her face up so she could better see me. "Oh, Eri . . . Lord Purvis came here. You looked for him in the south, and all the while he was here. He came looking for you. It was horrible, Eri, he—"

She babbled about Purvis's attack, and as I'd shut out the tastes of the fen, I shut out her words. I didn't need them. I knew full well what had happened. Purvis and his men had come to Mardel's Fen, the trees and walls of thorny growth had barred their way, then fought against them, some of the trees spearing the men with branches as deadly as a knight's lance. So Purvis had raged against the woods and found a way to set the damp trees on fire.

But the very heart of the fen hadn't burned.

"Where is Lord Purvis?" I interrupted Alysen's tale. "Where is he?"

"Gone, Eri, run off. The Nanoo joined their magic and kept the men from coming to the heart, killed men and horses. Two Nanoo died, and others were hurt, but—"

Nanoo Shellaya touched the top of Alysen's head, the simple gesture startling her. "We tended our injured, Eri, and theirs who seemed important by their manner. One . . . enemy still lives. One died this morning, despite our ministrations. We've wrapped him and will give him to the trees in a ceremony tomorrow. We have fallen brothers to honor then, too."

That meant let the animals and insects feast on the corpses. The Nanoo did not believe in burying bodies; they thought what remained of a person should feed creatures and fertilize the land. From time to time they collected bones they came across in the fen. These, too, were used, made into tools or ground up into a powder for various medicines.

"The dead man of Lord Purvis, where is he, Alysen?"

She shook her head, either not wanting to think about it, or not knowing.

"Here. Follow me." This came from Shellaya. Though starlight shone down brightly in the center of the Nanoo community, her features were so shadowed I couldn't read the expression on her face. Her shuffling gait took her from my side and through water that rose above our knees, past her cottage and to a spot where the canopy was thicker and I had to strain to make out anything.

I heard the incessant buzz of flies, and though I kept my wyse-sense in check, the stench of the body was strong enough to make me gag. It was wrapped in Galia leaves, tied with cords.

"The dead should not concern you, Eri." Nanoo Shellaya stood by the body, head bowed. She showed respect even for the enemy.

She'd used the word "enemy" earlier, a fact that made me even angrier at Lord Purvis. While many people in this world distrusted the witches and feared them, none had been considered an enemy before.

"Eri, the dead are beyond the cares of the land and face the dreamland or the desolation."

"The desolation for this one, I think." I sloshed to the body's head and pulled back the leaves. I heard Nanoo Shellaya retreat back to the heart of the fen. So difficult to see; I had to stare at his shadowy features, then run my fingertips along his cold, cold face. I'm not sure why I wanted to know this man, perhaps I just hoped it might be Lord Purvis. I felt the lips. Not Purvis. I felt around the eyes.

Celerad, the man I'd seen in the scry and the man who'd visited Bastien in what seemed like long, long days ago. I pulled a knife from the sheath and cut all the cords holding the leaves around the body. I hoped I hadn't broken a taboo or angered some Nanoo spirit. I felt around his waist and found his belt and buckle, unclasping it and tugging the belt free, jostling the body and disturbing the flies and other insects. A section of the belt was covered with dry, crusty blood, and it felt heavy in my hands because of the sword in the scabbard that hung from it.

I awkwardly worked the belt around my waist and buckled it in the farthest notch. Still big for me, it settled around my hips, and the end of the scabbard reached to past my knees and disappeared in the water. I turned the belt slightly, so I could get at both the sword and my two knives.

Satisfied, I did my best to replace the leaves and retie the cords, though I left a gap in the leaves around Celerad's face. A part of me wanted to make it easy for the vermin of the fen to feed off the Moonson.

30

TILLARD STOOD BY NANOO SHELLAYA'S COTTAGE, EYES ON MY hips where the sword belt hung. I didn't offer him an explanation of why I wore it. If he wanted to know, he could pull that from my mind easily enough.

"Shellaya said another man still lives. One of Lord Purvis's evil flock. I want to talk to him." My expression added, "Now."

Tillard gestured to a thick stringybark with a wide slash that served as a door. A peach-colored light glowed from within, and as I neared the home I smelled fruit tea brewing and something like camphor. Too, I smelled dried blood—a scent I'd become overly accustomed to.

He lay on a low cot in front of a small fireplace, his armor and weapons neatly arranged underneath the cot. No fire burned, but there were thick orange candles on a table, and these provided enough light to chase all the shadows from the one-room dwelling.

The sweat on his face announced his fever. Conscious, he watched me glide to his side, my wet boots dripping over the hard-packed dirt floor. I knelt by him only so I could get closer to his face and better see his wounds. There were bandages across his stomach, dotted with dark splotches of blood. I couldn't be sure what had injured him, but I suspected trees had speared him. I felt no pity, and I'd no intention to help tend him.

"Tell me of Lord Purvis." I made certain my words had an edge to them. "Everything you know."

His head pointed at the ceiling, he looked out the corners of his eyes at me. His mouth parted and he licked his lips. "Water, please."

I made no move to help.

Two Nanoo were in the room. Likely they'd been here all along and I'd not noticed them because I was so intent on the wounded Moonson. I saw from the tabard folded beneath the cot that he was of the order. I'd not recognized him, or the Nanoo, one of who raised the man's head so the other could pour water into his mouth. He drank thirstily, then gritted his teeth when they lowered his head back.

"Lord Purvis, I say. Tell me of him, Moonson."

He worked his lips and stared at the ceiling. "He directed us here days past. It was a mission of great import for the Empress, he told us. I was not privy to the nature of our mission, only that we would be fighting enemies of our Empress." He gasped, and the Nanoo gave him another swallow of water. "Three days past we started our assault."

"The woods kept them out of the heart of the fen for nearly a day," one of the Nanoo supplied. She was a young woman, I could tell from her hands and voice. But already she had the lined skin of her people, and her hue was dark like walnut.

"Then they did something to the outer trees. Normally, no fire could touch them."

"Lord Purvis has magic about him," the Moonson supplied. His voice cracked, and the young Nanoo wet a cloth and rubbed it across his forehead.

I did not understand her compassion for the enemy, but neither did I understand much about the Nanoo. I held my tongue until she was done fussing over him.

"Lord Purvis did something to the bark, cast a spell that coated the trees with . . . something . . . something shiny and sweet that made them burn. The fire, it wasn't magic, but what he put on the trunks . . . that sparkled like fresh snow."

I knew nothing of such a spell, but I saw the two Nanoos nod, as if they understood what he talked about. "The drying," I heard one of them whisper.

"They caught fire, the trees," he went on. "They didn't burn like we expected, the flames were small."

"But deadly enough to the grove," I whispered.

"We went in when the fire started to die. So difficult to breathe. Our eyes burned like they were on fire, too. We wanted to wait, but Lord Purvis—"

"He didn't want you to wait." I leaned closer, the smell of the Nanoo's medicine stinging my nostrils.

"No. He finally told us the precise nature of our mission. He wanted the girl."

I pressed a finger to his chest.

"The girl with pale skin, he told us. She would be singular in the village, looking like no one else."

"He knew of the Nanoo village in the very heart of this place?"

He nodded.

"Alysen, Lord Purvis called her. Alysen of the House of Geer. Said for the future of the Empire and the Empress we would have to kill her." He shook his head. "Against what we stand for, killing someone so young, but we'd sworn fealty to him. We'd sworn to follow him anywhere and heed his commands."

I applied more pressure with my finger, deliberately hurting him. At the edge of my vision I saw the young Nanoo step forward to protest. Tillard had come inside, and he stepped between the young Nanoo and the cot, holding his hands to his sides. He said something to her, but I didn't hear. I pressed a little harder and listened to the wounded Moonson.

"Celerad commanded us, our Pike."

A Pike of Moonsons was eighteen men, trained to fight on horseback with a variety of weapons.

"Lord Purvis had saved Commander Celerad's life two years gone, and Celerad—and thereby us—swore fealty to him. Such is our way. A blood-bond we'd forged."

"The one called Commander Celerad . . ." This came from the young Nanoo. I couldn't see her, Tillard was in the way. "He died this morning, though we tried our best to save him. The trees fought him, and an infection did the rest."

Tillard stepped to the cot and stared down at the man. Then he got on his knees and pulled out the chain mail, sword belt, and sword.

"And Lord Purvis wanted Alysen dead." I thumped the Moonson in the chest to get him to continue.

"Aye, said it was necessary. We'd sworn fealty." He paused and rolled his eyes. "We'd pledged the blood-bond and so we came into the woods, walking through water, fish dying at our feet from the heat. Hot as a dry summer, the place felt . . . though there was water everywhere. Hard to breathe, to think, to hear Lord Purvis. And then the trees, even the burned ones, came to life."

He recounted the battle, though I didn't need those details. I wanted to know about Lord Purvis, and if he'd died by the trees.

"He retreated, Lord Purvis, with those of us able to follow him."

"How many?"

He didn't answer me, licking his lips and eyes staring at the ceiling. I motioned for more water. Tillard gave it to him this time.

"How many men retreated with him?"

"Forty men, maybe. Forty maybe lived. Soldiers and oak brothers." He coughed, his shoulders bouncing against the cot. Once more Tillard raised the man's neck so he could drink. When he finished drinking, he went on. "Those of us who couldn't follow, the horrors we saw, the ground rising up and snaring us, vines like snakes, men with skin like the bark of old trees."

I grabbed his chin in my hand and turned his face so I could stare directly into his eyes.

"Tell me about Lord Purvis."

"He commands the Empress's army."

"I well know that." My spittle hit his cheeks and he closed his eyes.

"But he did not bring the army here, only some of his soldiers and our Pike. This mission was to be as quiet as possible."

"More—"

"He has been given a barony, Lord Purvis, and our Pike . . . each of us has been granted land south of his estate. Lord Purvis has done well for himself, especially after the Emperor's death. He has done far better than his father."

"His father . . ."

"A mere taster on the Emperor's board."

My fingernails dug into the flesh of his throat. "Taster?"

"His father tasted for the Emperor, died when the Emperor did, failing to find a poison that killed them both."

I felt the color drain from my face. "Lord Purvis is Rembert Lemblyre t'Kyros? Not possible!"

The man's eyes were wide with the new pain I'd inflicted on him. I'd cut him with my nails; thin trails of blood wet my fingers.

Steadying myself, I took even breaths. "Why is he called Lord Purvis? Tell me!"

"Wisteria?" Tillard touched my arm.

Without trying I tasted Tillard's curiosity, and I tasted the Moonson's pain and fatigue and resignation.

"Tell me, Moonson!"

"Rembert Lemblyre t'Kyros served with Lord Elgar Purvis's men from an early age, it was said. And when Lord Elgar died in a battle with bandits, Sir Lemblyre t'Kyros took his name. Lord Elgar had no children and had willed his estate to Sir Lemblyre . . . the new Lord Purvis."

"Rembert." I fell back, hitting my head against the hard floor and staring at the ceiling, the room growing dark around me. Shadows that I'd not noticed before reached up and swallowed me.

Rembert?

My brother, Rembert?

It had to be him, not another man with that name, as the Moonson had said he was son to the Emperor's taster. I tried to deny it, tried to put another man in his place. Another Rembert.

I dreamt in the darkness, seeing my brother when we were children, his face so smooth and the color of cream. Two years older than I, in him my parents found so little wyse that they devoted their magical tutelage to me. He hadn't seemed bitter then; I'd not tasted that foulness in him ever. But later, before I was sent to the Village Nar and he was sent south and later became a soldier to some lord, I remembered tasting a hint of anger.

Just a hint.

The original Lord Purvis? Was that the man my brother had joined?

I cursed myself now in my dream for not keeping track of my brother. My life had become the Village Nar, and the people who meant something to me were Lady Ewaren and Bastien, Willum, and all the others my brother had ordered slain.

How had a boy I'd played with, fished with, shared secrets with . . . how had such a boy turned into . . . a demon-of-a-man? There was no better word to describe Purvis.

Rembert.

My brother.

Demon-of-a-man.

The darkness I dreamt in was absolute and thick. Despite all the pain and misery I felt, the black formed a comforting

cocoon that I wanted to wrap tighter and tighter. I vaguely
registered that I felt light-headed and that my breathing was
becoming increasingly shallow. I heard a rushing sound strong
in my ears, and had no clue where it came from. I didn't care.
I cared only about my cocoon, which was taking the breath
from me. It wouldn't be so bad, I knew, to stop breathing entirely. I'd see no more ugliness, would no longer hear the
deeds of people being bad to one another, no longer have to
deal with friends dying, bloodoaths to fulfill.

If I let the blackness claim me, I would be released from
my bloodoath. I would not then have to face my brother . . .
Lord Purvis . . . the one I'd been calling the demon-of-a-man.
I would not have the last of my family's blood on my hands.
The darkness tightened, and my head spun. I barely breathed
now.

No pain.

I thought there'd be pain.

In the darkness something brightened, something pale green
spotted with red. Lady Ewaren's torn and bloody dress.

I saw her foot.

She'd felt pain.

When each one of her fingers was broken—on the order of
Lord Purvis—pain had stabbed into her.

Each finger.

Such pain.

Then the blessed darkness had claimed her, as I thought it
was claiming me.

What had happened to Rembert? Had bitterness settled
that deeply inside him when he'd been sent away? It was
done, sending children away. I to the Village Nar, he to Lord

Purvis—the man whose name Rembert would later take.

Power? Is that what my brother had craved? Is that what the Empress offered him?

But at the price of my father's death? And the Emperor's?

Could my brother pay that damning price?

I wanted the answers, but more than that, I wanted the blackness to smother me.

"Wisteria!"

I felt hands on my shoulders, and the blackness receded a little, again showing me the pale, bloodied dress of my House Lady.

Her foot.

The blood-soaked ground.

"Wisteria!"

Tillard's face came into focus, pushing away more of the darkness. My mind flashed with anger—how dare he take me away from the comforting cocoon!

His face was filled with worry. "Wisteria, come back to us! Don't do this. We need you, Wisteria! Wake up!"

I didn't need this world. I'd seen too much, felt too much. I needed an end to this.

"Wisteria! Please!"

His face was inches from mine, and the taste of his concern and determination overpowered me. I saw the peach-colored light shed by the candles. And I felt Tillard's skin against mine, the back of his hand feeling my forehead, his fingers brushing my cheek.

Then he worked a hand behind my shoulders and helped me up. I cringed. The back of my head throbbed. I must have hit it when I fell away from the cot and slipped into unconsciousness. My head was tender and warm to the touch, and I felt a softness where a lump had started to grow.

"Where is Lord Purvis?" I got on my knees and shuffled back to the cot. The man's head was tipped; he had watched me fall. "Your commander, Moonson. Where in the Nine Circles is he?"

He stared at me, unspeaking.

Alysen entered the cottage, leaving her boots at the door so she would not track water onto the floor. Crowded with me, Tillard, the two Nanoo, and now her, the room felt overly warm. She stood on the other side of the cot, across from me, looking down at the wounded Moonson, then at me.

"Nanoo . . ." She looked down at the man again, deciding to avoid my gaze. "Nanoo Shellaya says I should tell you, Eri."

"Tell her what?" Tillard brought a stool over and placed it next to me. I shook my head that I didn't need it, but he tugged on my arm, and so I got up and sat on it. "Alysen, what did Shellaya want you to tell Wisteria?"

The young Nanoo nudged Alysen aside and checked the Moonson's bandages.

"She said I should tell you about my scrying." She finally raised her gaze to meet mine. "Not the ones I'd been doing here in the heart, but the ones before. The ones I hadn't told you about."

An uncomfortable silence found its way into the cottage. I didn't prod her, knowing that since she'd come in here, she'd eventually say what she needed to. It might take her a few minutes, and I wouldn't mind waiting. The back of my head continued to throb, feeling like someone had struck a hammer against it. The floor of the cottage was indeed hard!

"I saw Lord Purvis with your father, Eri, in one of my scrys. I saw him talk to your father, but I did not hear any words. Scrying does not let you listen, only watch."

I knew that from my own scryings, but I had no intention of telling Alysen I'd learned how to proficiently use the magic.

"They talked, and your father seemed to know him, smiled at him. I almost looked away, as I found nothing interesting in their meeting. But then your father poured them wine and turned away to look at something on a desk. Lord Purvis put something in your father's glass. I thought this part interesting, and so I watched a little longer."

She ground the ball of her foot against the floor. "Then your father drank it and died. Tester for the Emperor, Eri, you'd think he would have smelled the poison."

Not if he suspected nothing amiss would he smell it, I knew. And why ever would he suspect his son of wanting to kill him?

"My scry followed Lord Purvis, down a hall filled with paintings of fancy people and through one room after another. So big the house he walked through! A palace, it had to be. He went into a fine, fine room with tapestries and paintings with gold frames, and a carpet so thick his boots sunk into it. Lanterns burned, ones made of gold and silver, everything so very shiny. The Emperor was there."

Alysen shifted back and forth on the balls of her feet now, and tugged at a loose thread on her skirt band. "He poisoned the Emperor, too. I saw Lord Purvis kill them both, Eri. And Lord Purvis saw me." She stuffed a fist in her mouth and fought back tears. Then she dropped the hand to her side. "I couldn't tell you before. I just couldn't."

"But you've told her now." This came from Tillard, who was sorting through the Moonson's belongings. He held up the chain mail shirt against his chest. A moment more and he shrugged into it. The sleeves were a little short and the shirt itself too big. Next he put on the chain coif. He looked quite different with his lion's mane of hair confined. "At least you told her, Alysen." Despite his words, his expression revealed he disapproved that she'd not revealed this information earlier.

Tillard picked up the tabard, held it to him, then decided against it. Perhaps he read my thoughts that it was akin to blasphemy to wear the garb of a Moonson if you were not an oak brother. Perhaps he did not want to wear something so bloodied. He folded it and replaced it under the cot. Then he strapped on the sword belt and wrapped his fingers around the pommel.

"Where is Lord Purvis now?" Tillard leaned over the cot and brought his face inches above the Moonson. "Where is he? Wisteria and I require this information."

"I don't know. By all that's holy, I truly don't know."

"Then let us find out." Tillard placed a hand on either side of the man's head. "Wisteria, watch with me."

Curious, as I am ever curious, I got up from the stool, my head swooning and threatening to spill me back to the floor. But I managed to stay on my feet. I edged closer and bent at the waist, putting my hands on the side of the cot to steady myself.

"Let's find out where your demon-man is." Tillard squeezed his eyes shut and brought his face so close to the Moonson's that their noses touched. When Tillard opened his eyes, I gasped. There, reflected in the right eye of the Moonson, leered a tiny image of Lord Purvis.

Tillard used the water in the Moonson's eye to scry.

"He'll see us, Wisteria. This demon-man is strong in the wyse. I can feel his strength. Look, his eyes stare into mine."

"Strong in the wyse," I whispered. Though he hadn't been as a child, I recalled. His talent must have developed in later years, and he kept that news from my father.

I had to move closer still, as the image on the eye was so very tiny. Lord Purvis stood on a black field, black sky above him, but stars shimmering down to make his armor shine. There were men with him, but I couldn't see how many or how many were on horses.

"He's near, Wisteria." I tasted dread in Tillard's words.

I stared at the diminutive image. The black field he stood on was a charred section of forest floor.

Lord Purvis—my brother, Rembert—was bringing his force back into the fen.

31

TILLARD RUSHED FROM THE COTTAGE, CALLING FOR THE NANOO to gather around him.

Alysen stared at me wide-eyed. "Are you angry with me, Eri, that I didn't tell you everything earlier?"

That she let me think it was my bloodline that had brought Lord Purvis to the Village Nar? That she had put the bloodshed on me? That she had let all of this eat away at me?

I walked by her, saying nothing. As she was little more than a child, I knew the burden of her scrying probably was too much for her to bear or to admit to. Now, no doubt, it ate away at her. She would find solace with time, especially because of her young age. But I knew in my heart she would never completely forgive herself for the scrying that had led Lord Purvis first to the Village Nar and now to Mardel's Fen. It would never let her forget how many people had died.

Perhaps forgiveness should elude her. But not redemption.

I joined Tillard outside. Nearest to him were five people I suspected were his parents, brothers, and sister. I had one member left of my family—Lord Purvis, my brother, Rembert.

I still thought about Alysen and everything she'd seen through her scry spells. Even if she'd not looked in on my father and the Emperor, they'd still be dead—the difference being no one would know they'd been poisoned.

The difference being the Village Nar would still thrive.

A shudder passed through my body. Lady Ewaren, Willum, they'd still be alive. But the treachery against the Emperor and my father, and whatever dark plans the Empress and my brother had, would remain hidden. What a horrible, horrible price had been paid to learn of the royal manipulations!

My thoughts continued to swirl as I watched the Nanoo gather around Tillard. Nanoo Shellaya pressed through the circle and joined him.

"Listen to brother Tillard," Shellaya said. She raised her hands and the whispering among the witches stopped. I heard crickets and tree frogs, and from somewhere in the distance I heard a splash, likely a fish jumping. I forced out the image of the dead fish I'd sloshed through to get to the center of the clearing.

"The man called Lord Purvis returns to the fen. In a vision I saw him. He marshals his forces and comes at us now. We must prepare for him, defend our home and protect our lives."

In fast, breathy words Tillard talked about the murders of the Emperor and my father and how Lord Purvis wanted to kill Alysen—and now all the Nanoo—to hide the crimes and stop news of his foul deeds from spreading beyond the fen.

"For our home," Nanoo Gafna said.

I stared in surprise. The fingers of her left hand flexed as if they'd never been broken.

"Fighting is anathema to us," Gafna continued. "But fight we will, with all the wyse in us and around us. We will . . ."

Her words trailed off, and the Nanoo in unison turned to the west.

"They come," Tillard said. He drew the borrowed sword and stalked through the ring of Nanoo. My head still throbbing, I followed.

I REMEMBERED THE FIRST SERIOUS HUNT BASTIEN HAD TAKEN me on. I was twelve, I think, and the quarry was a gengan. It was like a boar, but only in its form. Its size . . . Bastien had told me gengan were as big as a stout calf, and I'd had a hard time thinking a boar could grow that tall. But I realized his words were likely true when he bade me not tell Lady Ewaren just what we were hunting. He said she wouldn't approve his taking me out in the woods after such a quarry.

The gengan were scarce in our part of the world, hunted heavily, Bastien explained, because people feared them. Hunting parties would search for dens of the small ones, slaying them and fleeing before the mother returned.

Most gengan had wandered to the pine woods of the far, far north, where there were few villages and where the game they sought was plentiful. As we looked for spoor, Bastien described our quarry; I'd only ever heard about them on occasion, no doubt because those in the Village Nar wanted to avoid the beasts.

The gengan was the largest predator in the woods next to the fose-bear, and Bastien believed that the gengans did not fear even the great bears. Larger and stronger than any wild boar or the greatest of the winter wolves, one could weigh four to six hundred pounds, he said, and yet make no more noise than a leaf falling to the ground if it deigns to be quiet.

I'd tried to commit his words to memory, that the gengan's tusks could grow as long and wide as a big man's forearm, that its barrel-shaped body was muscle, not fat, and that it could speed through the thickest of woods faster than a tree-cat. And when a gengan runs, he told me, it does so low to the ground, massive head down and casting from side to side to uproot small trees in its path, back legs churning over the ground and sending up a storm of earth behind it.

The gengan eats only meat, Bastien said, and it kills by trampling its prey, goring it, then eating the soft belly-flesh and leaving the rest for carrion. In the space of a few heart-beats it is finished with its meal, disappearing into the woods so silently you cannot rely on your ears to track it.

That Bastien had known one was within a day's ride of the Village Nar puzzled me, but then I suspect he relied on some bit of wyse-sense to make the discovery.

I was pleased it was only the two of us on this hunt, as I didn't want anyone to see I was nervous. But excitement was thick in my mind, too, and that drowned out any real concerns I might have. I was too young to wholly appreciate the danger in what we attempted. And I believe Bastien was too proud and seasoned to realize this was not a hunt I should be part of.

We found its tracks before sunset, only spotting them be-cause the gengan had walked through a puddle and left its wide mark on the mud around the edges. Farther to the north-west, we found the carcass of a deer, the torn flesh of its belly glistening. There were few flies, and that told us the kill was very, very fresh.

We left our horses under a black walnut, far enough from the deer that they wouldn't be disturbed or spooked by small forest creatures that would be drawn by the kill. Then we crept along an overgrown game trail, Bastien pointing to the slightest signs that marked the gengan's passing.

That something supposedly so large could leave only the subtlest of signs made me curious, but I was too caught up in the hunt to ask Bastien about it. I would, however, ask him how many of the beasts he'd slain before, and then we would regale the Village Nar about how we'd slain this one.

We came to the edge of a clearing, circling to the west so we would be facing into the wind. Bastien clearly did not want the gengan catching a whiff of us. I wasn't worried that it would think us prey; we had knives, and Bastien had his sword, and I had my chain. But I was worried that we might spook the thing, and then I wouldn't get a chance to claim it as a trophy.

It was at the far edge of the clearing, opposite us, our faces hid by the weave of a tall lace-fern. Looking through a gap in the leaves, we saw it, or rather first the shape of it, as it was behind a spreading bunchberry bush. A dark shadow, it was, tearing at something behind that bush, snorting and wuffling and tamping at the ground.

I was not proficient at tasting yet, still I extended the tip of my tongue, hoping to sate my curiosity. I had to concentrate hard in those early days, and I squeezed my eyes shut, thinking that gesture helped. I tasted the fresh drops of moisture on the fern leaves, and I tasted hunger and anger, those two things slicing into me as surely as any well-wielded sword. I gasped at the sudden, sharp sensations, and my eyes flew open, straining to see beyond the fern and hoping the beast would move out from behind the bunchberry.

Finally, it did, part of it. Its great tusks were scarlet with the blood of the deer and whatever it had killed behind the bunchberry. Though not as large as the fose-bear I would see years later with Alysen in the woods, it was still massive. The largest of its kind Bastien had seen, he would tell me later. Its fur was the color of polished walnut, looking rigid in places, and I imagined it would be horribly coarse. I saw no irises in its eyes, only solid, shiny black.

The gengan was not the size of a calf, but the size of a well-fed cow or a bull, and its hooves were as large around as Lady Ewaren's serving platters. Though it wasn't chill this day, the beast's breath puffed away from its mouth. And without using my wyse-sense, I could smell the intense fetidness of it.

I shivered, no longer too young to understand the danger that stood less than fifty feet away.

My hands dropped to the chain and the handle of a knife. Bastien's right hand dropped to my shoulder, and his eyes met mine.

We backed away from the clearing, leaving the gengan to its hidden kill, taking care that we stayed downwind of it, and moving more quietly than we ever had.

I always wondered if Bastien would have fought the beast if I'd not been with him. I never thought to ask him. Or had he taken me on this "hunt" to teach me that some things are unbeatable and that sometimes a hunter should walk away from its quarry?

THE QUARRY I SEARCHED FOR NOW, IN THE HEART OF THE FEN, was more dangerous than the gengan or the fose-bear. It had a malevolent cunning those creatures did not possess.

And unlike those creatures, my quarry was evil.

"Brother," I whispered.

32

BEHIND ME I HEARD CHANTING, THE NANOO WORKING IN CON-cert to affect some spell.

"They give the trees life," Tillard told me. "Life beyond what they have now, and a measure of my sisters' and brothers' sentience. The Nanoo give all of the fen and the woods beyond a piece of their own lives."

I heard twigs snap ahead: Lord Purvis and his men. I heard sloshing behind me. I knew some of the Nanoo came with us. I'd spied them grabbing knobby staves and sickles that gleamed in the starlight.

"Spread out," Tillard told the Nanoo with us. "That is what Purvis and his men are doing. They are coming at us like a wave rushes to a beach."

Tillard had detected their thoughts! That's how he knew they were coming into the fen! No doubt the men with my brother shouted their thoughts to him, just as I did. Tillard held the sword high. I could tell he'd used one before, but where and when puzzled me. As he wasn't nobility, he couldn't legally carry one. Where had he traveled that he'd learned how to . . .

"In my early journeying, Wisteria, I served as a minor noble's guard. Three months I worked for him, and I picked this up in the process. He said it was for his own safety that he taught me how to use a blade."

"Where are they, Purvis's men?"

"Near, Wisteria. Too near."

So many things happened in the next instant that I had trouble sorting it all out.

The trees in front of us, the ones not completely charred, started moving, their branches dropping down and writhing like serpents. Between trunks I saw rows of thorny growths spring up. The crickets and tree frogs stopped their songs. But the swarms of gnats and flies, drawn by the bodies of men and horses, persisted.

One man, in Lord Purvis's colors, appeared between gaps in the branches. He waved his arm to get the attention of his unseen fellows, and he pointed at us.

"Lord Purvis!" he hollered. "Look ye there! Nanoo!"

Another man in chain mail, sword in one hand and shield in the other, stood in a beam of starlight. Others joined the two and saw us, all of them hollering now and charging forward, tabards hanging down in the water and whipping around their legs.

Tillard ran forward to meet the first man, his long legs easily hurtling the growing thorns. He glanced over his shoulder. "Wisteria, Purvis is behind these men. Circle their line if you want him."

He knew my brother's location from the thoughts of the

advancing men. I spun to the south and ran, knowing my sloshing steps could be heard, but counting on other noises to keep the men occupied.

Swords clashed to the west, wood groaned as limbs moved forward, stretching to grasp the trespassers. I fought to keep my wyse-sense in check, as I couldn't risk being overwhelmed here with the stench of death and all the wild emotions that I was certain filled the fen.

The chanting continued, as did the ringing of swords and sickles. I didn't want to look to the north, where I knew Tillard fought. I didn't want to see what was happening there. I feared it would be nothing good. Serving as a guard and learning sword skills during the course of a few months would not put Tillard at the level of Lord Purvis and his men.

Someone hollered in pain, someone else in victory.

Was either voice Tillard's?

I ran faster to the south, my steps in time with the pulsing throb against the back of my head. Faster still, then I was flying forward, my foot hooking in a submerged root and throwing me off balance. I slammed into the ground, all of me submerged, my lungs sucking in the water, then spitting it out when I pushed myself to my knees. I coughed until my chest ached, then I took in a great swallow of air and reached forward into the water, fingers fumbling until I found the pommel of Celerad's sword.

On my feet once more, I pressed against the trunk of an ancient black willow, its branches flailing all around me. Then the branches stretched away from me and reached out toward two men in chain armor. They were advancing, one of them in a Moonson's tabard. I couldn't see the features of the men's faces, and so I could not guess their ages or know their mettle. But without trying I tasted their fear, as the branches coiled around them and raised them far off the ground, hanging them and drawing the life from them.

I sped forward then, avoiding branches that could well snare me, too, then springing into the darkness, where the canopy above had not burned and so kept the stars at bay. I slipped past two more men, then found myself face-to-face with another.

I held the sword in front of me, just as Bastien had taught me so many years ago.

"I offer you your life," I hissed. "Leave the fen and Lord Purvis, and I will leave you alive."

He snarled and charged me, and I felt a chill pass through my arms, traveling from my fingers that wrapped around the pommel to my shoulder. It was a pleasant sensation, though it precluded a most unpleasant deed. It was the chill I'd felt during my first lesson with Bastien, the sensation that gave me strength.

I brought the sword back, feeling my muscles bunch then relax as the blade came forward, keen edge slicing into the links and going deeper. It made a grating sound, passing into his armor, then rasping against a rib. His sword fell, splashing against the surface of the water, then disappearing beneath it. The man fell to his knees, mouth open in surprise, but uttering not even a moan.

I sidestepped him as he fell forward, then I was running again, going north now, hoping my course would bring me around and behind the rest of the line of men and to Lord Purvis.

Fearing it would indeed bring me to him.

"Rembert."

I saw him heartbeats later, sword flashing and slashing against the lowest branches of a half-dead elm that was trying to skewer him. I saw, too, that smeared on the trunks of trees near him were patches of a slimy mixture that sparkled like new snow.

"No!" He meant to set more of the woods ablaze. "Rembert!"

He whirled as he slashed at another branch, cleaving it. His helmet was gone, and so all of his face was revealed to me. A ropy scar ran down his right cheek and disappeared into a thin beard. His hair was coppery, the same shade I'd remembered from our childhood, slightly longer than mine and wet with sweat.

"Rembert, stop this!"

He took a step toward me, sword raised, then he paused when some hint of recognition struck him.

"Who?" he mouthed.

"Rembert, please, by all you value, please call a stop to this. Have your men stand down. No more dying. Rembert, please."

His mouth worked, silent words spilling out, head cocking. Another step forward. "Wisteria? Sister?"

I gave a nod. "Yes," I added. "I'm your sister, Rem." I neared him, cautiously. Though I knew who he was, I truly didn't know the man he'd become. "Please have them stand down."

All around us the woods creaked with the arcane life the Nanoo had given them. Branches whipped at men out of my eyesight. Faintly, I still heard the clash of sickles and swords.

Fainter still, the cry of someone who'd been wounded, perhaps killed.

"Alysen doesn't have to spill words of your horrid deeds, Rem. And you don't have to kill her or any of the Nanoo." My speech to him was a lie, though, as in my heart I knew word had to get out about the murder of my father and the Emperor. And about the Empress's dark ambitions.

What was my brother's wyse gift? Could he read my mind like Tillard could?

He stared at me, seeming to look through me. I could tell he wasn't reading my mind.

"She's a child, Rem."

His sword lowered just a little, and he took another step. "Wisteria. By the Green Ones, Wisteria." He paused and swallowed hard. "I saw you earlier, watching me. You scryed on me. I didn't know it was you, didn't recognize you. Hadn't seen you, sister, since the day I went to the south and they sent you to a village."

"Nar." The village you slew, I thought. My home that you shattered.

"Nar." He dropped his gaze for a brief moment. "The Village Nar."

My free hand clenched tight, fingernails boring into my palm.

"She saw me, Wisteria? Saw what I did in that village?"

"I wasn't there, Rem. But I know what you did. She told me."

"The girl Alysen told you."

"Yes."

"She scryed on me. She saw too much."

"But she doesn't have to tell what she saw, Rem." Again I lied.

Rembert's shoulders sagged. "I can afford no witnesses, sister, no matter that one of those witnesses be a girl living with witches in the swamp."

A silence slipped between us, and in it I heard the *shush* made by branches waving against one another, the click of other branches striking at armor, the cries of the wounded.

"You can end this," I argued. "Have your men stand down." A heartbeat later, I added, "Or they will die, Rem. The Nanoo were the first people of the world to learn the secret. They have more wyse-power than anyone. A peaceful people, Rem, they will kill your soldiers and Moonsons. You give them no choice."

He shook his head and I saw the corner of his lip curl up. It was the familiar sneer from the visions.

"I should have brought more men with me, Wisteria. I will bring more men the next time. I command an army, you know. I should have brought them all. This would have been fast work for an army."

Was there madness in my brother's eyes and voice? I hoped so. I prayed madness was responsible for his acts of greed and murder and his taking a name that wasn't truly his.

"Next time, Rem?"

"Yes, sister, I will grant you that on this outing, I underestimated the power of the Nanoo. I will have to call a retreat, and . . ."

He paused again, and in the interval between his words,

I heard the screams of more men and the groan of wood. The fen and the Nanoo were winning, I could taste their victory. Too, I heard a great crack and then someone holler, "The ground opens. Like the maw of a beast, it swallows us!"

"Next time, sister." He bowed slightly to me, then took a step back, and then another, retreating in the direction from which he came.

"No!" *There will be no next time.* I closed my eyes for a heartbeat, seeing my House Lady's foot, her broken fingers, the blood thick on the ground. Nanoo Gafna's broken fingers. I opened my eyes and saw he'd backed farther away, keeping his gaze on me. "When did you develop your wyse talent, brother?"

He stopped for just a moment and offered me a slight smile. "A year after I'd been sent south. In boredom, I recalled mother's lessons about the world's secret."

"The secret that the wyse exists in each of us."

"Yes, to varying degrees. The magic of the world is in us and around us, and if we search deep in our souls, we'll discover what gift the Green Ones bestowed on us."

"Every woman, man, and child is gifted with the wyse," I said.

"Few of them know it or believe it, though," he returned. "Good for us, eh? Good that not everyone knows they have a gift." He bowed again. "Next time, Wisteria."

No next time.

The coolness spread from my chest and down my arms, swirling in my fingers that gripped the pommel of my sword. I felt strong and certain of purpose, my head no longer throbbing, and aware of everything around me. It was like the very first lesson Bastien gave me, when I discovered the sword was not so heavy.

I became aware of everything . . . the soldiers and Moonsons dying, some of the soldiers running north and beyond the grasp of the trees . . . the rent in the earth that swallowed half of my brother's forces . . . the thorny walls springing up either to drive men back or trap them.

Too, I became aware that Tillard still lived, directing the Nanoo and alternately helping those nearest him who'd been injured.

Aware of everything, I saw only my brother. My vision had narrowed to blot out all else.

"No next time!" I raised the sword and rushed him, feet pounding across the fen and sloshing water in all directions.

Aware, I avoided submerged roots and rocks.

Aware, I closed and brought my sword down hard against his. So very hard.

He gasped in surprise and jumped back, brought his sword to the side and swept it in a great arc, meaning to slice through my stomach.

I dropped below his swing and pulled a long knife with my free hand, then sprung up so close I felt his breath on my face.

I drove the knife forward, the blade sliding between a gap in his armor and going in up to the hilt.

His eyes wild, wide, and full of madness, he brought his sword above his head, pommel held in both hands. He howled and brought it down, but I'd moved.

His blade cleaved through empty air, even as my blades

rose and flashed in the starlight, the sword cutting through his right arm, and the knife lodging in his neck.

Blood spilled from his lips as he fell back, sword slipping from his dead fingers.

"Rembert. Oh, by the gods, Rembert." The chill faded slowly and the throbbing at the back of my head returned. "By the Green Ones, I am sorry. So very, very sorry."

33

THE DEAD WERE LEFT TO THE WOODS, THOUGH PIECES OF ARMOR, swords, and shields were gathered. The Nanoo didn't want the metal rusting in the fen and posing a hazard to those walking there.

Tillard never told the Nanoo that Rembert was my brother. Neither did I reveal that news, as it would change nothing that had happened and would benefit no one.

Alysen decided to stay with Gafna, though in truth she had no say in the matter. Too young to be on her own, too powerful to be left untaught, she needed a guardian. All of the fen witches would serve that role.

"People must know about the murders, Wisteria. They should know about how the Emperor and your father died. They have to learn about the Empress." Tillard sat next to me just beyond the fen, at the edge of a pasture where the vanner and his horse grazed.

I agreed, though I wasn't entirely sure how to approach it.

"We'll travel, you and I, to village after village, then to the great city in the south and to the lands beyond. Wisteria, we'll tell all the people about the Empress's doings, the murders."

"Work together."

"Yes, sweet Wisteria. My gift . . . I'll know who believes us and who among them will help spread the word. I'll know who needs more convincing and who is beyond convincing. The word will travel far and fast, Wisteria."

I nodded. "And unrest will spread."

"Better that than complacency."

"Perhaps our words will foment a war."

"If there is a war, we will win, Wisteria."

I looked at him, at his eyes so full of hope. I tasted his hope, so strong I could get drunk on it. And I tasted other emotions that didn't scare me any longer. I liked the company of this odd-looking man.

Who will win? I wondered. Who is this "we"?

He gestured across the pasture. In the distance I saw a curl of wood smoke from a fireplace.

"We will win," he repeated. "All the good people of this land."

"And in the process the wyse will grow stronger in this world." I believed the words, and I believed Tillard.

He took my hand in his and we watched the horses graze.

In the back of my mind, I no longer could picture the Village Nar.

The Green Ones favored me this day.